INDELIBLE

INDELIBLE

A Chris Honeysett Mystery

Peter Helton

This first world edition published 2014
in Great Britain and the USA by
SEVERN HOUSE PUBLISHERS LTD of
19 Cedar Road, Sutton, Surrey, England, SM2 5DA.

Trade paperback edition published
in Great Britain and the USA 2015 by
SEVERN HOUSE PUBLISHERS LTD

British Library Cataloguing in Publication Data

Helton, Peter author.
  Indelible.
  1. Honeysett, Chris (Fictitious character)–Fiction.
  2. Private investigators–Fiction. 3. Artists–Fiction.
  4. Bath (England)–Fiction. 5. Detective and mystery
  stories.
  I. Title
  823.9'2-dc23

ISBN-13: 978-07278-8423-7 (cased)
ISBN-13: 978-1-84751-529-2 (trade paper)

All Severn House titles are printed on acid-free paper.

Severn House Publishers support the Forest Stewardship Council™ [FSC™],
the leading international forest certification organisation. All our titles that
are printed on FSC certified paper carry the FSC logo.

Typeset by Palimpsest Book Production Ltd.,
Falkirk, Stirlingshire, Scotland.
Printed and bound in Great Britain by
TJ International, Padstow, Cornwall.

AUTHOR'S NOTE

Thanks to Juliet Burton, to everyone at Severn House and to Clare Yates for making this book possible. Special thanks to Jess Knowles, the guardian of my sanity. No thanks to Asbo the cat for kicking what Mr Helton laughably calls his 'USB backup' under the radiator. Aren't bagless vacuum cleaners marvellous, though?

'A successful artist would have no trouble being a successful member of the Mafia.'

Sir Sidney Nolan

'The job of the artist is always to deepen the mystery.'

Francis Bacon

ONE

I t is always like this. There are no warning signs, no omens in the sky and you won't feel any different. You'll get up in the morning just as you do most days, put too much quince jam on your croissants, congratulate yourself on the perfect breakfast egg and enjoy the aroma of your coffee. It'll be a fine sunny morning in early October, just like this one, and that high-pitched paranoid string music that would instantly have warned you that taking the Norton for a spin might not be a good idea today is simply not there. Such a fine day for it too, and you haven't done this for ages, not since Jake found you another old Citroën to drive around.

We were enjoying that rare and often wished-for phenomenon: the Indian summer, often predicted but rarely realized, at least in England. I had finished a painting only the day before and my haphazard private-eye business – Aqua Investigations – had nothing at all on the books. No shows to prepare for, no missing persons to pursue and Aqua Investigations' principle operative was taking the day off. Not that having nothing to do was something I could afford to celebrate for too long. I had recently been paid a decent amount of money by a TV company for looking after the presenter of their archaeology show – very decent in fact, considering what happened to him under my care. Another few grand had found its way into the Aqua Investigations coffers – well, more jam jars to be honest – via a successful insurance job. But Mill House, with its three acres of jungle, dilapidated outbuildings and the tottering barn at the top of the meadow, devoured money in large chunks. My father left it to me because he knew how attached I was to the place. In his suicide note he expressed the hope that the money needed to keep it going might put an end to my life as a feckless painter and make me get a real job at last, though the note was a lot less polite. Becoming a feckless kind of private eye was probably not what he had in mind, either. Money was still frequently short.

I shared house and studio with the talented Ms Jordan. A few

years ago, while she was in her last year at art college, Annis
had turned up unannounced at Mill House and before I knew
why, I had offered her a space to paint in the big old barn I use
as a studio. She started helping me with my private-eye jobs soon
after that. When I kept finding her sleeping in front of her easel
I offered her a room in my house and one thing led to another
– what did you expect? What you didn't expect was to find that
Annis was bestowing her favours in equal measure on Tim.

Tim Bigwood is the third member of my hapless little detective agency. He has quite an interesting back story, if cat burglary
and safe breaking is your kind of thing, though he had gone
straight by the time we met (or so he said) and worked for Bath
Uni as an IT consultant. How he could afford to always drive
the latest model Audi TT and live in his rather nice flat in
Northampton Street on what he earned, I never asked. Everything
to do with computers, electronics and the odd bit of lock-picking
that needed doing was Tim's department. That he completed
our triumvirate in more intimate ways too came as a bit of a
surprise to both of us. But then life is full of surprises, some
more surprising than others.

Like Annis's 1950s Norton starting straight away, for example.
Annis doesn't mind me taking the Norton out for the odd run.
She had a rather spectacular crash on it a while back and has
since stuck to driving her equally ancient and spectacularly tatty
Land Rover.

A few moments after I fired up the machine, Annis's
strawberry-blonde head appeared in the door to the painting
studio. She does like the exhaust note of the thing, which is
quite impressive even from eighty yards away. She waved and
went back to her enormous canvas while I thundered out of the
potholed yard and bounced up the rutted track. It eventually
brings you to the tarmacked lane that runs the length of our
little valley just east of the city of Bath. Left or right? I decided
on left and tootled off towards town.

I do like Bath, even though sitting in our quiet valley we like
to complain about its noise, the amount of tourists and the price
of fish. Bath attracts a lot of people and along with the good and
the great this brings in those that prey on them. Apart from the
usual contingent of ne'er-do-wells, the Georgian city is a favourite
haunt of pickpockets, fraudsters, con artists, marriage swindlers,

quacks and hotel thieves, all of which give employment to the police, insurers and the likes of Chris Honeysett, painter and private investigator.

No sooner had I made it into town, wearing nothing more elaborate than jeans, boots and my ancient leather jacket, than dark clouds came over the horizon, pushed by a westerly wind that I fancied brought with it the first faint scent of autumn and perhaps the smell of the not-too-distant sea. I did a leisurely tour of the city centre, pootled past the weir, through Orange Grove and past the Abbey, took another look at the clouds and turned for home. It was one of those events where later on you might think: *if only I had not wasted those three minutes, everything would have worked out so differently.*

I didn't fancy getting soaked so I speeded up a bit. Along Broad Street, past the Pig & Fiddle and up Walcot Street, over the mini roundabout and I was on the London Road out of town. In no time at all I had turned off the main road and was heading for the valley.

A lot of accidents happen within a mile of the driver's home, especially after long journeys. You're nearly there. You relax. You think of what there is to eat in the house, or of the bath you are going to run. You're still driving but your mind is already through the door and putting the kettle on. Mine was up in the barn, stretching a new canvas and wondering what to paint next. The clouds had not yet swallowed up the sunshine and I knew I would make it home before the rain. I was on the home straight now, the narrow single-track lane that runs through the valley, riding on autopilot, slowly and lazily in high gear. A classic Norton has no mirrors and I hadn't bothered checking over my shoulder for ages. The exhaust is so loud that other engine noises don't intrude on your ears until they're very close indeed, which meant that when I heard the sound of the car behind me it was already very close. I flicked a brief look over my shoulder, and behind me loomed every motorcyclist's nightmare: the undentable Volvo. It was coming up fast so I adjusted my speed, not wanting to hold up the driver, planning to let the car pass at the first opportunity. The Volvo kept coming. I checked over my shoulder but couldn't make out the driver through his sun-dazzled windscreen. The car swerved left, then right, then left again, trying to find a way past me in this ridiculously narrow lane. A sudden surge of its big engine alerted me to the fact that he had apparently decided to go through me. He sat just inches from my number plate and accelerated again. I opened the throttle wide. On a modern bike I would have outrun the car quickly but a sixty-year-old Norton has its limitations and even on a modern bike any traffic coming the other way would have meant instant disaster. I inched ahead of the Volvo. The turn-off to Mill House and safety flashed past – I was going far too fast to take it – and I had to flick the bike around a few potholes. The sunshine suddenly disappeared as the clouds overtook us. I was pulling away from the car's bumper but not quickly enough. I was now going too fast to take the bend which I knew was about to come up and yet I couldn't afford to touch the brakes. But before the corner, on the left, would be the entrance to Ridge Farm. I would ride in there at full speed like a missile and look for something soft to crash into. During the day the five-bar gate to the farmyard was usually open. Usually. If it wasn't it would cut me into equal portions like an egg slicer. Behind me the Volvo driver leant on his horn and kept coming. For a few seconds I managed to squeeze a tiny bit more out of the screaming engine to give myself a few more inches of space, then I went for it. I scrubbed off as much speed as I could without getting hit by the Volvo then threw the bike into the turn-off. The gate was open. I flew across the concrete yard, terrifying a couple of loose chickens into the middle of next week as I hurtled past the astonished farmer, a Land Rover and a vet with his arm up a cow's backside, before I managed to stop inches away from a very solid farmhouse wall.

In the lane the big Volvo yowled past, horn still blaring. Fifty yards further on it missed the bend, crashed through a fence, ploughed uphill across the meadow, hit a stone water trough and flipped on its side. It gave me a warm feeling of instant justice, the kind so sadly absent from most of our lives.

When I got there the wreck steamed, groaned, hissed and ticked like an evil thing. It had been a shiny silver motor only a couple of minutes earlier; now it was lying on the driver's side in a field, comprehensively junked. The Volvo's terminal velocity must have been something approaching sixty miles per hour. Just before it crashed I had distinctly heard it shift up a gear. Standing in the field I looked over my shoulder at the corner where it had

left the road. There were no tyre marks on the tarmac. Volvoman
had made no attempt to brake. It didn't feel right.

We had called for an ambulance and described where to find
the wreck – water troughs don't come with postcodes. In the
meantime I'd see what I could do. I still couldn't see the driver.
The windscreen had shattered into a million pieces but still hung
together, rendering it opaque. I gave the car an experimental pull
at a front wing; it looked precarious but had in fact ploughed
itself solidly into the ground.

Rick Churcher, who owned Ridge Farm and the Volvo-adorned
field, puffed up the hill, his noisy border collies dancing around
him. Rick looked just like you'd imagine a Somerset farmer to
look, especially if he frequently drank too much of his own cider.

'Anybody hurt?' he bellowed up the hill.

'Yes, I think so. It's a bit quiet for my liking. Give me a hand
up; I'll see if I can get the passenger door open.'

Rick obliged and I pulled myself up on to the wreck. Kneeling
on the side of the car I could get a look at the driver despite the
cluster of airbags. I couldn't see his face properly as his head
was hanging down towards the other side but I had an impression
of an elderly man. I knocked on the unbroken passenger window
and called, then tried the door. It was unlocked and I managed
to yank it half open, heavy against gravity. I called inside, helpless things like 'Can you hear me?' and 'Are you badly hurt?'
but got no answer.

I turned to Rick. 'Hold the door up for me, will you? I'll see
if I can reach him.'

Rick obliged again, one strong arm enough to take the weight.
I tied my hair back and dived in head first, dangling by my hips.
I found one fragile-looking hand, ink-stained and covered in liver
spots. I felt around for a pulse at the wrist but found nothing.
Next I reached down and tried his neck which was twisted
unnaturally away from me. I wasn't sure if I was doing it right
but there was nothing there either. It felt bad though, and it
smelled bad. It smelled of death. I wriggled painfully backwards
across the sill of the door and slid out of the car. I shook my
head meaningfully.

Rick shrugged and let the door fall shut like the lid on a
rubbish bin. Farmers are more used to death than most. 'How'd
it happen?'

'Don't know. One minute I'm cruising along, next thing I know this guy is driving around on my number plate. I had to stuff my bike into your yard to get away from him or he'd have had me – he was trying to drive straight through me. He leant on his horn, drove past your yard and ploughed all the way up here without touching his brakes.'

'Stupid arse.' Rick nodded in affirmation, now sure of the driver category. 'What is he, a kid?'

'On the contrary. Elderly, I think. I couldn't see his face but his hair was silver-grey.' Like his car.

'Don't mean much.' Rick ran a callused hand through what was left of his own hair, sparse and grey. Rick wasn't forty yet. That's farming for you. Or cider. 'You really think he's snuffed it then,' he said without a hint of regret. His dispassionate eyes travelled from the car-sized hole in his fence along the scar the vehicle had produced in his grass. Then he shook his head and gave the car a playful kick with his black wellington boot. 'I was fond of that stone trough. Nineteenth century that was. It's cracked right through.'

'I always thought Volvos were so safe. You'd have thought that kind of crash was survivable, in a car like that. It's got enough airbags.'

Rick widened his eyes at me, slapped a hand to his forehead and gripped it with fingers splayed wide, as though he'd suffered a sudden seizure. 'It's the brain, Chris,' he moaned. 'You got seatbelts and airbags to stop your body when you crash but your brain keeps travelling. It keeps going at the same speed your car is going when you crash and slap! It hits the inside of your forehead and twists and sloshes about. Human brain can't take it, you see? S'not meant to happen. Humans haven't evolved to go that fast.' He pondered this for a bit while his black-and-white dogs tore about, quartering the meadow. Then he wagged a decisive finger. 'Unless you fell off a mountain. You'd be going quite fast if you fell off a mountain. But then you'd be in all sorts of other trouble. The brain-slapping thing probably wouldn't come into it much.'

'Not for long.' There wasn't a lot I wanted to add to that so we just stood around and chatted about the price of chicken feed, the poor state of the lane and global warming, as you do. I absentmindedly accepted one of Rick's cigarettes, cheap, filthy stuff he got off the Portuguese fruit pickers who brought van loads of it with them each year when they came to help with the fruit harvest. The warm wind that had blown a grey blanket across the sky wafted the smoke away up the hill.

The ambulance snaked along the lane with its siren going, closely followed by a police car. The paramedics in their green uniform came up carrying their gear, quickly and purposefully. Two police officers took their time at the bottom of the field, talking, gesturing, while the ambulance people went to work. Rick told them they were wasting their time. 'He's snuffed it.' They cheerfully ignored him.

When the police officers came up I got to tell the story all over again, except they also wanted to inspect my bike and then they asked me the same questions for a second time. The paramedics confirmed Rick's expert diagnosis and the younger of the police officers went off to call a doctor to make it official.

The older one stayed with me, scribbling more notes in his flip-up notebook. He pointed his pen at the lane and knitted his eyebrows. 'There's no sign of tyre marks, no sign the driver made any attempt at braking.'

'Yes, I noticed that.'

'Well.' He tilted his head and half closed one eye. 'Then he either crashed deliberately or he was asleep or very drunk.'

'I think you'll find,' one of the paramedics said flatly, 'that he didn't brake because he was dead before he had his crash. My guess is he had a heart attack some time before this and the car kept going.'

The constable looked at me, nodding encouragingly. 'So when you say he started accelerating back there and driving erratically that means you were probably being followed by a dead driver. The car's an automatic. If he was dead but his foot remained on the accelerator that would explain why the vehicle speeded up and shifted up through the gears. He must have slumped on to the steering wheel in the end, which set off the horn.'

I gave an involuntary shiver, just as the first drops of rain began to fall. 'Great. You ride home minding your own business and along comes a dead guy in a Volvo and tries to kill you.' I spoke lightly but had a strong image in my mind of a dead man stretching an arm out from beyond the grave, trying to pull me over to his side, the other side. The older I get, the less I like the spooky stuff.

It only takes one car to block the lane and the police car managed it admirably. Soon an impromptu traffic jam convened and each driver trying to reverse ran into the path of the next one arriving. The young constable was busy trying to explain the situation and redirect people. When the pathologist arrived he had to abandon his car half a mile back and walk the rest. It was raining steadily now but he appeared unperturbed despite being hatless and having no umbrella. I was less happy about it. I scrounged another cigarette off Rick and stood under the incomplete cover of a solitary unhealthy-looking oak away from the mangled car.

By now the windscreen had been removed to make access to the victim easier and it didn't take the pathologist long to confirm the paramedics' diagnosis. When the doctor straightened up he handed a white envelope to the constable, who looked at it for a while, then looked at me for a while, from thirty paces away. He then talked into the radio clipped to his stab vest for a bit, listened, then talked some more while looking at me.

Then he walked over slowly and deliberately. 'You told me you didn't know the accident victim,' he said accusingly.

'So I did.'

'Strange, when he seems to have known you.' He lifted up the white business envelope so I could read the name and address that was written across it in a spidery hand: *Chris Honeysett, Mill House.* 'It was sticking out of the man's jacket pocket. The doctor found it.'

'Did he?'

'Yes. Would you care to explain it?' he said in a Sherlock Holmesian tone.

'I would but I can't. Thanks.' I stretched my hand out for the letter but he snatched it away.

'Oh, no, you can't have that.'

'It is addressed to me, therefore it's my post.'

'Ah, no, it's got no stamp on it. So it's not post. Hasn't been posted, see. Hence not post. Just a letter in a man's pocket.'

'But clearly meant for me.' I stretched my hand out for it again but he wouldn't have it.

'Perhaps. But I still can't give it to you. It could be evidence.'

'Of . . .?'

This seemed to throw Sherlock for a moment. 'I don't know yet.'

'This isn't the Maltese Falcon, you know?' I complained. We argued a bit more but he wouldn't budge on the issue. It really looked like the chap in the Volvo had been on his way to my house to hand-deliver a letter but died before he got there and then nearly ran me over after he had expired at the wheel. It was a bit out of the ordinary for a Tuesday, but then it wasn't as though he had staggered through my door with a mysterious note in his hand and a knife in his back. I trudged over to the car and got down on my knees so I could look inside. Now that the broken windscreen had been removed and the airbags deflated I could see the ashen face of the corpse. He looked pretty old to me now. I thought I might have seen the face before somewhere but couldn't place him.

'You still maintain you don't know him?' said the constable.

'Don't recognize him.'

'And yet it looks like he was coming to see you,' he insisted.

I shrugged. 'So what? Lots of people come to see me,' I said. Prophetically, it turned out.

TWO

At breakfast the following morning, Annis and I were still talking about the crash. I could see the Norton through the half-glazed kitchen door where the old bike sheltered from further adventures and the rain in an open shed, along with all manner of slowly rusting and obsolete machinery. The potholes in the yard were filled with muddy rainwater and my gleaming black Citroën DS 21 stood on the sole surviving island of cobbles, looking as fine as it had when it rolled from the production line forty years ago. 'I think I'll stick to the DS from now on,' I said and returned to the table to ladle more quince jam on to my croissant.

Annis gave a prolonged shrug. 'I was cured when I crashed into the bridge when the brakes failed.'

'I was feeling more than a bit vulnerable when that guy rolled up in his tank of a car.'

'What are the chances, though, of that kind of thing happening?' She plunged the plunger on another cafetière of Blue Mountain. I was continuously surprised we could afford the stuff.

I had fixed views on the Volvoman subject. 'He was trying to kill me. He didn't fancy crossing the Styx on his own and tried to take me with him.'

'Perhaps he wanted you to pay the ferryman.'

'It's just that I enjoy the acceleration of a bike,' I mused.

'Acceleration? On the Norton? Tell me, when did you last drive a modern car?'

'What do you mean?'

'Just what I said. Apart from your old Citroën and my old banger you haven't driven anything for ages. Talk about acceleration. Cars have changed, you know.'

'And what modern cars did you drive that you're such an expert all of a sudden?'

'Tim lets me drive his TT sometimes. The words shit and shovel spring to mind. Another croissant, slow coach?'

I had forgotten about Tim's shiny black Audi. 'He lets you drive that?' I felt an absurd pang of jealousy. Absurd, considering what else he let her drive.

Annis dropped another warmed croissant on to my plate. 'You should ask him to borrow it some time; you'd be instantly converted to the twenty-first century. Honestly.'

'Nah, thanks.'

'Why not?'

'Too many buttons. Computers . . .'

'Suit yourself.' She cut me short. 'What are you doing today? Are you painting?'

I had spent the evening poring through the summer's sketch-books and had finally settled on the image to work up into a painting. 'As soon as I've primed a new canvas.'

Annis's eyes hardened as she stared past me. 'I hope you're right, hon. Look what's coming down the track.'

One of the many things we like about Mill House and the way it sits in the landscape is that to get to it one has to negotiate one's way down a tortuous potholed and rutted track which allows its inmates to catch a glimpse of any visitor long before they arrive. I looked around. A large grey Ford saloon was picking its way down towards us. I couldn't see its occupants and as a car it should have been anonymous enough, but visiting grey saloons usually meant only one thing.

'What's he want now?' Annis wondered.

'Are you kidding? If I as much as breathe on the same day that someone dies in Bath, Needham pops out of the ground next to me.'

'Sometimes I think he just comes for the coffee. Sometimes I think he comes because he actually likes you.'

'Let's hope it's because of the coffee then.' I put the kettle back on the stove.

When the car rolled into the yard I could see he was alone. Had I been in trouble then even the formidable (and rather large) Detective Superintendent Needham would have brought backup. I do have a shotgun licence after all, and he suspects, with good reason, that I also keep an illegal World War Two Webley .38 which came with the house. Needham didn't make superintendent by being complacent.

His body language seemed to confirm that I wasn't in immediate danger of being carted off to the nick. Despite the drizzly rain he took the time to visit the Norton, huddled among the rusting remains of several lawn mowers in the open shed. Naturally Needham knew he was being watched from the house, so he made a point of having a good look around the ancient automotive junk in the yard before coming over to darken the door I'd been holding open for a couple of minutes now.

'Your coffee is getting cold, Mike.'

He sniffed the air in the hall. 'I thought I could smell it when I got out of the car. You do make good coffee, I'll give you that.'

'You'll give me that, will you? So what is it you won't give me?'

'Figure of speech, Chris, don't go off on one. It's just a friendly visit. Now lead me to it.'

Annis, already in her bespattered painting gear, came out of the kitchen on her way to the studio as we rounded the corner. She was carrying a steaming mug of the stuff.

'Morning, Ms Jordan. Is that for me?'

'Dream on, Detective.' Annis held the mug high out of Needham's fleshy reach as she danced past us.

'Never try and interfere with her coffee,' I warned him. Annis had a serious addiction going.

'Was her hair always that red?'

'Yes. Gets redder when she's angry. Is this about yesterday – the accident?' I busied myself at the stove while Needham pulled up a chair.

'Sort of. The man had this on him.' He pulled out the envelope with my name on it and laid it in front of him on the kitchen table, then laid a heavy hand on top. The envelope had been opened. The cheek of it.

I feigned indifference, though it was clear it contained something important enough to bring Mike out here during working hours. I put coffee pot and cups on the table and poured. Then I set the sugar bowl just beyond comfortable reach. Needham probably came to Mill House partly to escape for a moment from a life plagued by instant coffee, styrofoam cups, plastic stirrers and aspartame. He flicked the envelope across the table at me and I released the sugar bowl into his custody.

'You did know the deceased; you used to work for him when you taught drawing at his private art school. John Birtwhistle.' Needham didn't look at me. He had obviously allowed himself one spoonful of real sugar and was concentrating hard on balancing as many sugar grains on a teaspoon as the laws of physics permitted. 'It's an invitation. Probably cancelled now.' He avalanched the white poison into his coffee and stirred meticulously.

'That was Birtwhistle?' He had been the owner and head of the Bath Arts Academy when I covered for a sick tutor there for a few months. 'I didn't recognize him. He used to have flowing dark hair and a beard.'

'That was seventeen years ago.'

'Was it?' Mike had certainly done his homework; it was a figure I could not have pulled out of a hat.

'Post-mortem hasn't been done yet but it'll probably turn out he died of a heart attack whilst driving.'

'That's what the medic thought. I still can't believe I was being chased down the lane by a dead man driving a Volvo. That's all my nightmares in one basket.' While Needham slurped happily at his coffee I unfolded the letter.

Dear Chris,

My plan was to surprise you at your home and studio but since you are reading this that plan has failed. I also hoped that a personal visit might increase my chances of persuading you to contribute to my little project.

You might not be aware that the Bath Arts Academy is celebrating its 30th anniversary, which we are planning to mark with an exhibition of works by all the (more talented) tutors who ever worked with us, to be held next month in Studio One and various other parts of the college.

I'm aware that you only worked at the academy for a short time but we would be proud and indeed honoured if you would contribute a new painting and a sketchbook for exhibition, thus giving today's students an opportunity to view and understand your work. I am contacting as many ex-tutors as I can personally. I am also trying to persuade as many of you as possible, and I know I am pushing my luck here, to produce a work of art at the school itself, thus giving the students a chance to observe accomplished artists at work.

While this is not a commercial exhibition, we will try and meet any (reasonable) expenses. If you are willing to participate or have any questions before committing yourself please contact me or Claire Kilburn in admin, who will help me coordinate the show.

Yours faithfully
John Birtwhistle

I put the letter down. 'So you thought you'd play postman.'

'Yes, and why not?'

'Because you're a senior detective in the Avon & Somerset Constabulary and don't get paid to deliver the post.'

Needham smiled benignly across the table. 'I was in the area.'

'What, England?'

'Well, it's curious, isn't it? Dead man drives down the road and ends up nearly killing the person he was looking for. I mean, it would have been more curious if he'd succeeded, of course.'

'Sorry I spoilt it for you.' The truth was Needham had a suspicious mind. I was pretty certain that even a parking ticket with my name attached to it automatically crossed his desk. Mike disliked the notion of private investigation. Unless of course it confined itself to things like chasing after missing persons, for which the police, despite having a duty to investigate, now hadn't remotely enough manpower. No wonder my phone never stopped ringing. Not that I did many mispers; I usually passed them on to a much larger agency, Bentons of Bristol. They in turn sent me the deeply strange, bewildering and hopeless cases they wouldn't touch with a barge pole because there wasn't a hope in hell of collecting a fee.

Needham gestured at the letter. 'Looks like he wanted you to show some of your work at the academy. Posh little place. Are you going to do it?'

'No idea. I'll have to think about it, see if it's still on, with Birtwhistle dead. Why are you asking?'

'Because it's a strange death and it's to do with you and if you're involved that means things can only get stranger. It was "Birtwhistle" then?'

'What was?'

'Not "John".'

'See what you mean. No, it was John and we did get on well enough. I quite liked him, though I had little to do with him; he was busy running an art school and spent a lot of time in the print room. I was only there for a while. I had no teaching qualification, didn't need one then. I was quite unknown then, too. I just taught off the top of my head whatever I thought the students ought to know.'

'Are you quite well known now, then? Making money?'

'So-so.' I'd had a few good shows a while back and invested the money. It was just a dribble now but it kept us from starving. 'I get by,' I lied.

'Sounds nice,' Needham said, not believing it. He had finished the coffee and I could see he tore himself away from the coffee pot with difficulty. 'Well, I can't hang around here all day. *I've* got to work for my money.'

'Unlike me, you mean.'

'Call that work?'

I waved him off as he squelched his Ford out of the yard,

covering his normally immaculate car in honest Somerset mud, then I took a fresh mug of coffee up to the studio. I was greeted by a strong smell of Venice turpentine. I often wondered how we could afford so much of it, considering it cost a hundred quid a litre. Annis had been busy on her new canvas. After the mural she had recently completed at a rock star's mansion, no canvas seemed big enough for her. This new painting would be the largest she had ever attempted.

'It still leaks, you know,' she said, prising the mug of coffee from my hands. She pointed pointedly at the empty paint cans dotted around the floor into which the rain dripped melodiously.

'I quite like it.' After a passing storm had taken a fancy to the roof and made off with large bits of it, I had only been able to afford the most superficial repairs. For some reason most of the remaining drips seemed to fall in Annis's side of the barn, which apparently was *just typical*.

'What did Needham want?' she asked from the other side of the barn. Her canvas was so big she had to tramp to the outer reaches of the studio whenever she wanted to take it all in.

'To play postman with me.' While I slotted together a more modest eighty by seventy-two inch canvas – modest by comparison; just large enough to be impossible to ignore – I filled Annis in about the letter.

'Are you going to do it?' she called from somewhere.

'Not a chance. Have you been there? Batcombe House? It's a very strange place. Huge house, huge garden. But it's been an art school for thirty years so no one has done anything to it apart from occasionally sweep up, I suspect.' I secured the stretcher with cross bars and pulled eighty-five inches of medium canvas off the roll, which I then wrestled across to the long table at the gloomy end of the barn. How Annis had stretched her monster canvas was beyond me. 'It's a real warren, Batcombe House. From sub-basement to attic, it's got linseed oil, plaster dust and ceramic clay ingrained in its fabric. Not to mention charcoal. Absolutely freezing in winter but when it's warm it's OK, really. Students drawing outside or in the woods behind Batcombe. Late-night parties round Fiddler's Pond. There's always a few landscape painters among that mad lot too, who lug their paints through the valley.' I punctuated my words with the stapler as I

worked round the stretcher. 'Sculptors working on huge stuff in
the garden. I remember the old sculpture tutor, Lizzy Kroog, she
used to live and work in the old bothy. Smoked a foul pipe and
scared off all but the most determined students. I wonder if she's
still there.'

'Well, you'll find out when you get there tomorrow, won't
you?'

THREE

I t was without the slightest feeling of foreboding that I brought
the DS to a halt on top of the ridge. I had stopped in a narrow
lane beside a neglected drystone wall, to find myself ignored
by a small herd of brown cows beyond it. From here I could
look down into the little valley, on the other slope of which
nestled the tiny village of Batcombe, looking exactly as it had
seventeen years ago, perhaps a hundred and seventy years ago.
Sitting here, all it took was a small adjustment of the inner eye
for the twenty-first century to dissolve into the misty sunshine.
The clusters of freestone cottages, the comfortably sagging roof-
line of the Three Magpies pub and the ancient church flying the
flag of St George on its squat tower all wrote 'English village'
across the hillside in a firm, old-fashioned hand. From here I
couldn't see even a single car, which made the illusion of looking
back into a previous era near complete. I turned off the engine.
The distant bark of a dog and the squawks of pheasants nearby
were all the sounds I could hear above the ticking of the cooling
engine. The view plucked at me with a strange nostalgia for a
distant past, a past that wasn't mine. Then an RAF helicopter
tore across the valley and nudged me back into the present.

The Bath Arts Academy had its home at Batcombe House, a
substantial pile of masonry above the village, half hidden from
view by a protective arm of Summerlee Wood. I rolled to the
bottom of the hill, crossed the stream via the single-span stone
bridge and zipped up the other side, past the Three Magpies and
through the heart of the village, with its triangular village green
in a crook of the road and what looked like a real live post office

clinging on to the end of a row of low cottages. A few 4x4s were dotted about here and there, some with real mud on them.

Batcombe House hadn't changed much either since I last saw it. It was a very large house set in several acres of grounds that ran on into Summerlee Wood. The house itself was early 19th century, which had been added to in Edwardian times. All had aged well together. Ivy had been allowed completely to cover one wing and looked determined to swallow the rest of the building. As usual the wrought-iron gates were wide open and if they were a little rustier than the last time I drove through them I didn't notice it that day. A few cars were parked on the patchwork of concrete hard-standing in front of the house and a tangle of bicycles leant by the porticoed entrance.

Bath Arts Academy was a slightly overblown title for a small private art school that had never catered to more than sixty well-off students. It did not give out grades or award degrees and so did not attract the kind of government funding or scrutiny other art schools enjoyed. It meant that tutors could concentrate on teaching whatever they thought artists needed to learn rather than doing paperwork, but it also meant that fees were high. The BAA was expensive rather than exclusive, with a student body that consisted of a mix of ages and nationalities. That the college would have freely accepted working-class applicants, had any beaten a path to its brass-handled doors while carrying enough money on their person, remained an untested hypothesis. What you needed to get into the BAA was talent, passion, plenty of funds and a touch of the eccentric. I locked the car and crunched over the perishing concrete to the west wing of the building. An unexpected rush of memories made me want to have a quiet look around before announcing my arrival. From the left corner of the house towards the west you could see, on the other side of the decidedly tufty lawns, the sculpture sheds and the 'bothy' of the resident sculptor, sculpture having been banished from the house where less noisy and noxious art forms were taught. As a painter I had never been wild about sculpture but I approved of the big and noisy variety. A lot of it was standing around in the gardens, especially near the pond. I walked along the stone-flagged path skirting the west wing; every flagstone was cracked and chipped, some rocked underfoot; grass and weeds had made a home in the cracks. The French window of Studio One was wide open, yet the small forest of easels stood silent and leafless. From somewhere I could hear a voice, measured, melodious and with frequent pauses; even without hearing what was being said I recognized the familiar rhythms as an art history lecture accompanied by a slide show. The room above Studio One served as meeting place and lecture hall; sure enough, its four sash windows were closed and curtained. Further on, a long and ramshackle conservatory and the rooms behind it were home to the small ceramics department. Right now it presented a damp air of neglect which was wholly deceiving. By necessity potters, needing to fill kilns which would turn clay into ceramic, worked in batches and, in my memory at least, spent even more time reading novels on the lawn than the painters did. Then suddenly they'd all disappear when the opening of the big kiln yielded up excitement and disappointment in near equal measure.

Many of the conservatory's lights were cracked and much of the glass was almost as grimy as the windows of my own studio. Some split-bamboo shades and strung-up dustsheets helped with the gloom. I approved. Standing in the open door I could see only one solitary girl sitting at one of the potter's wheels. She wore a once-white, clay-streaked smock over a pair of jeans; her long, straight blonde hair was tied back into a ponytail with a gingham tea towel. The electric wheel hummed and spun. The girl looked up, registered me without apparent interest, then looked down at the wheel. She threw a lump of grey matter the size of a man's brain on to it and centred the wet mass. Her hands cupping the spinning clay, she looked across at me. Without taking her eyes off my face she conjured with the clay. A tall, narrow vessel grew from between her hands; for a moment it spun, perfectly rounded and upright, guided by her thin fingers, then she crushed the vessel back down into a dense, spinning lump. Her eyes blinked only once. Gas-blue eyes. 'Help you?'

'No. I know my way around. Where's everyone, at a lecture?'

'The Future of the Visual Arts in Britain.'

'You're not going?'

The clay on the wheel wobbled then stopped. The girl cut the clay off the wheel with a wood-handled wire cutter, wet her hands and re-centred the lump. 'No thanks, I have seen the future.'

'And what's it look like?'

She set her face into a narrow-eyed scowl and raised a

wide-mouthed vessel from the clay, then squashed it down so it spun misshapen and off-centre. She hammed up a tragic voice. 'Dumpy. The future . . . is dumpy.'

Perhaps she could read the future in lumps of clay. 'Thanks for the warning.'

I walked on to the next door: the Small Studio. A select, fanatical bunch of painters had received my equally fanatical wisdom concerning drawing in here. A few paces further brought me to another set of French windows: Studio Two, the large painting studio. I could not pass without sticking my head in. It was also devoid of students but crammed with paintings in progress, mostly large canvases on the walls and only a few smaller ones on easels. Some talented stuff here, with one or two exceptions, but nothing earth-shattering. I stood in the open French doors with the studio behind me and looked across the lawns that were surely in the process of returning to pasture. To the left I could see several large wood and metal sculptures standing close to the sculpture tutor's house, as though left there as giant peace offerings. There were the low sculpture sheds behind; further to the right and in the shadow of Summerlee Wood I could see Fiddler's Pond, so named because the shape of its dark waters used to be reminiscent of a violin, yet today its edges were ill-defined. Only the bravest students, or those propelled into the water by their contemporaries, swam in it.

I completed my first foray past some neglected flower beds that had been all but swallowed up by brambles and evil-looking laurels, and back at the front of the house I pushed through the glass doors into the cool entrance hall. To the uninitiated, the profusion of doors, stairs and corridors was either inviting or intimidating, depending on temperament. I remembered it all easily. To the left a corridor led to painting studios and ceramics, then the stairs that led to the next floor and the attic above, beside it another corridor and off that the steps leading down into the basements. All the paintwork had once been cream but all doors, doorframes, corners and even the banister bore a thirty-year patina of many-coloured finger-, palm- and even the odd footprint. To my right the door to the administrator's office stood half-open and I sensed movement in there, so that's where I headed. Inside, a large woman in skirt, shirt and sensible shoes was standing with her back to the door in front of three open filing cabinets.

She was pulling out file after file and laying them on an already tottering pile on the deep windowsill.

'Hello?'

She whirled around and laid one hand across her heart. 'Hoo! Haa. You startled me.' She took a deep breath and shook her head.

'Guilty conscience?'

'Oh, always,' she assured me. It was more than just the *hoo* that made me think of an owl. She was in her thirties but in defiance of current fashion had a pudding-basin hairstyle, wore large amber-coloured round glasses and dressed in greys.

'Sorry I startled you.'

'That's OK. Can I help you? Oh, wait, I know who you are . . . don't tell me, you're . . .' She held up her left hand and wiggled ringless fingers at me. 'Honeysett, right?'

'Right.'

'I'm Claire Kilburn, I do the admin around here. Trying to. I saw your picture in the Chronicle a while back. That thing with the iguana called Knut? *Amazing.* But you're also one of poor John's artists. Mr Birtwhistle's, I should say. You used to work here.'

'For a very short time.'

'Well, you must have made an impression because poor Mr Birtwhistle said he was very keen to get you here and teach again. Unfortunately he died in a car accident a couple of days ago. You probably heard about that? The police have been here twice already. Tragic, quite tragic.'

And could have been even more tragic had there been a head-wind. 'Quite tragic.'

'For the college too,' she said. 'He was a popular tutor and really the driving force behind the school. Sorry, that's not what you came here for, is it? We're all a bit distracted at the moment.'

'Had you worked for him for long?'

'No, not at all. I've been here a couple of months now. There wasn't much administration going on until I got here, to be honest. It was a little chaotic, shall we say.'

'I can well believe it.' I remembered this office looking like the dumping ground for everything from bundles of life drawings to plaster moulds and etching plates. A plastic skeleton usually stood by the fireplace. Now the place looked like a proper office.

Naturally I preferred it the way it was before. It reminded me of home. 'I'm not actually here to teach. Mr Birtwhistle wanted me to be part of an exhibition he was planning. Is that still going ahead?'

'Oh, but you're quite wrong there. Paul, our painting tutor, has gone and left for a teaching job in Queensland, of all places. Interviewed over the phone and the internet and went as soon as he got the job. John didn't want to stand in his way. It was you he had in mind as a replacement.'

'There was nothing about it in his letter. It was all about the exhibition.'

'Oh, I know; he was going to see you personally. He said he would try and sweet-talk you into it.'

'All academic now, I guess. What about this exhibition? Is that going ahead?'

'Oh, absolutely. I think it's even more important now. It was almost like it was his last wish, wasn't it?'

'I suppose so.'

'And naturally we'll include some of John's own images, to show just what an underrated artist he was.'

I had warmed to the idea of a mixed show at the college; some interesting artists had taught here in the past. 'Good. I'm glad. So, who else will be showing?'

Claire sat down behind the smaller of the two desks, opened a drawer and withdrew a sheet of paper, which she handed to me. 'It's not as long a list as John would have liked. Some could not be traced, one died, another went mad, one gave up painting for potholing. Much the same thing if you ask me. Anyway, that's how it goes.'

I ran my eyes down the list and recognized most of the names. 'So these are the ones that agreed to show? It should be quite . . .'

'Well, no, actually. Sorry.' She held up both hands in apology for interrupting. 'That's just a preliminary list, nothing has been finalised. John was going to see them all personally. I don't know how many he managed to visit. You might have been the first.'

It had been more visitation than visit. 'He died before he managed to see me.'

'Yes, the police asked me about that.'

'About what?'

'Whether John had communicated with me and had he mentioned that he had seen you that day.'

Typical, as Annis would say. Despite the fact that Birtwhistle had nearly killed *me*, the police hadn't taken my word for it that he died on the way *to* my house rather than *from* my house. I changed the subject. 'I've met one of the artists on this list, and I've heard of Greg Landacker, of course.'

'Ah yes, Landacker is quite a name; we are very keen to have him exhibit. I don't think he has exhibited anywhere for a while.'

'I think you're right. I like his stuff. Like it a lot. Dawn Fowling I don't think I have met; I only vaguely remember swirly canvases. And Kurt Hufnagel, he's quite good. I met him though he probably won't remember me,' I said modestly. Or remember much else of the evening, I thought uncharitably. There were five names here, including mine. My name topped the list.

Above us much chair-scraping signalled the end of the Future-of-Art lecture. I thanked Claire and wandered back into the hall, still studying the short list of names and addresses. There was something odd about it, I thought, but I couldn't immediately see what. I was distracted by the sudden onrush of students, all heading for the refectory. Somewhere among that lot was probably a tutor but the group was so mixed that no one stood out. They all passed through the hall in groups or pairs, ignoring me. Relative quiet once more settled on the hall.

'You're going to do it then?' said a voice right behind me. I turned around. The girl from ceramics stood there, still wearing her spattered frock, but she had let her hair down. She was standing about a foot closer to me than was conventional between strangers. Her eyes, perhaps more petrol- than gas-blue, were nearly level with mine, but she was looking just past me as though passing on confidences and checking for eavesdroppers.

'Yes, I think I will. You know about this then?' I held up the list. 'If the others agree to do it, I will. It sounds like a really good idea.'

'It is. Shame there's no potter on the list, of course, but apparently the last tutor went mad and smashed all his work. I know how he feels. Ah, here comes Dumpy.'

I turned around. A woman descended the stairs then clacked in noisy heels across the floor. She was about forty, I guessed, but didn't look like an art-school tutor. Only a tall, thin creature like Ceramics Girl would have described her as 'dumpy'. She was comfortably pear-shaped and unfortunately permed, certainly, and five foot if she was an inch, but she was sharply dressed in a Windsor-blue business suit. She made for the office door but changed her mind, swerved and turned towards me with a sigh. 'And you are . . .?' Her voice was tired and irritable.

There was only one possible answer to that. 'Chris Honeysett.'

'Yes, and . . .?' She suddenly mellowed, looking even more tired. 'Are you a parent?'

It wasn't something I felt like discussing, so I said, 'I used to work here, for a short while.'

'Oh, you're one of those. Sorry, my mind is rather full at the moment. My father's death has left me with an awful lot to sort out. I'm Anne Birtwhistle.'

I mumbled my condolences, which seemed to make her irritable again. 'You're here because of this exhibition my father had planned.' She looked around the hall and staircase. Both were adorned with student work, some of it truly hideous, and which had probably been there for decades where it attracted dust and caustic comments from later students, often scribbled in biro on the wall next to them. 'Well, a change of decor might not be a bad thing. But I'm afraid I'm far too busy to give it any attention now.'

'I received a letter from your father which said your admin-istrator . . .'

'Yes, Claire,' she filled in.

'That Claire would be organizing the show.'

'I doubt she'll have the time either. This place needs a complete overhaul since I've now been lumbered with it and with my brother conveniently bumming around in Asia. Or was it Sweden? I tell you what. You want this show, you get started on organizing it. We'll talk again after my father's funeral.' She nodded, tried for a smile and failed, then disappeared into the office and shut the door behind her.

A familiar smell of refectory food came wafting up from the basement. I checked my watch: lunchtime. The school had always provided breakfast and lunch, free to tutors and at reasonable prices for students. Meals – quite edible meals, as I seemed to remember – had been cooked almost single-handedly by a reassuringly large woman called Mrs Washbrook; could she possibly still be down there? It certainly smelled familiar, I thought when I followed the echoing stone steps down into the basement. Of course I was neither a student nor a tutor but if she still ran the place I would throw myself on Mrs Washbrook's mercy.

The place was busy. Strip lighting ran the length of the low vaulted ceiling, and I did not remember the walls being lemon yellow, but there she was, thinner now and the hair under her cook's bonnet had greyed completely, but it was without doubt the same woman, bustling about at twice the speed of her younger and thinner assistant. She didn't remember me at all. 'No, sorry. How long did you work here, love?'

Not long, I had to admit. I paid a ludicrously small sum for an edible-looking beef stew in gravy, with a mountain of mashed potato and an avalanche of peas. I was looking for a place to sit down when a familiar face looked up and waved me over to her table. She was sitting by herself in the furthest corner.

'Glad you could make it, Honeypot,' she said. 'Dine with me. No one else dares come near.' It was Elisabeth Kroog, the resident sculptor. 'I knew you were around, saw your old car. Not many of those around any more. You're a man of some taste.'

Time had not been kind to Kroog, or perhaps she had not been kind to herself. She was probably in her late sixties now but her face was so wrinkled she could easily pass for eighty and her skin looked as though granite dust was ingrained in her pores. On her nearly bald head perched a black skull cap embroidered with faded gold thread and the few teeth she had left were stained a deep amber from constant pipe-smoking. Even now the long, curved church warden pipe lay next to her plate of sausages and mash.

I started by making the appropriate conventional noises about John's death but she cut me short with the wave of a forked sausage. 'You know what a workhorse John was. He had a couple of scares in the last two years but refused to slow down.'

'That was exactly how he went in the end. He died at the wheel but kept on accelerating.'

'Very fitting. And now the bastard has left me here all alone, stranded in the twenty-first bloody century. I never thought in a million years I would end up on the wrong side of the millennium.' She decorated the length of her sausage with mustard and bit it in half. 'I'm glad you decided to come back. You and

Washtub,' she pointed her half sausage at Mrs Washbrook, 'are the only familiar faces round here now.'

'You're the second one who thinks I came to teach here. I never spoke to John, of course, and in his letter it didn't say anything about teaching.'

'He knew you'd poo-poo the idea if he wrote to you; he wanted to go and *charm* you into it. It's only until we can find a more permanent lunatic to work here for free meals and jelly beans. To replace Paul who followed the mammon down under to teach the colonials. I pray his plane will crash and burn.'

'I can't teach here; I've got things to do,' I said and quickly shovelled some stew in my mouth.

'Oh yeah? What?' Kroog paused, clapped a paper napkin over her mouth and coughed bronchially into it. Then she looked into the napkin and said 'bugger' under her breath before crumpling it up. 'What's more important than teaching the next generation to recognize the difference between real art and real crap? Or in my case the next-but-one generation. I'm sure you can sacrifice a few weeks at the altar of the only true religion left on earth.'

'I can't believe John wanted me to teach again. He fired me.'

'Not really. Everything else has stopped working properly but there's nothing wrong with my memory, lad. You two were drinking too much French plonk by the pond and got into a ridiculous drunken argument about Matisse of all people. You both talked yourselves into a corner and you, as I clearly remember, said, "If that's so then I don't see how I can continue teaching here," and John said something like, "If that's how you feel, old boy, you should find something better to do," and that was all. John never fired you. He *liked* you.'

'I'm really not cut out for teaching,' I said lamely. I didn't have anything on my books and no show coming up until – hopefully – a spring show at Simon Paris Fine Art, and with a rising panic I found that I couldn't for the life of me think of any excuses.

'Rubbish, you'll be fine. Write your own timetable, studio space, free room at the Bothy and free grub courtesy of Washboard here and I might even get round to paying you.' I looked up from my plate of food. 'Don't look like that. I was deputy head. Now John has deserted us I'll have to drive this ship of fools. I could really do with some help.' She patted my hand and nodded. It was all decided, apparently.

'How long until you find a new painting tutor, d'you think?'

'Oh, no idea. We'll advertise. After John's funeral. Good, great. Have a look at the timetable. Start just as soon as you've got over the shock of having a job to go to.'

FOUR

'*T eaching?*' Annis nearly fell off her painting stool in her haste to silence the clockwork radio. 'You're winding me up.'

'Lizzie Kroog talked me into it,' I lamented. I looked around the studio. I must have been mad to agree to that.

'She must have bewitched you. You always said you *hated* teaching. I remember distinctly you saying that teaching art was completely useless. What was it again? "You can't teach art; it's like trying to teach the taste of chocolate." Your very words.'

'It was John Birtwhisle's dying wish, apparently. Or nearly.'

'Rubbish.'

'I didn't want to let them down. It's not going to be for long. And I've got a couple of days before I have to start. In the meantime Kroog wants me to see if I can find any of the people on this list of exhibitors and twist their arms. Fortunately none of them seem to have moved very far.'

Annis pulled a doleful face. 'Probably can't afford the bus fare.'

'One of them's Greg Landacker; he could afford the bus company.'

'Good luck with asking him. I hear he's an anti-social bastard.'

'Most painters are anti-social.'

'Well, you'll just have to curb your baser instincts for a while, won't you?' she said gleefully and turned the radio back on.

Annis was probably right about Landacker being a hard nut to crack; people said his sudden success had gone to his head, that he never answered questions about his work and had cultivated a *mysterious loner* act, while really craving admiration. He sounded like a right barrel of laughs. Which is why I would start with a slightly softer target, someone I had met before: Kurt Hufnagel.

Not that I thought it would be that much more enjoyable, but Hufnagel should be easier to persuade. I had met him before and he struck me as someone who would respond well to vague promises of money or publicity as long as he wasn't too hungover. The last time I had seen him was at a private view of some of his work at Simon Paris. Then his clothes had needed ironing, perhaps even airing, and he had drunk the red wine on offer at an alarming rate. He had irritably pointed out to me that his name was pronounced *Hoof-nargle*, as though that should have been obvious to anyone with a modicum of intelligence. I had seen a couple of red dots, enough to keep him in cartons of Bulgarian plonk for a few months. Most of his paintings depicted the chaotic interior of his painting studio with the obligatory woman posed naked for no good reason amongst the clutter. Come to think of it, there had always been a naked girl somewhere in Hufnagel's paintings. Even as he got older the girls in his paintings appeared not to age and all were of a similar physical type, though he seemed to have no preference as to hair colour. It occurred to me that being a painter he could of course paint them with green hair if he had a mind to.

His address was on the list but since I didn't have sat nav in the DS, 'Honeysuckle House, near Stanton Prior' would have to do. Stanton Prior was a tiny village north-west of Bath. After criss-crossing the countryside around it for a while without success, I started looking for people to ask without having to knock on doors. There was nobody about. I wondered how the English countryside could be so empty of people considering how small an island this was, then I realized that the almost complete absence of shops and jobs might have something to do with it. Eventually I came across a farmer in blue overalls and black wellies who was securing a load of sawn logs to the trailer behind his Land Rover; it appeared they had bounced off into the road. I picked up a stray log and lobbed it onto the trailer. The mention of Honeysuckle House drew a blank.

'It's owned by a painter. Kurt Hufnagel,' I ventured.

'Ah. People will rename houses,' he said, shaking his head. 'It's unlucky. Him, yeah, bizarre chap. But I dare say it takes all sorts.'

'Do you?'

'Yeah, you can't miss it.' He gave me 'unmissable' directions involving a multitude of left and right turns. 'What was the house called before he renamed it?' I asked as I walked back to my car. 'Do you remember?'

'Horseshoes.'

Unlucky for some. After about three turn-offs I had forgotten the rest of the directions but found the place anyway. It was a drab and dispiriting house standing forlorn by the side of the narrow lane. Un-cared-for dusty hedges encircled the untidy property; there was a garage with torn tarpaper roof, a largely glassless greenhouse, a tottering shed and an ugly cement-brick extension at the back of the house with a corrugated asbestos roof and rust-streaked skylights, which had to be the man's studio. In between it all lay a wilderness of crud, including two old chest freezers, a half-burnt sofa and a slimy-looking slant of flimsy timbers. The car parked in front of the doorless cluttered garage was a cack-coloured eighties Fiesta with balding tyres. On the low garden gate, squeezed between the hunched shoulders of the hedge, a barely legible sign with blistering paint proclaimed the name of the house. Hard as I looked, I could see no honeysuckle anywhere. The area just outside the front door was crowded with tied-up carrier bags bulging with rubbish. The place gave off an air of depression that made me hesitate at the tatty wooden gate. When I pushed it open it squealed mournfully. The sound made me shrug deeper into my leather jacket. If there were more than two bottles of milk at the doorstep I would call social services and leave it to them to explore the place.

There were no bottles of milk at all, just more crud. I could hardly reach the bell button without standing ankle deep in unwholesome-smelling stuff that scavenging animals had ripped to shreds. When I depressed the button I didn't hear it ring. I picked my way round the side of the house. Towards the back was another dark and narrow door. No knocker or bell. I tried the handle and it opened. It led into a shadowy corridor. First to my left was the kitchen. From deeper inside the house I could hear what sounded like Led Zeppelin being played at quite a volume.

'Hello? Shop!' I made some noise for form's sake but it was clear I wouldn't be heard above the din unless Hufnagel was hiding in one of the cupboards.

The kitchen was easily identifiable as belonging to an

old-school painter, one who saw it as an extension to the studio and trudged paint and left smudges everywhere. It also desperately needed to be cleaned, preferably with a pressure hose, and it smelled as if something needed emptying or, better still, incinerating. Every square inch of surface had empty foil containers and other rubbish lying on it, in several layers.

I followed the noise along the shadowy corridor to a broad door which I realized led into the cement-brick annex and behind which Led Zeppelin were working on 'In My Time of Dying' at the appropriate volume. The door knob and surrounding area were a familiar symphony of paint smudges so I knew this was Kurt's studio. I knocked, knocked again, got no answer, and opened the door.

I had guessed right. It was a long, open-beamed studio space crammed with the kind of stuff self-referential figurative painters like to stick in their paintings when they paint pictures of their studios – theatrical props almost, a hangover from the nineteenth century. Flower stands, pretty jars and bottles, a stuffed pheasant, a chipped bust of Mussolini, reams of fading velvet curtains thrown over sticks of furniture, that kind of thing. Hufnagel himself was standing with his back to me, working wild-haired on a large canvas secured to a couple of radial easels. He was working on another studio still life, though there was also the obligatory naked girl who was posed, almost incidentally, in a tattered armchair beside a stovepipe parrafin heater. Even though I was in her line of sight, the model, being utterly professional, completely ignored me.

'Hello!' I tried again and waved. It was the movement of my hand rather than my voice that finally alerted Hufnagel to my presence. He whirled about quickly, startled, staring at me through round, black-rimmed spectacles with intense painter's eyes.

'What the . . .' He came towards me, making shooing motions, still holding a loaded brush and not afraid to use it. He made no move to silence the paint-covered midi-system. His painting gear consisted of an old-fashioned suit which was almost completely covered with paint at the front, as though he had suffered a head-on collision with a freshly painted canvas. He checked back over his shoulder but the model held her pose regardless.

'Sorry, I did knock,' I shouted. 'I don't suppose you remember me. I'm Chris Honeysett . . .'

'Yes, yes, I know that,' he said irritably. 'Outside. I'll come out. The sitting room. No, the kitchen, actually.' He gently but forcefully pushed me through the door. He turned to the model. 'OK, take a break, love. I'll bring you some coffee in a minute.' He closed the door firmly behind him then stared at me wild-eyed in the corridor. 'How did you get in here? No, I mean, how did you get here? Hardly anyone knows where I live.' He seemed genuinely unnerved by suddenly finding me in his place and fluttered alongside me into the kitchen. Here he filled a whistling kettle at a sink so cluttered with dirty dishes he could barely fit it under the tap. He then crashed the thing down on a two-ring camping stove connected to a gas bottle by what looked like a bit of garden hose and a twist of wire. 'Bloody electric kettle caught fire. And the bloody stove burnt out.' He waved a tragic arm at a melted lump of black plastic on a work top and at the encrusted hulk of an electric cooker sulking in a corner yellow with grease. 'It's a bloody conspiracy.' He opened and closed cupboards, looking inside as though he had found himself in someone else's kitchen. His face betrayed extreme consternation.

'Look, I can go away if you want to get back into the studio,' I offered. 'I know how it is.'

'Do you really? Well, bollocks to that, you're here now. Only the irritated oyster makes a pearl and all that. That's me, the original irritated bloody mollusc who cannot find any sodding *coffee*!' He slammed another cupboard door. 'Tea all right?' He smiled sweetly, looking almost normal for the first time.

'Sure.'

He briefly held my eyes, as though testing my sincerity and nodded a few tiny nods, then went on a hunt for tea that looked worryingly like the previous coffee hunt. 'Ah!' He extracted a couple of limp teabags from what looked like a half-collapsed shoebox that stood beside a bird cage containing a suspiciously quiet and motionless budgie. If the rest of his domestic arrange-ments were anything like this then the irritable Hufnagel ought to have pearls to spare. While he furtled about I edged closer to the bird cage. The bird on the wooden perch was plastic. The bird shit in the bottom of the cage was real.

I also had time to notice that Kurt's hair had gone thinner and wilder since I had last seen him and he seemed to have aged a lot in other ways too. The skin on his face was dry and flaking and his stubble practically white. The taut skin on his hands looked translucent. I began to wonder whether the nests of empties everywhere didn't have something to do with it. Supermarket whisky, most of it. With the odd bottle of single malt among them. Feast and famine, which is usual for painters – mostly famine of course, some of it doubtlessly brought on by the ever-rising price of single malt.

'So what do you want?' Hufnagel said as he willed the kettle to boil. 'Who's died? I mean, it's got to be an emergency for you to trek out here after nine years.'

'Nine years?' He sounded as though I had walked out of a relationship with him. I had only met him a couple of times.

'Nine years is when we last talked. I remember it, my show at Simon Paris.'

'Mixed show, if I remember rightly.'

'Yeah, all right, no need to rub it in. So who died?'

'John Birtwhistle.'

He stopped dead by the now singing kettle. 'Oh shit! Figure of bloody speech, I didn't really mean *who has died*. I mean. Shit. Old Birtwhistle. Shame. Mind you, he was no fan of mine. But a good bloke, really. I used to teach up at the old whatsit, BAA. Didn't last all that long.' He reanimated himself and went looking for the teapot. He found it straight away, took off the lid and looked inside. 'Crap! Everything goes mouldy in this sodding place.' He dived down into an old tea chest and came up with a stack of hideous pink and baby blue teacups. 'I bought a job lot of crockery at an auction last month. Worked out a penny a piece. Saves on the washing up. They just need . . .' He blew the dust out of a couple of them and put them on the table. 'There. And no, you can't have a saucer, I used them all for mixing paint. You know how it is. So you came here to bring the sad news? Old Birt and I didn't exactly part as friends. What did he die of?'

'Had a heart attack at the wheel of his car and crashed it into a field. Missed me by a whisker when he did.'

'Dramatic stuff.' He dropped a teabag into each of our cups and splashed hot water over them. The dank cavern of a lightless fridge yielded a carton of milk. He shook it, presumably to test how lumpy it was.

'I'll take it black, thanks,' I said hastily.

'Probably wise.'

'What about your model?'

'Oh yeah, forgot.' He blew the dust out of another cup, adding teabag and water. 'I'll just take Sophie that.' Lucky girl.

When he returned from the delivery he paused at the door. He looked gaunt. Hollowed out. 'So why are you really here?'

'Didn't I say? It's a show. At the college. Birtwhistle wanted past tutors to show their work. When he died he had a list of artists on him and you were right near the top. It's thirty years of BAA, apparently. The show's meant to be for the benefit of the students.'

'What, so that students can see what a real painting looks like? Sod that. You mean it's a charity do.'

It would probably work out that way but that was not how I was going to bill it. 'Not necessarily. Rich students have rich parents.'

'Hadn't thought of that. Are you sure Birt wanted me there, though? He did fire me.'

'Did he? Me too. But he was keen you should show. Your name's at the top of the list. What did he fire you for?'

'Fraternising with the enemy.'

'Shagging a student? Not the done thing. Unequal power relationships.'

'I know, I know. I only meant to console her. She'd just been dumped by her boyfriend and all that. One thing led to another. Birt went mental. Unhelpful, unwarranted, unethical. A lot of uns. Fired me on the spot. Landacker took over from me. I was gutted. Cushiest job I ever had. I even had a room at the Bothy with scary old Kroog. Crap wages but it kept me alive while I was painting.'

'That's how I felt at the time, though I didn't have a room – they were all full of students then.'

'So what did you get fired for?'

'Not sure. We just had an argument and both refused to back down. I think we were possibly drunk. I talked to Elisabeth Kroog and she thinks I just talked my way out of the job.'

'Lizzie Kroog, is she still there? Now that woman is scary.'

'I think some of her social-skill components have burnt out, but everything else works. She talked me into teaching painting until they find a new tutor. It took her five minutes to do it.'

'Yeah? Where's the old tutor buried?' He slurped unconvincingly at his tea. It was clear soft drinks weren't really his thing.

'Are you going to contribute to the show? If you say no I might have to send Lizzie round here.'

'Who else will be showing?'

I dangled the list. He tried to take it but I whipped it away, not wanting him to see I had lied about him being top of the list. 'Greg Landacker, Dawn Fowling, you, me and someone called Rachel Eade.'

'Not sure I remember the last one.'

'Don't know her at all. The current tutors will be contributing, I expect.'

'Yeah, I'm in. Can't really afford to turn anything down at the moment.'

'Not selling much?'

'I've gone out of fashion a bit. The last ten years have been quite grim. I sell enough to stay alive. Or so it is rumoured. If I hadn't been left this place by a mad aunt I'd be stuffed.'

'Can't you get another teaching job?'

'Do you think BAA will have me back, now Birt has handed back his brushes?'

'Don't know, ask Lizzie, she's taking over from Birtwhistle.'

'Not a chance.'

'There are other art schools.'

'Are you kidding? They no longer use artists to teach artists; they use teachers. They know all about teaching and sod-all about art. Of course we knew sod-all about teaching.'

'Possibly.' In view of my recent re-appointment I quickly changed the subject. 'We're allowed one piece each but it must be accompanied by a sketchbook to show how your images develop. It's supposed to be educational. If you can paint it at the college you'll get brownie points and free grub.'

'Really? There might be a problem with my model.'

'I'm sure they'll let you use their model. Or you might paint something without a naked girl in it.'

'What would be the point of that?'

'OK, I'll let you know all the details and how I got on with the rest of the list. What's your email address?'

'Ah. I don't actually have a computer as such.'

'All right, give me your phone number.'

'Same problem there. The phone people have become quite unreasonably strident in their demands lately and I told them what they could do with their landline. And I did get a mobile but it doesn't have any credits. Or leccy. The chap who sold it to me forgot to give me the charger.' He gave a little-boy shrug, looking for understanding. 'It *was* only a tenner.'

'I'll send a pigeon.'

He walked me outside, more relaxed about me now, but as soon as he actually set foot in the outside world his mind went back to Def Con 3. We squeezed past a sea of plump carrier bags stuffed with festering refuse. Kurt took aim and kicked one hard; it soggily refused to budge. 'The *bastards* won't take the rubbish away unless it's in sodding black bin liners.' He opened his arms wide like an Old Testament prophet, standing by a sea of crud, inviting it to part. 'Where do they expect me to find *bin liners* in the wilderness?' I was already at the gate. He stumbled after me. 'Hey, you haven't got a spare can of petrol in the boot, have you? I got home on fumes.'

'Sorry, Kurt, not a drop,' I said truthfully and got into the car.

He remained standing just inside the lopsided gate. 'Typical,' he said hotly. 'Bloody typical. It's a *conspiracy*.'

FIVE

*T*here but for the grace of God – or perhaps Annis, was what I thought when I saw Hufnagel shrink to an angry blob in my rear-view mirror. If that was his usual frame of mind then I didn't envy his life model.

Annis was amazed. 'How on earth did he manage to persuade her to visit him on his island in the crud?'

'It's a mystery,' I concluded. 'It doesn't look like he has any money and he couldn't possibly have charmed her into it.'

'Must be blackmail then,' she said darkly and went back to her painting.

'Yes,' I agreed uncharitably. 'I wonder what he's got on her?'

The rest of the day I wandered about the place in a daze. *Teaching*. Teach them what? I had been working away on my own paintings for many years now and even though the next painter was never more than twenty feet away – and frequently a lot closer – I couldn't remember having discussed painting for ages. Painters never talk about their work. They talk about the price of paint, the rent for their studio and about sales, if any. In other words: money. I couldn't possibly tell the students what I thought of their actual prospects out there in the real world unless I wanted to send them headlong into depression. (*Bath Art Students in Mystery Suicide Pact.*) The last real talk about art I could remember was when after a few weeks' drawing in Corfu I announced that I was giving up abstract art for figurative painting. Annis had said it was like giving up composing symphonies for writing dance tunes and Simon Paris had promptly cancelled my autumn show at the gallery. Annis had since changed her mind and Simon had tentatively offered me a spring show but it meant I wasn't exactly brimming with confidence. While I moped around the mill pond, getting a damp bottom from sitting in the meadow and cobwebs in my hair from rummaging in the outbuildings, I gave it some thought and by the evening I had come up with a reasonable teaching strategy.

I was going to wing it.

By the next morning my enthusiasm for teaching art was at a very low ebb, if it had ever flowed at all. Elisabeth Kroog had made it sound like the easiest thing in the world, but then she had been doing little else since the beginning of time. *Write your own timetable*, she'd said. *Start when you've got over the shock of having a job to go to.* I piled an obscene amount of sticky rose petal conserve on top of a hunk of croissant. *Teaching*. What had I been thinking? I managed to manoeuvre the whole piece into my mouth without getting half of it all over me and the taste took me back to what now looked like the carefree days of a legendary spring in the hills of Corfu. I definitely hadn't got over the shock yet, so I'd be starting tomorrow at the earliest. Perhaps the day after, to be on the safe side.

I looked down at the list of exhibitors. I had ticked off myself and Hufnagel, which left the (allegedly) arrogant Landacker, a painter called Dawn Fowling and a sculptor called Rachel Eade. I wasn't in the mood for Landacker this early in the morning, and I never quite know what to say to sculptors (apart from 'Would you mind doing that outside, please?') so if I wanted to keep up the illusion that I was doing something useful it would have to be Fowling. Problem was there was no address, unless 'Bath' followed by a question mark now qualified. I sent Tim a text: could he find me an address for Dawn Fowling, probably in Bath? I had just managed to dispatch my second croissant when he called me back. Sticky-fingered I answered my mobile.

'You're up early,' he said. 'Welcome to the world of work.' Tim sounded disgustingly awake.

'Haven't started yet. Did you find her?'

'Yes, what's she done to deserve your attentions?'

'Taught at the art school once. On my list of exhibitors.'

'Ah yes, Annis told me. You're suddenly quite busy. Teaching, painting, exhibiting.'

'I'm glad there's no PI business at the moment.'

'There's none because you never answer your phone or check your messages. If it goes on like that people will cease to believe you're real.'

'I'm waiting for something interesting to come along. Can I have that address, do you think?'

'Sure. It's just around the corner from me. Dawn Fowling. Sounds like something you do early in the morning with a gun . . .'

'A fowling piece.'

The address turned out to belong to a block of council flats hidden between Julian Road and Lansdown. Fowling's name was sun-bleached into doubtfulness but I could just make it out as one of twelve on the battery of bell buttons. I rang, waited, rang again.

'Hello?' An incredulous voice from above. I abandoned the intercom and stepped back to look up. A tousle of blonde hair at a tiny third-floor window. I heard a very tired 'Yes?'

'Hi. I'm Chris Honeysett. Are you Dawn?' An underpowered moped with two kids on it prattled past. I wondered if I had been heard because the woman looked up and down the street before answering.

'Yeah, what of it?'

'It's about a show at Batcombe House. You know, the art school. You used to teach there.'

'I know.' She continued to stare down, perhaps thinking, perhaps going back to sleep. 'Erm, look, I'll come down.'

Good, because shouting up to the third floor was giving me a pain in the neck. I could not remember having met her but thought I remembered her work. If I was right, then Fowling was the creator of romantic abstractions that were based on cloud patterns in the skies above the British Isles. It allowed her to range through an enormous spectrum of colour, from slate grey to rosy pinks, or Payne's Grey to Geranium Lake if you care for that kind of language.

It seemed to take her forever to get downstairs, long enough for me to smoke half a cigarette, cough for a while, then finish the other half. Almost without noticing I had started smoking again, ever since I had accepted the offer of a cigarette by the side of Birtwhistle's crashed car.

When she tumbled out of the front door Dawn was apologetic. 'Sorry,' she croaked. 'Wasn't dressed yet.'

'Couldn't find a brush,' she might have added. She was either suffering from serious bed-head or female hair fashion had taken an unexpected turn. I suspected a monumental hangover was in progress. The clothes she had been able to find however were an agreeable jumble of paint-spattered jeans, washed-out checked shirt, tatty biker's jacket and purple Doc Martens. She gave me a not-too-unfriendly sideways look from tired blue eyes as she stomped past me down the road.

I fell into step. 'Where are we going?'

'Mangia Bene.'

My Italian had always been a bit shaky. 'Eat well?'

'Is that what it means? Deli around the corner. You speak Italian then?'

'Nah, don't have the time.'

I took a breath to start explaining why I was here but she stopped me with a spooky little gesture of her hand. 'Please. I'm no good before coffee.'

I thought she and Annis might get on well if they ever found themselves awake at the same time. We remained silent until two cappuccinos had been delivered to our little pavement table outside the deli in St James's Street. She took a sip, furtled a cigarette from my pack and lit it with a Zippo produced from her jacket. She exhaled smoke through her nose. 'OK, shoot.'

'Ex-tutors exhibiting their current work at the Bath Arts Academy. Thirtieth anniversary, apparently.'

'Are you an ex-tutor?'

'Ex and current again, though just until a new painting tutor can be found.'

This had a more invigorating effect on Dawn than the cappuccino; I now had her attention.

'When were you there?' I asked.

'Gosh. I left twelve years ago. I wasn't there for very long either. I was . . . seduced away. I wish I was still there; in retrospect it seems idyllic now, compared to what goes on at the big colleges.'

I thought I already knew where this story was heading. 'Is that where you went?'

She growled and nodded. 'The money was better and the other so-called benefits looked good.'

I nodded sagely. I kept quiet in the pause that was developing. I could hear the bitterness in her voice and thought Dawn could probably do with telling it just one more time.

'Within a year they fired us all and made us re-apply for our own jobs on completely insane terms. Short-term contracts, no holiday pay, term-time only and a huge cut in salary. The students didn't care, didn't even blink, the selfish little gits. I stuck it for two terms then got "replaced".'

'Did you ever try and go back to BAA?'

'I did talk to John. There wasn't an opening at the time. And he did say about having been disloyal and all that, and he was right. I was stupid. I made lots of stupid decisions round that time.'

'I have a portfolio of those,' I assured her.

'Your own or other people's? So, anyway, I wouldn't have thought Birtwhistle would be keen to have me there.'

'On the contrary, your name's at the top of the list.'

'Really? That's very decent of him, considering. And he sent you?'

'In a manner of speaking. I forgot to mention – John died. Last week, in a car crash.'

'I didn't know. Shame. He was a decent guy. Not quite of this world, even when he was alive.'

I wasn't quite so sure about John's otherworldliness. When he was alive, that was. 'I think he just didn't care for the way things were going, the direction art education was taking, and he created his own world around him. And even within that world he was happiest hiding in his print room with his smelly inks. But he did make time for his students. So perhaps he was a bit disappointed that you followed the money.'

Dawn nodded. 'I'm surprised he wanted me to exhibit there.'

'I was surprised to find myself on the list too, but he probably didn't choose us because he thought we were particularly nice people or good teachers, even. He chose us because of the kind of work we do. He was thinking of the students again, exposing them to the kind of art he thought they ought to look at. Not at people turning lights on and off in empty rooms or other lazy nonsense.' It appeared I had pressed a button there because Dawn reeled off a string of names, all prefixed with the same derogatory adjectives, of people who were currently making easy money from a gullible art world entranced by the emperor's new clothes. I was almost sorry I mentioned it. With difficulty I managed to change the subject. 'Is your studio near here?'

'You want to see it?' She stood up, ready to go. 'When did you last sell a painting?' she asked.

'In spring,' I admitted rashly.

'You win. You get to pay for the coffees.'

We didn't have far to go. Her studio was in fact a converted double garage in a nearby mews. The doors had been bricked up and faced with Bath stone so that it became nearly invisible.

'The entrance is through here.' She led me through a tiny gate by the side of a row of garages with painted wooden doors. Dawn's studio was the last one. A door had been set into the back wall which faced on to a tiny courtyard, separated from substantial town house gardens by a ten-foot wall. As she opened the door I could see that a long skylight had been fitted into the roof along one side. 'There's no toilet but that's never been a problem; there's a pub round the corner.' Apart from a paint-encrusted hostess trolley that held her palette, brushes and oils, and a small shelf unit crammed with paint tubes, every bit of space was taken up by paintings. Dawn Fowling had either been extremely busy or hadn't sold much for a while. I suspected a bit of both. There was no easel; she fixed her canvases to the wall via a wooden framework screwed into the brickwork. When I closed the door behind us the light seemed just right.

'A perfect little studio. Good lighting. I could work well in here. Does it have heating?'

'Don't get excited. I've been given two months' notice. They're turning it back into a garage.'

'What? Why?'

'So some sad git can keep the rain off his Porsche.'

'They must be mad.'

'Where have you been? They're going to get rid of the skylight and put the doors back in and turn it into a lucrative black hole. The rent is going up by five hundred per cent. They already advertised and got over a hundred replies.'

'What are you going to do?'

'No idea,' she said bleakly. 'I looked but there's hardly anything and what there is I can't afford.'

Not for the first time I counted my blessings. Dawn agreed to produce a painting and sketchbook for the anniversary exhibition. I in turn promised to get in touch with the details and to keep an ear open for any affordable studio spaces.

I had returned to the car fully intending to drive home, perhaps pick up some food on the way and, at most, do a bit of drawing, but a vague yet strangely familiar feeling had started nagging at me. After a while I did recognize it from my school days. It was the 'uncompleted homework' feeling. I started the engine and drove out to Batcombe.

Apart from meal times, when students and tutors emerged from wherever they had been lurking to make their way down to the basement refectory, the Bath Arts Academy, despite being a hive of creative activity, could be very quiet and at times feel almost deserted. Batcombe House and the grounds were large enough to swallow all of the students and tutors. On cool, cloudy days like today when rain was threatening, there was not a soul to be seen outside and only the odd student could be heard walking from A to B.

I could hear a voice from the office door, which was ajar as usual. I knocked and went in. Claire was behind her desk on the phone, nodding at me and feeding *ahas* and *yesses* into the receiver. She pointed at a chair, presumably as an invitation to sit, but it was piled high with files and I declined.

'The funeral has been postponed,' she said after she had hung up. 'That was Anne. She didn't say why but she sounded furious.'

'Has the body not been released?' Out of habit my criminal mind immediately imagined dark findings at the post-mortem.

'No, it has, it has. His daughter made it sound as though the postponement was somehow poor John's fault, but she didn't elaborate.'

'Stressful time for her,' I murmured inanely and changed the subject. 'I contacted two of the would-be exhibitors and they both agreed.'

'That's marvellous. Who agreed?'

'Fowling and Hufnagel.'

'Excellent. But do have a go at Landacker.'

'I will.'

'I can't tell you how much I appreciate you doing this. Anne has just about tripled my workload. She wants a complete over-haul of everything, a complete inventory, all the files up to date, everything ready for her inspection at a moment's notice. She thinks of herself as a new broom, I believe.' Claire pushed her glasses disapprovingly up her nose.

'I don't know her at all. I didn't even know John had a daughter. She's not an artist herself?'

'Ha!' I had scored a direct hit on a sore spot. 'Anne Birtwhistle wouldn't recognize a work of art if it fell on her. Which is entirely possible in a place like this. No, she's an estate agent. Or works *for* an estate agent,' she said pointedly.

'I'm glad you two hit it off so well. It appears that quite apart from helping with this exhibition I'm now also the relief painting tutor.'

'Told you,' she said.

'Can I see the timetable?'

'It's behind you,' Claire said, panto style. Beside the door was a wall chart of the term, divided into weeks and days and morn-ings and afternoons, which listed in inch-square boxes the times of 'student – tutor contact' (what used to be called teaching) for all subjects. 'Just look for Paul and substitute Chris and you have it,' Claire said. I studied it with foreboding but found that it was unlikely that Paul had deserted his post because of the excessive workload. Formal teaching, in the form of lectures, happened once a week. All students had a tutorial once a month, and I had two tutorial afternoons a week. Otherwise my twenty-five painting students would be working on the projects I was planning to set them as well as doing their own work and it was up to me to chase after them and find them wherever they were painting or drawing. Nothing had changed there, neither had the system that set it very much apart from other art schools. At the BAA there were no divisions between the 'years'. It was a three-year course but all were taught together and picked what lectures and projects they wanted since there were no exams and no grades awarded. Under John Birtwhistle the system had become so lax that one student had stayed for six years before anyone noticed. She was later successfully released back into the wild.

I was still trying to find a scrap of paper to copy down my 'contact' times when Lizzie Kroog pushed through the door. She wore her trademark brown leather waistcoat, the only kind of garment that didn't regularly catch fire from welding sparks and from pocketing her smouldering pipe. 'Saw your car, Honeysett. Leave that for the moment; no one takes much notice of the timetable anyway. Come on, I'll introduce you to your students and to the rest of the staff if we can find anyone.' She grabbed me by the sleeve and pulled me away. Stealing a look over my shoulder, I could see that Claire was smiling happily as she went back to her paperwork.

Kroog marched me straight over to Studio Two. The large and airy studio – in long-forgotten times a well-proportioned withdrawing room – was large enough for more than a dozen painters to work in, either on radial easels or with their canvases fixed to the wall. The rest of the students were either working outside or had found space somewhere else in the building. Only about ten students were there. They had all turned towards us. Kroog always somehow managed to get attention long before she opened her mouth. 'Let me introduce you to your new painting tutor, Chris Honeysett. I know he sounds sweet but don't expect him to be as wet as your last tutor. Chris has taught here before so I know he is a bit of a slave driver and a workaholic and expects you all to pull your finger out.' They all stared at me as though I had three sixes tattooed on my forehead. I widened my eyes at Kroog but she managed to step firmly on my toes under the pretence of looking around all their faces. 'Projects will be handed in complete, essays on time and attendance will be one hundred per cent or Honeysett here will come down on you like the proverbial. You might want to pass the message on: your holidays are truly over.' Kroog turned and swept out again.

'As you were,' I said and followed in her wake down the corridor. I caught up with her at the next door. 'Was that kind of intro really necessary?'

'Of course it was. They've been half asleep since Paul left. They were nodding off even while he was still here. I expect you to introduce some drama into their lives. Right, drawing,' she said with her hand on the battered doorknob. 'You realize you're teaching that too, of course. General drawing and life drawing.' She ushered me into the Small Studio, which was mainly used for drawing of all kinds. Small was a relative term, however. Fifteen artists could easily draw in here at the same time. Among the groves of easels and nests of drawing boards were just three students grouped around a female life model. She had her ash-blonde hair held in a short ponytail and sat posed on a spartan chair.

'Your new drawing tutor,' Kroog introduced me. 'The life model is Petronela, who is from Poland and who I hope is getting enough breaks,' she said, looking reprovingly at the students. She then told me their names, which I immediately forgot again, but I recognized the types: fanatics. Fanatical about drawing, especially from nature. All three of them had faces streaked with charcoal and wore black clothes from head to toe, but judging from the thickness of charcoal dust around their feet those could have been any colour before they started. We'd get on just fine.

'Actually would be nice to make break now,' said Petronela and stretched. 'I am thinking my leg is making thrombosis and I need cigarette urgent now.'

'Half an hour maximum without a break,' I told them. 'You,' I pointed randomly at one of the students, a thin chap with glasses, 'are in charge of time keeping.' It appeared I had finally started work.

We exited through the French doors and I followed my guide through a fine rain into the ceramics department via the conservatory. Several students were about, including the pottering girl I had met when I first arrived. Kroog turned to her. 'Abbi, is Dan about?' The girl just pointed at the ground. 'Downstairs,' Kroog said to me. 'Follow me into the bowels of the bat cave.' Down a steep flight of stone steps we descended into the basement. It smelled damp, wet even, and clay seemed to have seeped into the fabric of everything down here, floor to ceiling. Only the odd bare low-wattage bulb was dangling from the ceiling here and there, providing minimal lighting. Kroog found what she was looking for in a shady room lined with slatted wooden shelves crammed with every type of unfired clay object. The quite unnecessary sign on the door said *Damp Room.*

'Chris, meet Dan Small, the ceramics tutor.' Dan Small was anything but what his name suggested. He had a physique that lent itself well to humping huge bags of clay about. His large hands were caked with the stuff, his hair and facial stubble sand-coloured and his eyes a watery blue. 'This is Chris, who's taking over from the treacherous Paul.'

'Welcome aboard.' He wiped a hand on his blue overall before he allowed me to shake it. 'Yes, fancy wanting to give up all this to teach under a cloudless sky. And for a mere three hundred per cent pay rise.'

'It does rain in Queensland too, you know,' said Kroog. 'But it comes all in one lump. Do you mind giving a talk to my sculptors again sometime this term, Dan? Remind them that there is such a thing as ceramic sculpture.'

'Sure, I'll dust off last year's lecture notes.'

'Don't you dare. Find something new to say. Whatever you told them last year didn't work.' Kroog led me out along a corridor where a student was lifting slabs of grey clay into a dumb waiter. 'Handy, those things. They had the kitchens down here originally. Dan's a good man, likes to get his hands dirty and get right in there. In stark contrast to the next and last inmate I'll introduce you to.' When we regained ground level we found ourselves in the east wing and our feet echoed past the stairs to the refectory until we came to a half-glazed modern door. 'Graphics,' was Kroog's terse explanation. She walked right in. In one long room sat a few students, mostly staring at computer screens. 'Stott about?' she asked the room.

'Printmaking, I think,' said the closest student, the only one who wasn't wearing earphones and had therefore heard the question. He was very smartly dressed and had a fashionable haircut. His desk was strewn with gleaming gadgetry. I took one look at him and knew I could chase him screaming around the house with a single stick of charcoal.

'Upstairs then,' Kroog said and swept out of the room again. Up a set of back stairs the tour continued. 'Stottie has been volunteered to take on the print department as well, now that John has gone to the big print room in the sky.' She pushed through a set of double doors into a room with two enormous printing presses, several very long tables and endless wooden cupboards and plan chests. A woman wearing spotless vinyl gloves and a brand new blue cotton apron stood in front of an open cupboard, staring inside. 'Catherine, I want you to meet Chris Honeysett, the new painting tutor. Chris, Catherine Stott, graphic design and now printmaking.'

The woman looked at me without much interest. Catherine was in her early forties, had fine dark hair, cut at a slant and ending in two points on either side of her face. Her ears supported large, modern silver and rose quartz earrings and a matching inch-wide band of silver encircled her neck. 'I won't shake hands,' she said, holding up her vinyl-gloved hands. 'It took me ages to wriggle into these.'

'Where are all your students?' Kroog asked her.

'I set them an essay so they're out of my hair until I find my way around this chaos. Nothing is where you'd expect it to be in this place; it'll take me ages to put it in some kind of order. I don't know how John managed to find anything.'

'Just ask your students, I'm sure they can tell you where everything is.'

Stott gave her a distasteful look. Kroog left her standing there miserably and walked slowly across the room, running a finger over a polished wooden handle on an old-fashioned printing press that looked like it might literally weigh a ton. 'It's a miracle they haven't fallen through the floor yet,' she said thoughtfully. 'When they do they'll wipe out the entire graphics department.' Then she let her eyes travel across the room as though she might never see it again.

'Don't mind Stottie,' she said when we were on our way back down. 'Bit of a dry stick. She never expected she'd be having to get her hands dirty again at her age. I remember her portfolio, she was very good at printmaking but got seduced by the dark arts and disappeared into her computer. Must be a shock to the system, having to use real colour again.' Kroog cackled happily and pulled out her pipe. 'That concludes the tour. The staff room

is where it always was and not even the sofas have changed.'
We were heading towards it when we could hear a voice echoing
down the corridor that I recognized as Anne Birtwhistle's.
'Through here,' Kroog said and abruptly pulled me into an empty
study room. She closed the door behind us, opened the sash
window, climbed through it into the garden and marched away.
'Come *on*, coffee at my place.'

We made our way through the fine drizzle across the gardens,
passing some truly outlandish student sculptures on the way. A
few of them were worked in stone but the majority of it was
welded rusting metal or enormous wood sculptures that stood
like patient giants in the rain. One appeared to be a machine that
looked like a ten-foot tall, eight-legged metal spider full of electric
motors and trailing wires.

Now my place is messy. Did I mention that? I admit Mill
House is a bit of a tip. Much that should be in the studio migrates
down to the house: small paintings, drawings, sketchbooks, rolls
of paper, that sort of thing. But this was something else. Kroog
walked straight in, the door apparently unlocked. I had never
been inside 'The Bothy', as this six-bedroomed nineteenth-
century house was so wittily called. It really consisted of two
substantial cottages knocked together and it would more truthfully have been named 'The Warren'. I presumed Kroog had
lived here for the last thirty years since it would have taken at
least that long to create this richness of clutter and chaos. The
front door led straight into a large sitting room. The two cottages
had not been completely knocked through but were connected
by doors upstairs and down. Standing as they were on the wooded
slope that ran all the way down to Fiddler's Pond meant that
three steps led down from one front room to the next, with a
similar arrangement on the floor above. Dark and narrow wooden
stairs led to the first floor from each end of the double sitting
room. The windows were small and almost completely blocked
by overgrown shrubs on the outside, magazines, books and
typescripts on the inside, casting the interior into perpetual
gloom. What at first I had taken for a person standing in the
shadows turned out to be a dressmaker's dummy wearing an
embroidered kimono and a straw hat. Between towering piles
of books, magazines and newspapers stood five-foot-tall rolls
of drawing paper, bundles of files and countless balls of

scrunched-up paper. Artworks stood, hung and leant everywhere, some finished, some perhaps abandoned or in progress, though most of them were in the form of maquettes, small-scale essays, some of which I recognized to be the forerunners of their life-size cousins on the lawns. Ashtrays were conveniently placed at three-foot intervals; the ceiling between the beams had gone beyond nicotine yellow towards burnt umber. Apart from one moth-eaten chair in front of a cluttered desk, all furniture designed for sitting on – sofa, chaise longue, armchairs – were piled high with *stuff*.

Kroog disappeared through a narrow doorway into an unevenly stone-flagged corridor, the flags worn concave by the centuries. 'Come through to the kitchen; you may find it less challenging,' she said before launching into a rumbling cough.

She was right. The kitchen was rustic, with a solid scrubbed oak table and an enormous stoneware sink full of piles of unwashed pots and dishes, but there were chairs to sit on and the table was empty apart from an ashtray and a lidded jar in the centre. Kroog set the kettle on to a Rayburn that made my own at home look positively space age.

I declined the offer but Kroog poured a measure of brandy into her own coffee, then filled her pipe from the jar on the table and lit up. I lit a cigarette for myself and for a short while we just sat there wreathed in unfashionable smoke.

'John's sudden death must have been quite a shock for you,' I suggested. 'You've known him, what, thirty years at least?' She nodded. 'You were close, I expect.'

Kroog leant back in her chair and narrowed her eyes. 'Very close for a while, after his wife died. That seems a long time ago now. I think we both thought of each other as fixtures and fittings at Batcombe. John barely left the place in thirty years, certainly never took a holiday. Lived in it, worked in it, lived *for* it. At least I usually have a hundred and fifty yards distance from the place.' She nodded the back of her head in the direction of the 'big house'; the kitchen windows looked grimly the other way, towards the wood and the pond. 'And just recently I thought John was getting just a touch too . . .' For a rare moment she seemed lost for words. 'Perhaps he was getting a bit confused, but he kept saying the place had become strange.'

'In what way?'

'I hardly dare say it; you'd think he'd gone senile. I'm not so sure he hadn't. He said he could feel *something evil at the house.* When I asked him what the hell he meant by that he said it was a feeling he had. As though the place was haunted. He said something was stalking the corridors at night. There are sixty-five prank-filled students and no locks on the windows and he thinks something is stalking the corridors? They've always managed to climb in somehow to start mischief. So I laughed at him. I said it was probably just Stottie's desiccated spirit looking for nourishment, but he was serious. Something spooked him. In a house where he knew every ceiling crack and floorboard! And he insisted that someone had come into his rooms at night and gone through his things. I think that's another reason why he wanted you here, because of the private-eye thing. He wanted you to keep an eye out for anything strange.'

'So that's how I ended up on the list of exhibitors,' I said, a little miffed now.

'No, that's not why. But that's how you ended up at the top of the list.'

I now realized what had been a little odd about the list: it was alphabetical, except for my name at the top of it. 'But you have no reason to believe there really is anything strange going on?'

'Strange? *Here?*' We shared a smile, then Kroog turned serious again. 'I don't know. Strange things have always happened at Batcombe House. It's an art college, not a school of accountancy. We've had a fox trying to get into the kitchens last week. We've had sheep wandering around on the first floor. Stottie had her tyres let down one day, then slashed the next. Not very nice, but hardly the work of an evil presence. She just annoys people, always has. I have felt pretty haunted myself since John died. I spent the first forty-eight hours drunk, I'm afraid.' Her pipe had gone out and she re-lit it. I reached for another cigarette from my pack. Kroog looked at me, then leant in towards me as though she had suddenly thought of something. 'Only complete idiots still smoke, you know that, don't you?'

SIX

'Shouldn't you be at school?' Annis, incredibly, had not only woken up before me but had got up, showered, gone downstairs, made breakfast and plonked some on a tray for me while I was still asleep having teaching nightmares. In my dream I had given a PowerPoint presentation at BAA where all images turned out to be pictures of me, aged four, playing naked on a beach in Devon. I was uncharacteristically glad to be woken up.

'I'm pacing myself. Don't want to overwhelm the students. What's this?' I surveyed the breakfast offering.

'Hot waffles, blueberries, crème fraiche and maple syrup.'

'You're getting the hang of this breakfast lark.'

'Tim likes it. I thought it might work on you, too.'

'You're now testing everything out on Tim first, is that it?' What else was she trying out on him first?

'Yes,' she said, getting up from the bed and making for the door. 'It's safer because he's more grateful when I do.'

'I'm grateful!' I called after her, probably a bit late. 'Truly thankful,' I added and fell on my waffles.

I had decided to have another stab at the exhibition list. Once I knew who was showing, when, where and what, I'd feel more settled and would bestow my decades of painting experience on the BAA students in unthreatening, easy-to-digest lumps, first making sure I had loaded the right images for my slide show. There were two more artists on the list who might agree to show and one of them could turn out to be the trickiest. He didn't give out his phone number to mortals, had a website but no friendly 'contact me' button and his address was no more precise than Hufnagel's. Landacker lived at 'The Old Forge, Motterton'.

Motterton was a one-eyed Cotswold village not all that far from Batcombe. As I drove through villages and hamlets on my way there I noticed that here most things were 'old': The Old Mill, The Old Vicarage, The Old School House, The Old Post Office, all closed down and converted. How long, I wondered, before people were living in The Old Pub, The Old Church, The

Old Phone Box? Conspicuous by their absence were The New
Pub, The New School House, The New Post Office.

Landacker had done well for himself if he could afford to live
around here. In fact I knew he had done well, keeping a jealous
eye on one's fellow painters' careers being a favourite pastime.
Landacker had given up teaching after a dramatic shift in his
painting had produced a sell-out show that had established him
at one stroke as one of the more collectable painters outside
London. Since then he had had several, usually long-awaited and
successful shows, some of which practically sold out even before
the private view. He rarely even turned up to his own private
views, which made me doubt that I might persuade him to come
and contribute to the Batcombe exhibition. Yet his painting
persona as a mysterious and intriguing recluse had to be pure
fabrication. I had met him years ago, before his work had taken
off, at some do at the Holburne Museum, and he had struck me
as a normal, slightly boring and even fusty guy who was perfectly
able to hold a conversation after a couple of glasses of red. Of
course anyone could have a sudden brainwave that transformed
one's work but no one became suddenly enigmatic and
interesting.

When I got to Motterton I made the mistake of trying simply
to drive around until I might spot the house, always assuming it
was happy to advertise its name. But the lanes were narrow and
after being forced to turn around for the second time I did the
sensible thing and asked directions – at The Old Post Office, as
it happened. A young woman opened the door and told me to
keep going to the bottom of the winding lane until it joined the
stream. The Old Forge would be on my left. 'You can't miss it,'
she said, not having met me before.

As it turned out I had driven past it once already, probably
because the house was so far removed from my naive idea of
what a forge looked like, an idea that had been formed by a
surfeit of black-and-white westerns in my childhood. Now I
remembered that smiths, along with millers, used to be important
people in the village economy. The Old Forge turned out to be
a large house made to look even more substantial by being
completely surrounded by a freestone wall that looked the part
but was almost certainly a modern addition. It sported a double
wooden gate wide enough to admit a Waitrose delivery van and

it was wide open. On the generous teardrop-shaped drive stood a silver BMW. The driver door was open. Next to it slumped a 'bag-for-life' supermarket carrier that had disgorged some of its content on to the ground. I left my own car in front of the gate and walked up the drive.

The house was a squat and solid two-storey building with a massive converted barn right next to it. From the pointed end of the teardrop drive, dark hardwood steps led up to a wrap-around terrace. The converted barn, if Landacker had any sense at all, housed his painting studio and probably had north-facing skylights on the other side. On this side it only had one high window and a half-glazed door with its glass smashed through. It was ajar. I briefly paused by the shopping bag; French butter, Parma ham and a mango had slid to the ground, while strawberries, lamb chops and cartons of cream remained safe in the bag.

I am not one of those unfortunate private eyes who keeps stumbling over dead bodies, but even once is enough to make one forever a little sensitive to this kind of still life, which the French so fittingly call *nature morte*. So far it looked very much like Landacker had arrived in his Beemer (3-series, nothing special, I'm told), dropped his shopping when he spotted that his studio door had been mutilated and rushed in to investigate. It was only natural that I should follow him inside so I could catch a glimpse of the man's work in progress. Picking my way gingerly across the vestibule strewn with broken glass and past the house brick that had presumably been used to break it brought me straight into the inner sanctum. 'Hello?' I had been unprepared for the sight that greeted me.

Our studio at Mill House being a wholly *unconverted* barn, my imagination had badly let me down when it came to envisaging what one might do to a barn with a few spare quid. Especially a few ten-thousand spare quid. A spiral staircase to a balustraded mezzanine hadn't featured. Hardwood floors and Persian rugs had been completely missing. Conspicuously absent had been two leather sofas facing each other across a glass coffee table. On the table sat a modern glass ashtray, a heavy silver cigarette lighter and a glass container full of hundred-millimetre cigarettes. I slid one out and lit it to steady my nerves for the rest of the tour. The most studio-like part was at the far end where there was a rosewood studio easel with brass crank, perfectly lit by the north-facing skylights and by a bank of adjustable daylight lamps. It held a large canvas that by the looks of it had just been started, next to a custom-built painting table on castors full of expensive French oil paints. Further back, on another table, sat some kind of projector, scanner, printer and an Apple computer.

'Hello?' I climbed the cast-iron spiral staircase to a gallery that was one third of the width of the floor below. From up here, close to the ceiling beams and skylights, the place looked even more impressive. Apart from a writing desk and an armchair, the gallery housed several bookshelves crammed with coffee-table art books, journals, files and some bronze nick-nacks. At the back of the gallery was a shiny black door with a Yale lock but no door handle. I walked up to it and listened for a moment, then I knocked tentatively but got no answer. Ah, well, I'd try the house then. I clattered back down the spiral staircase and ran smack into a podgy fist that smashed straight into the side of my face.

'Ow, you *bastard*!' howled Landacker, cradling his fist in his other hand and sinking at the knees in pain.

I was pretty busy being in pain myself so I went easy on the sympathy and stood well back. He'd missed my nose but I just knew I would have a spectacular black eye tomorrow. 'Landacker, you moron, it wasn't me who broke in here!'

He nodded. 'I didn't think so. Too nonchalant. Who the hell are you and what's the idea of just wandering in here?'

'Honeysett. Chris Honeysett.'

'The painting detective? Lord have mercy,' he said, still wincing.

'We met once, quite a while ago.'

'Really?' He looked me up and down and shook his head. 'I don't recall. Heard of you, obviously. A chameleon, wasn't it?'

'Iguana.'

'Ah yes, called Knut. I read about it. Quite a story.'

Greg Landacker had put on a bit of weight since I'd last seen him – hadn't we all? – and had gone greyer. He had small ears and a narrow nose which seemed to overemphasize the few pounds he'd gained. But he was immaculately turned out in brogues, designer jeans and shirt and wore a hefty gold signet ring on his right hand. The one he'd thumped me with. 'I'd appreciate some ice,' I said, still holding my face, which already felt like it was swelling up. I was glad his swing had missed my nose and teeth.

'Yes, me too, actually,' he admitted, wriggling his fingers experimentally. 'I never hit anyone before. You have a hard nut.'

'I think I should warn you, they're all like that.'

'Let's go in the house; I'll find some ice and you can tell me what the hell you're doing going through my studio.'

Like a complete idiot I even helped him pick up his shopping from where it had spilled: he was probably the most important artist on my list, he had just had his studio broken into and had simply overreacted, I told myself.

It didn't work. If I hadn't been desperately keen on Landacker at our first meeting, just seeing his studio had put me in a bad mood. Its antiseptic affluence had put my back up the moment I crunched inside. What kind of painter had Persian rugs in a painting studio, and right by the entrance, too, making it the first thing you'd notice? A painter who needed to impress people. Or perhaps wanted to impress himself.

I was relieved when I found I disliked his house as much as the man. His studio had made me green with envy but what the architect had done to the forge didn't make me want to live here. The interior had been trashed, walls removed and features obliterated with designs that would have been more appropriate in a newly built house. There were glass doors everywhere, a large, space-age kitchen that made me shiver with cold and a lot of 1990s chic that, predictably, now looked dated. To the left of the entrance and running the length of the house was another gallery but this time made entirely of glass. Even the stairs leading up to it had glass treads, etched with a swirling design, and rails made from glass or other see-through materials. There was a large Landacker canvas over what had once been a fireplace but was now full of candles and ornaments; enormous hi-fi speakers towered either side of it and uncomfortable-looking chrome and leather armchairs stood facing them. I just knew they would squeak if you tried to sit on them. In the futuristic kitchen, Landacker dropped his shopping on the table and then sluiced cold water over his hand at a Belfast sink.

'Ah, yes, ice for you. Just as well this makes crushed ice, isn't it?' His enormous American two-door fridge dispensed iced water

as well as crushed ice on the outside of the left door. He filled
a freezer bag with ice and handed it to me, then started putting
his shopping away.

'Was anything stolen?' I asked.

'No,' he said firmly.

'Nothing at all?'

'Not a thing.'

'Strange. Plenty of valuable stuff there for a burglar. You must
have surprised them when you came back. Didn't see anyone?'

'No one. I checked the studio, then checked in here. They
didn't try and get into the house. Too many alarms, I guess.'

'And your studio isn't alarmed? Why?'

'Never got around to it. It was finished long after I'd finished
the house.'

'Called the police?'

'No, what's the point? All I'll get is a lecture. I think it was
actually 1983 when they last caught a burglar and got someone's
stuff back.' He poured a couple of punnets of strawberries into
a glass bowl and set it on to the polished black kitchen table. It
looked good there. 'I called the glazier and locksmith – they
damaged the lock before they decided to go through the window.
Right, now tell me in three short sentences what you want.'

'I've come with a request. It is an invitation from beyond the
grave. Which means you'll find it hard to turn it down.'

'And did he?' Annis asked later.

'Did he what?'

'Find it hard to turn it down?'

'He did indeed. I think the thought tickled him straight away.
And he went all nostalgic about Batcombe House.'

'Fancy that.'

'As soon as I mentioned it he went and made tea, in a glass
teapot of course, which I had to drink at a very chilly kitchen
table from a glass cup. How he persuades water to boil in that
place is a mystery. He actually said he owed a lot to BAA, and
by extension to John. So he agreed to contribute.'

'Excellent. Just one more to go.'

'He did go a bit weird when I said John insisted on there being
a sketchbook to accompany the finished work. He tried to get
all mysterious and "oh, I never let people see" etcetera until he

remembered that I was a fellow painter and wasn't going to fall for it.'

'You didn't like him much, then,' Annis concluded.

'He hit me!'

'A natural impulse. But apart from that,' she said and pretended to wring another drop of wine out of the bottle we had emptied over supper.

I leant back and pulled another one from the wine rack under the kitchen counter. 'He's too . . . antiseptic. No painter should live like that.'

'Like what? With money to spend?'

'All that architect-designed opulence. Walk-in smegging fridge. Häagen and Dazs hi-fi. It's not natural.'

'But I bet he doesn't start hyperventilating every time a gas bill lands on his hall table.'

I poured more wine. 'I'll open it tomorrow,' I said. 'I promise. I've got a job now.'

Starting a new job with a multicoloured shiner was embarrassing. The next morning Annis rummaged among our large and interesting collection of out-of-date medicines, yellowing bandages and curled-up plasters and found me a black eye patch that covered nearly all of the affected area. I slipped it on and asked her if she thought I now looked rakishly piratical but she was too busy laughing to answer the question. I didn't get far in the car with the patch on. How did one-eyed people drive? I nearly rear-ended the first car I came across. I only slipped it back on when I turned off the engine in the Batcombe House car park, hoping that, if not rakish, the eye patch would look more dignified than the display of a black eye. If anyone asked me I'd just shrug it off as some minor accident.

Kroog was the first person I encountered. She was standing in the entrance as though waiting for me, with a saucer-less cup of coffee in one hand and her long pipe in the other. Next to her stood one of her acolytes, a young sculpture student called Alexandra who emulated Kroog's style of dress and smoked fat roll-ups made with brown liquorice paper. 'I'll see you at the house later, Alex,' Kroog said to her and Alex disappeared without a word. 'What happened to you?' Kroog asked me.

'Landacker. The bastard hit me the moment he saw me!' There was no point lying to Kroog; she'd never accept polite gloss as an answer.

'Was that before or after you asked him to exhibit?'

'It was before I had a chance to say who I was.'

'Did he stop hitting you when you did?'

I told her about my encounter and what followed. I didn't hide my envy of Landacker's financial success nor my disdain for his taste.

'Yes,' Kroog said, knocking her pipe out against the heel of her work boots. 'Greg always was quite conventionally minded. Which makes the direction his painting took all the more baffling. It has an edge that I could never find in the man himself. Mind you, look at Matisse, what an innovator, but you couldn't have found a man more bourgeois. Do you think he was shagging his secretary?'

'Matisse? I hope so.'

'But bourgeois or no I'm glad Greg has agreed to contribute. You did tell him that it has to be a new painting, done especially for the show and all that?' I nodded. 'All right, good. Have you given some thought as to what you'll be doing with your students?'

'I was just on my way to inflict myself and my ideas upon their cosy existence,' I said, nodding my head at the glass entrance door.

'Good, that's what I hoped you might say. Let's approach them from the garden,' she added. 'They won't expect an attack from there.'

As she pulled me away I could see through the glass behind Kroog that Anne Birtwhistle had appeared in the hall. Perhaps Kroog had seen a reflection in the half-open door or else she had eyes at the back of her head. 'I get the distinct impression that you are avoiding John's daughter.'

'And I suggest you do the same. It's hard to believe she sprung from John's loins. She doesn't have one artistic bone in her body. She's only been here a few days and people have already started calling her the Dementor because she manages to suck all the happiness out of you if you let her talk to you. I fear she may be a bean counter.'

'I expect there must be a lot of those to count in a place like this.'

We had walked along the west side of the house and reached the doors of the studio. 'It always depends what kind of beans you're counting. There are many types. Well, good luck in there. Give them hell, they're half asleep. Oh, erm, here.' She thrust the empty cup in my hand. 'Drop that back at the canteen for me, will you?' Then she looked left and right like a burglar climbing from a window and walked quickly towards the sculpture sheds, using the various sculptures on the lawn to give her cover across the open ground.

Since I'd already been introduced to many of them, the majority of students turned expectantly towards me as I slipped inside. I told them to keep on working while I had a look around to see them individually and I would talk to them collectively once I had an idea what they were all doing.

Looking at other people's paintings and listening to their ideas sounds like a pleasant way to spend a day, but it is surprisingly hard work. These were students, not fellow artists, which meant that by extension all their problems now became my problems. The students who have the biggest problems are usually the ones who don't know they have problems. This group was as mixed a bunch as you could wish for; male and female, British and overseas, enthusiastic and blasé, of average talent or superbly gifted, organized or sloppy, prolific or sleepy and various combinations of the above. I was glad to note that there was no 'school of Batford House', no house style that so often lays waste to students' talents as they try to conform or please an admired tutor. I tried to remember the persona that Kroog had tried to build up for me; she had apparently spread rumours that I was a fierce critic and a slave driver possessed by a strict work ethic and would brook no nonsense when it came to handing in projects or essays, arriving late for tutorials or other slack behaviour. As I made my way around the studio I noticed that my arrival had indeed a certain electrifying effect on most students. One of the painters I recognized as the skinny bespectacled charcoal-obsessed draughtsman from the life-drawing session. He was in fact working on a painting of Petronela, posed nude in a drab and dimly lit environment. His name was Ben Creeling. Being useless at matching names to faces I drew a pair of spectacles next to his name on my list. Everything about Ben was dark, and that included his eyes and hair, his charcoal-rimmed finger-nails and his painting. He was serious, humourless and apparently spent all his waking hours painting and drawing. He was also very good at it. 'I am trying to strip away all that is incidental and unnecessary from my drawing and painting so I can reveal the truth about my subjects,' he told me in an urgent voice while fiddling with a paper knife.

Always having been nervous around people who proclaimed to have seen the truth while fingering knives, I managed to make him admit that it was a very subjective truth and might benefit from the odd reality check. What I didn't tell him was that as far as I could see the truth about Petronela as he depicted it in his painting was that she was very bored with sitting on a hard chair.

After chatting to a number of students about their painting, some good, some average, I found another painter who stood out, in more ways than one: Hiroshi Takeyama. I would have no problem matching his face to the name. Japanese, six foot tall and with a carefully groomed triangular beard and a long ponytail, he stood in front of his enigmatic painting like a magus and pointed his paintbrush at me like a wizard's wand, perhaps hoping to make the intruder disappear. His painting was of a forest scene, eight foot tall and nearly as wide, and contained both vague mists and close details of forest flora – trees, leaves, roots. Hiroshi spoke good English with a pleasant accent and with a precision that was also present in some of his brushwork.

'Where is this forest?' I asked.

'It is Summerlee Wood, right at the centre of it.' He pointed his brush at the window in the direction of the trees. 'I always work from real subjects.'

'Did you paint this out there?'

'No,' he admitted, 'but I took these out there.' He handed me a bulging sketchbook full of six by four photos of forest scenes, details of twigs, leaves and of forest floor. 'I take reality and then improve on it in my painting,' he said modestly.

'And once you have done that we'll see if we can improve your painting,' I said mildly.

When I had finished making my round of the studio I still had a small number of students to visit who were either painting *en plein air* (sometimes also called 'outside') or who had found nooks and crannies elsewhere in Batcombe House where they could avoid the distractions of a shared work space and perhaps hope to escape the attentions of one-eyed tutors, reputedly possessed of a fierce work ethic. I still knew my way around and had soon winkled out most of those in the house: in a small room near the print department on the first floor, under a skylight in the tiny library and other odd corners and one in a forgotten but bright bathroom on a landing.

The last spot I visited was at the end of a rarely visited corridor where an oriel window with lead lights provided an interestingly lit work area for a girl with pale grey eyes, short hair dyed in red and gold stripes, and aggressive flowery perfume. She wore a boiler suit and walking boots and didn't look up from her painting until I was close enough to decide that she had dowsed herself in jasmine.

'You're Mr Honeysett,' she said. 'I went to one of your shows.'

'Yes, I'm Chris,' I said.

'I'm Phoebe.'

I found her on my list: Phoebe Snow. I sketched a tiny oriol next to her name as a map reference.

'I really like your work,' she said. 'I'm not just saying that.'

'Thanks. I'm afraid I've gone figurative,' I confessed.

'Really?' Her paintings were joyful and confused abstracts that tried to make up for what they lacked in structure by exuberance and brightness. A quick trawl through the painters whose work she rated, now that I had turned traitor, revealed that she was a great fan of Greg Landacker's. She even had a couple of postcards of his paintings tacked to the wall.

'Landacker will come and contribute a painting to the anniversary exhibition; I spoke to him yesterday,' I confided, though didn't mention that he gave me a black eye.

'Brilliant. I know he used to teach here, shame he's not any more,' she said, pulling a sad face.

Thus put firmly in my place, I decided I had seen enough of students for one day. There was still one exhibitor to find, the ex-tutor and sculptor Rachel Eade. I had googled her and found very little – a few things shown at art centres around the country, though nothing current or recent.

Kroog and I arrived at the same time in the refectory and shared a table again. '*She*'s on the list?' she asked when I mentioned where I was going next. Kroog was so unbelieving, she demanded to see it. 'Rachel Eade taught here when I was in hospital having this and that removed and as I convalesced I had to watch helplessly from my window as she filled the heads of my students with rubbish. I can't believe John wanted her to show here,' she fumed.

I gathered that Eade came from a rival school of sculptural thought. 'She's there in black and white,' I insisted.

Kroog grunted dismissively. 'Let's hope she's too busy dreaming up conceptual crap to attend. What did you think of the current crop of painters?'

'I haven't seen all of them yet but mostly above average, with a few exceptions.'

'Did you meet Roshi?'

'Hiroshi? Japanese?'

'The others call him Roshi, for short. He's one to watch, I think, in more ways than one. The other one with real talent is Ben Something-or-other. He's quite obsessive though and needs to loosen up. Paul worried about him. The last thing we want is another student having a breakdown.'

'Yes, not exactly a barrel of laughs, but he has talent.'

'Never stops drawing. Last year he used enough charcoal to roast an ox over. Probably needs a girlfriend.'

The refectory had filled up with students and tutors. Behind Kroog I could see that Claire, the admin secretary, and Catherine Stott were sharing a small table. Dan, the ceramics tutor, was sitting dustily at a table by himself, attacking a huge pile of spaghetti and meatballs. I had plumped for the same and was still twirling the thick spaghetti round the sauce when Anne Birtwhistle came in. At the counter she piled her plate full of salad and quiche, then stood for a moment, looking for a place to sit down. 'Don't look now,' I warned Kroog. 'Bean Counter at three o'clock.' Dan had noticed and was making inviting gestures at the chair opposite him but Anne pretended not to see. There were a few seats left at larger tables that were taken up by students but none of it seemed to appeal and she carried her plate out of the door and up the stairs. 'Panic over, she's taken her food upstairs.'

'Phew,' said Kroog. 'That woman makes me feel young. I'm scared I might throw the cruet set at her head. She's in a right tizz about John's funeral.'

'It can be a difficult time, of course, arranging a loved one's funeral.'

'Loved one? Anne didn't care much for her father and vice versa. *I* cared for John. It isn't that at all. John gave very clear instructions as to the disposal of his body and if she wants to inherit she'll have to abide by his wishes. He's to be cremated. Within a week his ashes are to be scattered in Fiddler's Pond during a party.'

'What's so odious about it?'

Kroog gave a gap-toothed cackle. 'It's fancy dress and torch-light. All who attend have to dress as famous artists or artworks.'

'Excellent. You can come as yourself.'

'Flattery will get you everywhere, Honeypot. Can you spare a meatball, do you think?' she asked, fork in hand.

SEVEN

There was no need to ask Tim for help this time. Rachel Eade, the last exhibitor on my list – or rather the last one I looked up – had not moved at all. She still lived in Limpley Stoke, an affluent village south-east of Bath. I found her place easily. It was one of the newer, larger houses, with a double garage and a brand-new Mini Countryman in sensible black and white parked in front of it. There had been a phone number on my list for Eade but I wanted to have a chance to stoke up my prejudices before first impressions got in the way. There was not much of a front garden, just a couple of stone planters full of bright annuals, a foot scraper in the shape of a hedgehog and a door knocker in the shape of a lion. Rebel country this wasn't. Whatever kind of sculpture Rachel Eade was making, she wasn't making it here.

The woman who opened the door was tall, slim and had very short, very blonde hair. Early forties, in a simple knee-length black dress and strappy sandals. She was also in a bit of a hurry and still fastening a silver watch to her wrist as she frowned at me.

'Rachel Eade?'

'The same.'

'I'm Chris Honeysett. I work at BAA in Batcombe.'

'Oh yeah?' she said, to rhyme with 'more fool you'. 'Come in, close the door. And what do you want with me? I must warn you, I'm in a bit of a hurry.' She looked at her watch. 'No, I tell a lie. I'm actually late already.'

I followed her into the sitting room – tastefully modern but straight from the catalogue – where she started rummaging through a large cream handbag and began throwing things into a smaller black one. 'We are organizing an anniversary exhibition, thirty years, which the now-late John Birtwhistle had planned. It's still going ahead and you are one of the artists who he wanted to invite to exhibit.' I then had much the same conversation I had had with the others. All but Landacker were surprised to be invited to return to the old school and, like the others, she hesitated.

'I'm a sculptor,' she said. 'I'm an installation artist.' She checked her watch again, sighed, then motioned me to sit down and did the same.

'Showing anywhere at the moment?' I asked unkindly.

'Not at the moment.'

'But you're working on something.'

'Naturally.'

'Where's your studio?'

'I don't have a studio *as such* at the moment. My work is always very site-specific. I prefer to work at the location, let it tell me what the place wants . . .'

Stuff, apparently, was what most places wanted. I had seen pictures. Drifts of leaves in corners, scribbles on walls, found objects scattered on the floors. I wondered who bought it. 'Here's your chance. The date hasn't been set but the condition is that it is a piece done specifically for the exhibition, with accompanying sketchbook.'

'Why not? I'm in. Send me the details. And now I really have to go.' She grabbed her bag and walked me to the door in haste.

'Oh, just one more thing,' I said. 'You'll have to do it outside.'

John Birtwhistle was quietly cremated on a Monday, at Haycombe crematorium, a 'close family only' occasion, which probably meant just Anne, unless her wayward brother Henry had put in an appearance. The scattering of the ashes, as stipulated in John's will, was to take place within a week and was planned for Saturday evening. As John had undoubtedly expected, students were spending less time thinking of the loss of their elderly tutor and more about 'what to go as' – work of art or artist, contemporary or classical?

The exhibition was to open three weeks later. 'That's not very long for new work to be created,' I suggested to Anne. 'Some painters, like Landacker, might take far longer to produce an image.'

'Rubbish. I've seen pictures of his stuff and if it takes more than an afternoon I'd be very much surprised. Tell them all to get on with it or I'll cancel,' she said and clacked irritably upstairs to her father's rooms where she had been staying since her arrival.

I left messages on Rachel Eade's and Dawn Fowling's answer phones but Hufnagel and Landacker would have to be told in person, one because he was too posh to give out his number to a mortal like me, the other because he was too poor to afford a working phone. I decided to get Landacker out of the way first. He had managed some kind of apology for the welcome he had given me but we hadn't exactly parted bosom buddies and I found him just a little self-obsessed.

I squashed my car into the shade of the hedgerow opposite The Old Forge. It was another warm day and the weather was set fair until the end of the week. The Old Forge was at the edge of the village and standing in the lane I noticed how quiet it was; all I could hear was the purling of the stream and a few birds. I also noticed that Landacker had had another unwelcome visitor. The broad gate had been mutilated at the side of the lock so that it would no longer close properly and someone had deeply scored the wood with a tag of some kind, in the shape of two triangles facing each other: I><I. It could, with a stretch of the imagination, depict a stylised butterfly. Last time I was here the gate had been open; had it already been mutilated then? I tried to picture it in my mind but all I could see was Landacker's BMW and shopping on the drive. Pressing the bell and waiting produced no results. I pushed gingerly at the gate until, through the resultant gap, I could see Greg's car parked in the same spot as before. After pushing a little more I slipped inside.

I needed no reminder beyond my eye patch of how my unannounced visit had been received the last time so I had every intention of making myself heard before entering studio or house. Like a good detective I laid a hand on the car's bonnet to feel if it had been used recently – it was cold to the touch. The door to the studio had been repaired with a new shiny lock and a new tinted window that did not allow me to see inside.

It probably did not allow anyone to see much looking out either, because while my fist was still raised to knock at the door it opened and Landacker came out, obviously unaware of me, because seeing me made him jump. 'It's you again!' he said accusingly.

'I was about to knock.'

'Glad to hear it.' He was wearing what I imagined was his painting gear: paint-smeared black t-shirt, designer jeans and Nikes. He awkwardly pulled the door shut behind himself.

'The date for the exhibition. Three weeks on Monday.'

'Three weeks. Righty-ho.' He didn't move. Neither did I but no invitation to come into the house or studio was forthcoming.

'John's body was cremated but there is a scattering-of-the-ashes party at the college early Saturday evening. John left strict instructions.'

'Eccentric even beyond death.'

'Yes. Everyone's to dress as a famous artist from history or a famous work of art. And his ashes are going in the pond.'

'And why not.'

'Your gate. I don't remember it looking like that last time I was here.'

'Bloody vandals.'

'They managed to force the lock. Did you have another break-in?'

'No, that's all they did.'

I was going to ask him if it didn't worry him but I could already that see Landacker looked worried. 'And I don't suppose you called the police about this either?'

'I'm thinking about it. But anyone can get over the wall anyway; it's only eight foot high in most places.'

'Yes, but they can't drive away your car unless the gate is open.'

'Damn. I hadn't even thought about the car.'

It seemed like Landacker was quite prepared to keep us standing on his drive so I said my farewell and left him to ponder his incomplete security. As I drove back towards Bath I came to think about the security at Mill House. It didn't take me long. We didn't have any.

Visiting Kurt Hufnagel at his honeysuckled shambles was to be my next good deed of the day and involved a stopover at the supermarket. It was partly the thought of his poor life model having to subsist on cut-price teabag tea and lumpy milk in dusty cups, but mainly the thought of having to sit down to another cup of it myself that made me do it.

When I let the DS roll to a stop outside Honeysuckle House it looked exactly the same. A pair of crows waited until I had pushed open the creaking gate before they abandoned their attack on the festering rubbish bags and lazily flapped away to wait on the roof of the garage until I had carried my shopping to the back door. No loud music this time but I could hear intermittent banging from somewhere inside. I did some myself, loudly, on the door and when I got no response I tried the door handle. This time the door was locked. Only after some more knocking did I finally hear movement on the other side.

Hufnagel opened the door a crack and peered through it. He was holding a claw hammer. 'It's you.'

'Father Christmas,' I said, swinging my shopping bag.

'Enter, friend.' Hufnagel gave a courtly bow and ushered me into the kitchen. Nothing had changed in here.

I indicated the hammer in his hand. 'Building a glider?'

'Some weird shit is going on, Chris. Why am I surprised, eh? Try and lead a normal, quiet life and turn your back on the madness out there? It can . . . not . . . be . . . done,' he said, tapping the kitchen table with his hammer for emphasis. 'Some bastard broke into the house last night. While I was asleep. Through the sash window in the living room. They cut a hole into a pane, reached through and released the catch.'

'Did they take anything?'

'No. I disturbed them, I think, when I got up to go to the loo. I heard a little noise below and shouted down the stairs. Not sure it's what you're supposed to do but it seemed to work. I heard someone clamber out, then I heard a car drive off.'

'Sash windows are always vulnerable unless you have proper window locks,' I said wisely.

'I nailed the bastards shut,' he said, holding up the hammer.

'All of them. No more Mr Nice Guy. Not sure they came to nick anything, though. They'd gone through the entire place; I could tell where they'd been from stuff they moved about, drawers opened, cupboards. I mean I don't have much to pinch anyway, look around. But they must have been here a long time to go through every room. It really gave me the creeps when I realized. But that's not the worst of it. The worst is what they did outside.'

'What?'

'They put petrol in my car.'

'You what?'

'I tried to start it this morning, thought it might just manage to cough to the garage up the road, and found the tank was a quarter full.'

'Could it have been your model? The petrol?'

'Sophie? No, impossible. Trust me,' he said when he saw doubt in my eyes, 'she doesn't even drive.'

'Perhaps they wanted to pinch the car,' I said and unpacked the shopping.

'Have you seen my car? Anyway, they *came* by car; I heard them drive off. You brought bin liners, what are you, my *mother*? Oh, coffee, good thinking.' He whipped the packet away.

'I only came to tell you the date's been set for the exhibition, three weeks on Monday. And John's ashes are being scattered on Saturday – thought you might want to come.'

'Why would I want to do that?' he said, spooning coffee into a pot. 'Why didn't you bring instant? Now I'll have to find a strainer.'

'You'll come because you're so grateful to have been invited to the show?'

'Oh, all right, I'll think about it.'

'Have you thought about what kind of painting you'll contribute?'

'It'll be a studio interior.'

'With Sophie in it?'

'Yes, why?'

'How much does she charge an hour?'

'Ah, she won't sit for anyone else. Will you look at that? A tea strainer, we're in business.'

'That's not what I asked. How much are you paying her?'

Hufnagel squirmed a bit. 'We have an arrangement. Look,' he

said, pouring murky coffee into two freshly dusted cups, 'thanks for bringing coffee and that but don't interrogate me, OK?'

Annis was busy shooing two black-faced sheep out of the studio door and back into the meadow. We borrow them from Rick at Ridge Farm to keep the grass down. 'They must be the only two curious sheep on the planet. Shoo!' The sheep scooted side by side downhill for a few yards then trundled resentfully on. 'Two break-ins? Nothing taken from either of them?'

'Worse. Hufnagel was out of petrol when I first went to see him. The burglar put petrol in his tank.'

Annis's eyes took on a ten-mile stare. 'Now *that* is creepy. Why would anyone do that?'

'Who knows? It's probably a faulty petrol gauge and he only imagined he was out of petrol.' Annis stood in the door, her ten-mile stare directed at the house and outbuildings below. 'What?' I asked.

'I was thinking of how safe we might be from that kind of thing.'

'People putting petrol in our cars? Very, I should think. You mean burglars? We've never had any problems . . .' I saw Annis go cross-eyed. 'Well, apart from that one time, but that was different, they weren't regular burglars, it was the forgeries thing.'

'Hon, if we had a burglary at the house or the studio we could hardly describe it as a break-in, could we? It would be more of a walk-in.'

I had to agree. We never locked doors or windows, the outbuildings were falling down and the studio had a latch on a nail, strictly to keep it from blowing open. 'But what could they possibly steal here unless they bring a truck and take away the Rayburn and the fridge? We don't even have a telly. We haven't got any money, your jewellery is worth tuppence—'

'Thanks for reminding me.'

'And the shotgun's in the gunlocker under the stairs. They'd need a gas axe to get in there.'

'There's a lot of expensive oil paint.'

'True. OK, we'll stick the cobalt violet under the pillow, it's thirty-five quid a tube now. They could have kitted themselves out for life at Landacker's studio if they were after oil paints. I've never seen so much art material outside a shop.'

'The Norton!' said Annis, electrified. 'They could have that away easily. We'll take it inside.' She jumped off her painting stool and marched down the hill towards the sheds.

I'm only telling you this so you'll know why I have a sixty-year-old motorcycle standing in my sitting room.

Now that all exhibitors had been informed, the date set for the opening and for the scattering of John's ashes, I could sit back and start worrying. What was I going to paint for the Batcombe show and what was I going to dress up as on Saturday? I spent the evening sitting in an armchair surrounded by drawings and sketchbooks, planning my new painting while the room filled with the unmistakable aroma of petrol and of engine oil dripping occasionally on to a newspaper under the Norton. It was no good. After an hour of deliberation I announced that I was going to do the brave thing: I would start from scratch with fresh drawings and work up at the school so the students could see how I worked.

'Of course it'll be quite a job to get all my paints, oils, solvents and varnishes up there. My glass palette, can't work without that, and I'd want to use my own easel; I wouldn't feel comfortable using someone else's. But it's got to be done,' I said, trying to sound upbeat.

Annis wasn't fooled. 'It's completely mental.'

'I know.'

'You'll regret it.'

'Probably,' I agreed. 'And now I have to decide what to go as on Saturday. Got any ideas?'

EIGHT

Saturday morning and I experimentally opened one eye. Then I remembered: no teaching on Saturdays. It was safe to open the other one. No sign of Annis, which meant her painting was going well and she had got up early to get going again. In the kitchen I found a note propped against the empty cafetière: 'You have an appointment for urgent Aqua business at eleven at Pizza Hut. Client's name is Susan Byers.'

This couldn't be happening. Just when I had thought it was

safe to get up. And to be told bad news before breakfast. Hang on . . . *Pizza Hut*? But I had nothing to wear!

I shoved the kettle on the stove and looked for fortification in the shape of a hearty breakfast. There was leftover pancake batter in the fridge. I slid a knob of butter into a pan and set it on the stove. Once the butter had melted I ladled batter into the pan, swirled it around, then went to find some smoked mackerel. I flaked an indecent amount of it on to my rapidly setting pancake then flipped it over and went to make the coffee. I even managed to get the pancake out of the pan and on to my plate without savaging it. A huge dollop of horseradish sauce would go well and help wake me up. Did people really eat shredded wheat?

I hurried up the meadow to the studio carrying coffee and complaints. 'I really didn't need this now,' I told Annis, waving the note accusingly. 'I'm busy.'

'She sounded really worried.'

'They're always worried.'

'She came up specially from Southampton.'

'Why didn't you tell her we were too busy?'

'If you keep refusing jobs you'll get a reputation for being unavailable as well as expensive and you can't afford that. Your teaching job is only temporary, you never asked them how much you'd be paid and you can't yet know if your new style of painting will sell.'

'You've given it some thought then,' I grumbled, recognizing a superior argument. 'But I can't possibly meet her in *Pizza Hut*, I'm a food snob. What if I like it?'

She grabbed me by the shoulders and squeezed them. 'Be brave.'

I don't keep an office in town and never meet clients at home. Usually I arrange a meeting in the Pump Rooms of the Roman Baths; it's quite civilized and gives my prospective clients the appropriate foreboding of the kind of fees I expect. Pizza Hut was mysteriously crowded; the main attraction appeared to be bread covered in tomato paste and melted cheese eaten mostly without the aid of cutlery. Annis must have described me well because as soon as I entered, a woman waved at me from a table at the back; so did her eighteen-month-old daughter. The table was heavily fortified with shopping bags plus a pushchair. After some sorting a space was found for me. 'This is my daughter,

Mel,' said the woman. 'Say hello to Mr Honeysett,' she coaxed.
'Go on. She can, you know, if she's in the mood.' I was meant
to be impressed by this.

Everything about Susan Byers was pink, from her outfit to her
daughter. This was of course an illusion. But there was enough
pink to give this impression: her eye shadow, lipstick, earrings
and V-neck top were pink. Her handbag, carry-all and daughter's
dress were pink. So were the girl's shoes and her drink. The
Byers females were pale and blonde and pretty.

'So how can I help?' I always like to say this in a reasonable,
reassuring tone, while my more realistic inner voice screams,
'*What is it now?!*'

Susan Byers took her time. When she spoke I realized that
she was choosing her words carefully because of the child. 'It's
my better half. I have a suspicion that he is playing away.'

'*Away* being here? In Bath?'

'Yes, we live in Southampton. Don't we, Mel?' The kid ignored
her. 'He works for Mantis, it's a computer company. They have
offices in Southampton, Manchester and Bath. He started off in
Southampton but for the past year and a half he's had to spend
more and more time in Bath. Most of the project he's working
on is being developed here for the MOD. He goes up to
Manchester too but mainly it's Bath.'

'Bath,' repeated Mel.

'The company is paying for him to stay here while this goes
on. First they paid for a hotel room – it must have cost a
fortune – now they have rented him a tiny studio flat. This latest
stint was only meant to last for a few months at first but it's
been dragging on. He can't really refuse; it's a very competitive
market and he's lucky to have a job. He comes home whenever
he can, some weekends, sometimes for a whole week or so
while he does some work in Southampton. But at the moment
he is mainly here.' She took a long draught from her glass of
fizzy orange, then tried for the third time to stop her daughter
from smashing everything on the table to bits with her empty
drink bottle.

I had already decided not to take the job. Sitting outside
people's houses trying to catch them commit adultery is the most
tedious kind of investigation work, unappreciated by either party
and utterly predictable. The little girl had taken to hammering

her bottle against the side of the table instead. 'You think there is someone else. What makes you think so?'

'I don't know. Don't look at me like that.'

I quickly shifted my face into neutral from wherever it had been. 'Like what?'

'Like I'm a silly little woman and you're bored out of your brains listening to me. Stop that, Mel.' The girl halted in mid-swing, then gave it one more experimental bang against the side of the table. Susan confiscated the bottle. The girl burbled something which her mother no doubt believed were words.

I decided I'd have to work on my professional facial expressions. 'Did anything concrete happen to make you think he's playing away?'

'It's just a feeling.'

'Describe it to me.'

Susan tilted her head in thought, looking past me. Her daughter meanwhile had laid her head on the table and was murmuring to it, obviously gone insane from boredom. 'He's changing,' Susan said. 'Things are different. It . . . I don't know. It smells different.'

I perked up. 'Smells different how?'

'Not literally. It's an atmosphere I'm trying to describe. And he, he . . . *does* things differently. If you know what I mean.'

I said I thought I probably did, having enough experience in it myself. 'How different?'

'*You* know . . .' She semaphored with her eyebrows and shifted uncomfortably in her seat.

'I don't mean *different how* but different to what degree.'

'Enough.'

'For . . .?'

'For it to make me think he's also doing it with someone else.'

'He's a man alone, away from home. Could he be watching . . . stuff?'

'I hadn't thought of that.' She turned her empty glass around and around while she mulled it over. 'No, I think it's a woman.' Mel made a gurgling sound. Her mother said: 'No, darling, we're going in a minute.'

'Does your husband know you're in Bath?'

'Oh yes, we saw Dad earlier. Didn't we, Mel?'

I wasn't sure what kind of answer she expected from her

daughter and Mel wisely ignored her. 'Is this unusual?' I asked.
'Did you try and surprise him?'

'We don't come up often, but no. No, he knew we were coming
but something went wrong at work and he had to go in even
though he had taken the day off. They're working through the
weekend; there's a deadline. It's often like that.'

'You went to his studio flat?' She nodded. 'Describe it for
me,' I said.

'Well, it's in Circus Mews, so it's very central. It's also very
small. In Southampton we'd call it a bedsit. It's got some of his
stuff in it but it's temporary so it's quite impersonal, even after
all this time. You know what men are like.'

'I think I do. So no sign of the feminine touch. You didn't
find anything unusual there?'

She shook her head. The little girl slithered off her chair and
began to whine so Susan picked her up and promised her they
were leaving.

I decided to start wriggling myself. I began by warning her
about my fees, which can be quite unreasonable if I feel like it,
when she cut me off. 'I need to know. I'm . . . having another
one.' She hugged her daughter to herself. 'But certainly not if . . .'

'Ah. You haven't shared the good news yet?'

She shook her head. 'And he might never find out.' Her face
hardened and she became quite businesslike. 'I thought it would
be cheaper to hire someone local rather than go to an agency
back home.'

'That's almost certainly right. Still. Let me ask you a question.
Have you considered asking him?'

'I did. A couple of months ago. He denied it. He said I was
being stupid. He was quite offended.'

'You didn't believe him?'

'I did at first. But then he seemed too relieved. And he was
too nice to me after that. Too attentive. I think he felt guilty. And
so the feeling came back.' Susan seemed to sense that I was less
than keen to take up her cause. She stroked her daughter's head.
Mel craned her neck to look up at her mother. Susan knitted her
brow and continued looking at me. Mel followed her gaze and
also looked at me. Together they gave me some kind of ju-ju
stare that made me say: 'Fine, great, I'll just need some details
off you then.' I scribbled them down and hurried out of there.

Pizza Hut *and* ju-ju was more than I could handle. I drove home quickly. I had an important appointment with some curling tongs.

'Bloody Béla Bartók. My father tortured us with it when we were children, now he is dead and he's still doing it.' Bartók's Concerto for Orchestra was booming across the grass from the direction of Fiddler's Pond where a sound system had been rigged up by running electric cable all the way from the nearest sculpture shed. Anne Birtwhistle was staring out from the French window of Studio One at the students that were sitting, walking, talking and, of course, drinking around the reed- and weed-fringed edge of the pond. She was dressed in her usual business suit in Prussian blue and a top in shimmering Payne's grey. Knowing that she had to walk to the edge of the pond later, she had exchanged her heels for dark court shoes. Her only concession to the dressing-up rule which, according to Kroog, she was unable to dodge if she wanted to inherit her share, was a Dali moustache drawn on with black eyebrow pencil. 'I don't mind telling you, I feel like a complete idiot looking like this.' The oblong container holding her father's ashes stood plain and sombre on the floor by her feet.

Studio One had been cleared of easels to be available for exhibitors who wanted to work at Batcombe House for the benefit of the students. Whether the students agreed that one long-haired tutor's ten brushstrokes a day was enough benefit to make up for having to find other places to paint in remained doubtful in my mind. So far I was the only exhibitor to paint in here, which made me feel quite guilty and put even more pressure on me: it had better be good. I checked my watch: it was eight o'clock, the sun had only just set. 'The scattering isn't for an hour yet. Why don't you go out there and have a couple of drinks? It'll make it a lot easier.'

'You're trying to get rid of me, I know.' Anne had come into the studio unaware that I was still standing in it, still frowning at the beginnings of my painting while the celebrations had already begun.

'Well, I'm going out there to have a drink or two in John's honour,' I said encouragingly. 'Come out with me. You can leave your father's ashes here and pick them up later when it's time.'

'I'm staying here until half past,' she said now in a voice that had regressed a little towards stubborn-teenager tones. 'It's bloody ridiculous. Look at them all. It's not a funeral, it's a carnival.'

'It's what he wanted.' I went out through the French doors, leaving them open in case she wanted to follow after all. Bartók's Concerto had come to a hectic end and had been replaced with an eerie piece for piano, percussion and celeste. Dusk was now settling over Batcombe and shadows were creeping out from the eaves of the forest, and as I skirted the giant mechanical spider and the sentinels of other rusting sculpture the first wax flares were being lit by the pond. With her painted Dali moustache Anne was not going to be alone; almost immediately I saw two more Dalis, though they had gone to a little more trouble than merely pencilling a moustache under their noses. I did not immediately recognize all references: a heavily drinking man in densely bespattered painting gear could have been Jackson Pollock – though the original hardly ever got paint on himself – and he was chatting up a floor-length Klimt painting with gold hair. Some costumes were more elaborate than others; I saw two Van Goghs and an Andy Warhol, which didn't require much work, but the girl that came as Van Gogh's ear must have beavered away all week in the sculpture shed for her all-enveloping fleshy costume. Claire the administrator had come as a seventeenth-century Flemish scullery maid and was talking earnestly to a young Rembrandt.

There was a bar, itself trying to look like it had sprung from a Manet painting, where I bought a bottle of Newcastle Brown from the nineteenth-century barmaid. 'Good costume,' she said as she handed me my change. I managed to find Kroog leaning against a brutalist abstract wood sculpture that had been cut with a chainsaw from a large tree trunk and had since split down the middle. It had a sputtering wax flare stuck in one of its cracks. Kroog was puffing her pipe and nodding approvingly at me as I approached. Next to her stood the tall Alex, keeping pace with Kroog's drinking and smoking. Kroog wore no costume, and as far as I could see, neither did Alex.

'Glad you made it,' Kroog said. 'Self-portrait with cushion, quite convincing.'

'And you have come as yourself after all.'

'Sheer arrogance, I know.'

I turned to Alex. 'What have you come as?'

Alex spread her arms out at right angles, revealing a fringe of twelve-inch rust-coloured tassels hanging from her sleeves. 'Angel of the North.'

'Witty and economical.'

Alex accepted my appraisal with a slight bow and indicated her empty wine glass before strolling away towards the bar. For a while we just stood and passed occasional comment on the various efforts. Catherine Stott, the graphics tutor, had made a surprising effort as the Girl with a Pearl Earring. Dan Small, the potter, was one of several Picassos. The student pulling along the The Death of Marat in a plastic bathtub on wheels stopped every so often to explain noisily to people that he had come as 'THE SCREAM!' by Munch. Stars were appearing in the darkening sky. Bartók's eerie music and the quiet conversations everywhere made this the strangest student party I had ever attended. Then a sudden hush spread from the direction of the main building right at the edge of the pond.

Anne had appeared on the lawn. She was flanked by two torch-bearing students in near identical Dali costumes. I thought that for someone reputed not to have an artistic bone in her body, Anne certainly had a flair for the dramatic. She carried the cardboard urn of her father's ashes before her with exaggerated dignity and slowness, which lent her procession a degree of absurdity she probably had not intended. Yet it had the desired effect on the students: a corridor was cleared for her so that she could walk straight towards the edge of the pond to deposit the ashes in its dark waters. But even before she could enter the now quiet circle, a sudden movement in the darkness beyond the reach of the flares caught my eye. Something was approaching from the dark, and it was huge.

The giant metal spider was on the move. Ten foot high, with eight horned and spiky legs that protruded from a body consisting of electric motors and two banks of car batteries, it crept forward towards our gathering in jerking, juddering movements. It had yellow headlamps for eyes and was a terrifying machine.

'Boris!' Kroog exclaimed beside me. 'But Boris hasn't moved for years!'

It was moving now, with a shocking speed for a machine so large and complicated. And it scuttled straight towards Anne Birtwhistle. The torch bearers deserted her and fled in opposite

directions as though it had been choreographed. For a moment
Anne stood and stared with disbelief at the giant sculpture
bearing down on her, then she ran towards us. Motors whirred
and limbs clanked as the spider changed direction with astonishing alacrity to try and cut her off. Anne saw it and changed
direction too. Collective gasps of fright and astonishment accompanied every move, as though from an audience watching a
high-wire act. With a wild and frantic scuttling motion the
menacing machine pursued Anne towards the edge of the pond,
getting closer with every jerk. When its spiky legs were hacking
at her very heels Anne flung herself into the water of the pond
where for a moment she half submerged, holding the urn clear
of the water, then fought to get to her feet, utterly drenched.
There was suppressed laughter here and there but most were as
shocked as I was at the sudden transformation from funereal
tableau to Hollywood horror. The mechanical spider took a
couple more steps towards the dripping Anne but finally seemed
to run out of strength, motors whirring uselessly, with its legs
stuck in the muddy bank.

Anne tottered and fought for balance in the muddy pond. For
a short moment, before several students rushed in to assist her,
she stood still, silently dripping, her head lowered like an animal
about to charge. If this had been a cartoon, which it so clearly
resembled, steam would have escaped from her ears and nostrils.
She accepted with bad grace the help of a couple of students in
getting back to dry land. There she stood for a moment, dripping
with anger, one shoe lost. She turned, wrenched the lid off the
urn and flung the ashes in a wide arc across the water of the
pond. Then she pointedly let the urn drop to the ground and
hobbled unevenly but erect with head held high towards the
house. Students retreated before her wrath.

'What just happened here?' I asked Kroog, who was calmly
refilling her pipe as though nothing had happened.

'Boris. Kinetic sculpture. A few of my students built him a
couple of years ago. It's got solar panels on top to charge the
batteries. But it hasn't worked for ages. Remarkable.'

Students were now crowded around the thing, trying to pull
the creature from the reeds. Anne meanwhile had disappeared
into the dark.

'But . . . the thing knew where it was going!' To me it had

seemed to be possessed of a will and intelligence and had changed direction several times.

'Oh yes, I'm sure of it.'

'It definitely followed Anne.'

'It picked on the one non-artist in the gathering, how uncanny,' she said and lit her pipe with a match from a big box of kitchen matches. 'It's remotely controlled, like a toy car. I haven't seen the remote for years, I don't think. I wonder who found it. Oh look, there's Greg. We *are* honoured.'

At the edge of the lit area I could see the feeble effort of a straw-hatted Van Gogh that was one per cent Dutchman and ninety-nine per cent Landacker. Someone had furnished him with a glass of wine which he sipped with visible distaste; he probably hadn't drunk anything this cheap for many years.

'Why do I get the feeling you are trying to change the subject, Lizzie?'

'Not at all. You want to talk about kinetic sculpture, go ahead. Ask me anything. Though I might need another drink before I can make any kind of answer.' As if telepathically summoned, Alex appeared and wordlessly handed Kroog a fresh bottle of beer, then walked on without comment to watch the spidery rescue operation. I couldn't help noticing that rather more students were helping to pull out Boris than had offered to help Anne Birtwhistle.

'Someone just attacked the school's owner and you seem very calm about it.'

'You're over-dramatizing, Honeypot.'

'But you said yourself that the thing was remotely controlled.'

'A student prank. I don't think Boris would have hurt her if he had caught up with her. As it is, I think the intention was probably just what did happen, to chase poor Anne into the pond. I'd be surprised if John wouldn't have approved. He did think Anne was a bit of a dry stick. He always preferred Henry. Henry is chaotic but fun.'

'A bit like this place, really, if you don't mind me saying.'

'Not at all.' She clinked her bottle against mine. 'John always liked a good shambles, as long as it was a creative shambles.'

Now that the ceremony was definitely over, the music changed from Bartók to dance music and the character of the gathering changed to something more akin to a normal art student party.

Kroog and I strolled in step to the outskirts of the action. Claire overtook us, walking towards the house. 'That went better than expected, don't you think?' she said neutrally.

'Perfect,' said Kroog, which reminded me that she probably felt the loss of John Birtwhistle more keenly than anybody and that the chaotic scattering-of-the-ashes ceremony had lacked any kind of dignity, even though Anne's dip in the pond had momentarily cheered her.

'You have made a start on your painting, I hear. Very brave of you to paint under public scrutiny. How are you finding it?'

Three days earlier I had established my new, temporary workplace in Studio One. The operation had been, as Annis had predicted so eloquently, *mental*. During many years of working in a spacious shambolic studio I had accumulated a phenomenal amount of outlandish home-made oil and varnish mixes, mediums made from exotic resins and a hundred and one other things, which I discovered, while packing, that I couldn't possibly work without. My glass palette, for instance. Which had set solid into twenty years' worth of dried oil paint that had solidified into multicoloured swirls and ripples. This meant taking the entire table. Which had, on closer inspection, stuck itself to the floor by the same method as the palette to the table. I wanted my own studio easel, naturally, and cratefuls of bottles, from Venice turpentine to Damar varnish; every tube of paint I owned (including the spares or else I'd worry); armfuls of brushes of which I would use probably five but I would feel uncomfortable if the other hundred and twenty weren't standing in their buckets; oil rags, of course, and a stretched canvas. Lastly, my painting stool, which was just the right height for sitting in front of an unfinished painting in an attitude of quiet despair.

Mental.

'I told the students they could drop in any time they feel like it if they want to talk about something, or even just to watch.'

'And have they?'

'I leave the doors wide open most of the time but so far only Phoebe has come to watch me paint. She sat for hours.'

'Good.'

'She sniffles. Hayfever.'

'Does it disturb you?'

'Drives me up the wall.'

'Good, good.' We had reached the front of the house where two feeble bulbs in grimy lanterns nearly illuminated the car park. 'It was certainly a memorable send-off,' Kroog said as we stopped and looked back towards the figures dancing by the pond. She broke into a richly rumbling cough that went on for some time. 'I must have a think about my own funeral sometime,' she said when it had subsided. 'I think I'd quite enjoy being scattered here. Not cremated. Just . . . scattered, you know?' She walked off towards the bothy, in front of which I could dimly make out the black silhouette of the angel of the north, her wings spread wide.

NINE

'**M**usic is the most completely abstract art form there is. Even though some pieces of music may be directly inspired by events or places, in no way can they be said to be directly descriptive of a place.'

A charcoal-blackened hand shot up. 'But what about music like Finlandia, for instance?' The drawing-obsessed Ben looked defiant near the French windows. Studio Two, where I was hectoring my students, was crammed with painters sitting on chairs, stools, pots of primer, on the floor or else were leaning against the wall and each other.

'True, it's called Finlandia,' I admitted. 'But if I'd never heard it before and you played it to me, would you expect me to say "Oh, yeah, that's Finland, that is, just east of Kristinestad"? Possibly not. The point I am trying to make is that while music has mood and tone etcetera and can be called abstract, that doesn't mean it's just a collection of pretty notes played one after another or at the same time.' Appreciative nods here and there. 'It is rigorously structured. It has rhythm, it has a form, often a well-known form like the sonata or the symphony.' The odd sigh. *Yeah, yeah, we know all that.* 'And music isn't composed by mooning around at the piano, striking keys at random to see if anything comes up. Abstract painting needs structure. It almost always benefits from being anchored in something tangible out

there in the real world. And it definitely benefits from preliminary
colour sketches.' Some uncomfortable stirrings. This sounded
like work. 'Painting is work. Playtime is over. There's no reason
why you shouldn't enjoy it but great art will not miraculously
pour forth from your brushes by pushing paint around and hoping
for the best.' I could see a few faces drop. 'Of course the figurative painters among you will find this project a breeze. So go
out there and produce twenty-five drawings and sketches, I don't
mind what of, but stay within half a mile of here.'

'Why?' Phoebe wanted to know. 'Why within half a mile?'

'Because you may have to lug an easel there later.'

General groans. I could see that Hiroshi seemed particularly
put out. His forest-inspired painting was entirely based on photographs and he hadn't reckoned with having to take pen and paper
out there. I could also see that being taught, being told what to
do and being given projects to complete came as quite a shock
to many of my students. My predecessor must have had an
extremely *laissez-faire* attitude, as Kroog had hinted. After the
way she had introduced me to the students I now had a reputation to live up to. If any of them ever found out what I was really
like I would probably end up in the pond.

'We've talked a lot about abstract art,' Hiroshi said, 'but you
yourself have recently moved from abstract painting to figurative
work. Why?'

'Because I'm *a very strange man*,' I said and walked out of
Studio Two into Studio One to look at my own work and to try
and fathom just how strange my painting had become. I had
revived a method I had first hit on in my own art school days. I
would go and find something to draw outside, then take the
drawings to the studio and start work on the canvas. Periodically
during the painting process I would dash outside again with my
sketchbook to draw the same thing or place from various angles,
then take the treasure of drawings and sketches back to the studio
until my inspiration needed topping up again. Then I had been
painting multilayered abstract paintings, now I was engaged in
doing the same but in a way that recognizably depicted a locality.

I had chosen a spot deep in Summerlee Woods, in a small
circular clearing where I had stumbled on an abandoned kiln. It
consisted of a round tower-like structure, roughly made from
local rocks of all shapes and sizes, set into a bank of earth.

Leading into it was a brickwork tunnel with a domed roof. The arched opening was littered with broken pottery and the area in front of it deeply stained with charcoal. Nearby lay a large woodpile of yard-long logs as thick as my arm but it was clear that the kiln had not been used for a long time. The whole place had become overgrown with ferns and brambles. The opening of the tunnel was just wide enough to admit a person at a crouch but nothing on earth could have persuaded me to squeeze myself inside.

Apart from a few thumbnail sketches to work out the overall structure of the thing, I had only made one detailed drawing, of a storm-damaged oak that had fallen across the clearing next to the kiln. This I had begun to render in oils on my canvas but it felt wholly inadequate now. I would have to go and snatch another piece of reality with my sketchbook to drag back to the studio. The fact that there was method in my madness would only become apparent if I pulled it off. I had brought a shoulder bag in which to carry my drawing kit for my field studies. I chucked in a sketchbook in landscape format. But my painting was in portrait format so I threw one of those in as well. I had a bulging pencil wrap of graphite pencils of various grades, from H to 6B, something I had never bothered with as an abstract painter. I packed a knife and sandpaper for sharpening; also a soft white eraser and a hard plastic one for cutting highlights. Naturally I would want to do one or two colour sketches too. For this I packed a twenty-four-colour watercolour paintbox and some brushes and a tube of white gouache; a small(ish) block of watercolour paper went in as well. I added a bottle of masking fluid to preserve highlights in the watercolour sketches and another of granulation medium which would come in handy for the textures. Some kitchen roll to wipe my brushes on completed the kit. No, wait! I would need water for doing watercolours. I filled a litre bottle of water at the paint-encrusted Bristol sink in the corner. A couple of old jam jars to pour it into. There, I was ready. Or would have been if I could have lifted the bag. It weighed half a ton. 'This is ridiculous,' I said to the studio in general.

'That is why I use a camera. Mine weighs two-hundred grams.' I had not noticed Hiroshi come in, even though at six foot tall and with his broad shoulders he ought to have been easy to spot.

'Yes, but your camera lies to you,' I said distractedly as I stared into my bag looking for the housebricks that had obviously concealed themselves in there.

'How so? The photograph does not lie.'

I decided to leave one of the sketchbooks behind. But which? 'The camera does not see even remotely like the human eye does. Look at my face,' I demanded. 'Look into my eyes.' He did as I asked. 'Your field of vision takes in half the room, with me in the centre. Behind me on the wall is a printed notice. Without taking your eyes off my face, read it.'

'I can't.'

'A camera could. But humans can only focus on one tiny area at a time, everything else is completely blurred. Where we focus, that is where our attention goes and then our emotions get to work on it, helping us decide what is important and what isn't. The camera has no idea what is important and what isn't. Depth of field is a lie. Humans don't have any. You may stop staring at me now.'

'Thank you, *sensei*.'

'*Sensei?*'

'It means "teacher",' Hiroshi said with the slightest of bows.

'You don't have to call me teacher, call me Chris.'

'Does the painting never lie?'

'The painting always lies. That is its function. The truth doesn't lie in the painting; it lies in the making of the painting. The rest is up to the people who look at paintings. Once your painting is finished it is an honest object, just pigment on canvas, but it is capable of many lies. People want lies. It's what they look for in a painting.'

'You are a philosopher, *sensei*.'

'I've been called other things, too. I see you have your sketchbook, are you ready to go out there and draw?'

'I am.' He produced a pencil stub from his jeans pocket as evidence.

I dived into my bag, pulled out my little landscape sketchbook and grabbed an HB pencil stub off the table. 'Me too.'

Outside the weather was beginning to change. It had become overcast and the dark edges to some of the clouds made me glad I was wearing my leather jacket and boots as we ambled across the tufty lawn. 'We'll both be drawing in the forest,' I said. 'It'll be interesting to compare our different approaches to painting the same subject.'

'Ah, but I'll be drawing in a different part of the wood. Very different.'

'You know Summerlee Wood well?'

'Very well. I can tell from your painting that it has its source in that part. Near the old kiln.' He pointed to the right of Fiddler's Pond. 'But my painting originates in there.' He pointed to the left, where the fringe of wood reached out to embrace the sculpture sheds and Kroog's cottage, and he struck out in that direction. I walked the other way, remembering precisely the way to my chosen spot; it was along this bit. Or maybe that bit. The faint paths, trampled by generations of student feet, soon petered out and disappeared into the undergrowth. After ten minutes of frequently changing directions and a rising feeling of irritation I did find my spot again. Gratefully I sank down on to one of the fallen limbs of oak and lit a cigarette. Naturally, after five minutes' rest I regretted not having brought all the painting gear out here. No matter; I would do it tomorrow. Perhaps I could put wheels on that bag. And an engine. I picked an area of my painting on the diagram I had drawn earlier and started drawing.

Drawing devours time. Once you are engaged in recording what is in front of you with a pencil or a stick of charcoal you start to get pulled into the making of the drawing to such an extent that time simply disappears. Then you look up and think 'how strange, hours have passed'. Or in this case 'how strange, I feel like someone is watching me'.

The feeling had been growing on me until I could not help but halt my pencil in mid-scribble and look around. Summerlee Woods was dense all around me. The trees had grown close together; some of them were covered in ivy and the fallen limbs of the ancient oaks were richly overgrown with mosses. Clumps of fern and brambles meant that I could not see far from my little clearing into the wood. Now I imagined I could hear a rustling sound nearby. What of it? I had told the students to get out and about, so I had to expect a few of them to be in the woods. I returned to my drawing. In my haste to pretend to Hiroshi that I could work in Zen-like simplicity with nothing but paper and one pencil I had omitted to bring a knife for sharpening and was now trying to record fine detail of bark and

stone with the bluntest pencil in art history. I looked around
for something to use as a sharpener. Never a squirrel around
when you need one. The light began to fade down here under
the dense canopy. I picked up a shard of broken pot – it was
useless. I picked up a stone and used it like sandpaper to sharpen
my pencil; it restored a point to it but one so short that it
disappeared within two minutes. Useless. A raindrop fell on
my drawing. That was it, enough for today. I had got quite a
bit done. I stood up.

A rustling and crackling behind me meant I had definitely
disturbed some kind of critter, but when I turned around my view
was blocked by the bramble growth and all I saw, or thought I
saw, was something shadowy close to the ground. Now the patter
of raindrops, slow and heavy, began to drown out the patter of
hoof or feet I thought I could hear. After taking a last look at
my drawing and comparing it with the area I had concentrated
on, I struck out in the general direction of Batcombe House.
Several times I stopped to gather up a handful of stones to make
a tiny cairn or to lay out fallen branches in the shape of rough
arrows to help me find my way more easily to the locus of my
painting next time. It was getting dark with cloud and rain now
and the sound of the falling drops was all around me, but I still
managed to hear it: a cracking sound as from someone treading
heavily on a twig. I whirled around and saw it. I wasn't at all
sure what it was I was seeing at first, but then it became clear.
It was a human figure, naked, pale in the gloom and with wild
hair. The man was moving quickly away from me through the
undergrowth. At least I thought it was a man, and before I could
decide whether to call out or pursue it the figure was gone,
disappeared into the gloom and the rain. A naturist? An amorous
student in pursuit of his love object? The wild man of the woods?

Whatever it was, I would definitely make sure that next time
I came out here I'd have my pencil sharpener with me.

TEN

'Not a chance, hon.' Annis burrowed deeper under the duvet.

'It's not fair.'

Muffled defiance from under the sheets. 'Don't care.'

'But it's your turn.' I yawned.

Annis wriggled her head free, holding on to the edge of the duvet for dear life. 'Not at half six in the morning, it isn't. I'm a painter; those numbers aren't on my clock.' She turned over, taking much of the duvet with her. 'You want to go detecting at sparrow's fart, you make your own breakfast. My private eyes are firmly shut.'

I couldn't actually remember when I'd last been victorious in one of these squabbles, so I pushed my reluctant carcass out of bed and Neanderthaled towards the shower. Why on earth had I agreed to do surveillance on Susan Byers' husband? Why, when my tongue had already touched my palate in the forming of a firm 'no', had 'OK then' come out? Probably for the same reasons that it was my turn to make breakfast again.

I would keep half an eye on Martin Byers today and hopefully it wouldn't take long to establish whether or not he was cheating on his pink Southampton spouse. Yesterday I had got extremely wet on my trek from Summerlee Wood to the shelter of Studio One at Batcombe House. Quite possibly all of my students had also been soaked by the sudden rain that had brought with it a definite autumnal air. I was certain the Wild Man of the Woods must have felt it too. Now it looked like more rain. I was hoping that following Martin Byers about wouldn't mean getting soaked standing at street corners like so much private-eye work does. If I was really lucky, I would be there to see him leave his place covered in lipstick marks with his mistress waving him off as he left for work: case closed. Which reminded me, I needed to take my camera since a quick pencil sketch would presumably not be acceptable as proof of guilt. I dressed quietly and picked up my watch and rings from the bedside table.

'Can I have quince jam with my croissants?' Annis mumbled through a nest of strawberry hair.

'I thought it was too early for you,' I protested.

'Well, now that you've woken me up, I might as well have breakfast. By the time you've made it and brought it upstairs it'll nearly be breakfast time anyway,' she elucidated with the kind of impeccable logic that I find impossible to defend against before I've had my first coffee. 'And don't let the egg go solid again, I hate that.'

I stuck the kettle on the stove, whizzed some beans in the annoying little coffee mill, and primed the cafetière. There were no croissants, not even in the freezer. This was not a good start. Then an image of Kurt Hufnagel's kitchen floated before me and I counted my blessings. I soon lost count, in fact. I found bagels in the freezer and cream cheese in the fridge, but no cucumber. Hufnagel would have called it a conspiracy. And he'd have been right. There were plenty of eggs from the happy hens of Ridge Farm, though. I went straight to the Honeysett default setting triggered by any *now what?* kitchen situation: Scrambled Eggs With Everything. Tim would have been proud of me. Frying pan, olive oil, chopped onion, chopped coriander, as much Indian spice paste as you think your victim can swallow, and slide in the scrambled eggs. Keep it moving round the pan until the bread pops from the toaster and divvy it up. A generous dollop of the inevitable brinjal pickle rounds it off nicely.

'This is boys' food,' Annis complained while she shovelled golden forkfuls of it into her mouth. 'What's wrong with cornflakes?'

'Cornflakes and brinjal pickle? Are you mad?'

She stabbed my arm with her fork. It left an orange tattoo. 'So it's the old hubby-playing-away-from-home scenario. How tedious for you.'

'Yup. Can't say my cup runneth over with excitement.'

'Speaking of which, any more coffee?'

I topped her up. 'According to Nabokov, infidelity is the most conventional way of breaking with convention.'

'The bloke who wrote *Lolita*? He should know.'

'Except Mrs Byers says she's pregnant again, though she's not showing yet.'

'She told you? Why did she tell you that?'

I shrugged. People like telling me things. Mostly lies, of course. 'I don't know. To make me take the job, I guess. Her husband doesn't know.'

Annis handed me her empty plate. 'Thanks, hon, that was gruesome. Only kidding, it was nice, just a bit spicy for breakfast.' She let herself flop back on to the pillows. A split second later she sat up again like a demented toy. 'She told you but not her husband? Did she mention abortion?'

'Obliquely, yes. She thinks she might not have it if it turns out he's cheating on her. Fair enough, I suppose.'

'Fair enough? Not if you're the baby, I should think.'

We were entering difficult terrain here, a possible minefield I was not prepared to enter this early in the morning. 'Anyway, it's just a weird feeling she has. It's not like there've been strange phone calls or she's found unexplained knickers in his laundry. She just feels he's changing. He might be squeaky clean.'

'Yeah, and I'm a hobbit.'

'What makes you say that? You don't know the guy.'

'Instinct,' Annis said firmly.

'A *woman's* instinct? Don't give me that. If women had instinct there wouldn't be millions of them hanging around with useless men.'

She widened her eyes at me and her eyebrows rose dangerously. Me and my big mouth. 'Hey, who just made breakfast?'

'A fiver says he's cheating on her. No, tell you what, I bet you a whole month of breakfast in bed if he's kosher.'

'Done,' I said.

Rash.

As I drove into town I was already coming to regret the wager. But surely there had to be plenty of devoted husbands out there working away from home who never looked over their shoulder and who dreamt of nothing so much as to return to the bosom of their families? A month of breakfasts in bed! What were the chances of him not cheating on her? The woman said he was doing things differently. He'd obviously been *practising*. But was he still?

Due to my complicated breakfast duties, I was running later than I had planned. Traffic on the London Road was practically at a standstill. I tried to imagine it in the days of the horse and cart, when it had been built, and wondered what had been considered busy then. I was already missing my biking days, when I had been allowed to whizz past stationary traffic in the bus lane. But the first raindrops were coming down and I began to appreciate being warm and dry and being able to listen to the radio. By the time I had found a parking space in Rivers Street it was raining steadily and by the time I had walked to Byers' address in Circus Mews a familiar private-eye mood had settled on me like a cold mist. The mews was too narrow to sit around in a parked car. I'd have to stand around in a neighbouring doorway while I kept an eye on his.

This is what most private investigations amount to: standing on street corners and in doorways while your feet get wet or, if you're lucky, sitting in a warm car with your brain sliding into atrophy while you wait for someone to turn up at an address, leave a house or move a curtain. Then, after endless hours of nothing, a frantic scramble for your camera and *click*, you've missed it.

I used to hand over grainy 6 x 8 photographs; now increasingly it's video footage. The pain, I imagine, is the same. And if you think you would never spy on your spouse then they're probably spying on you: more than fifty per cent of divorces involve a private detective.

I checked my watch. It was ten to eight, much later than I had hoped to arrive. I lit a cigarette and stood, ostensibly looking down the road but really just keeping his front door in my peripheral vision. After a while that gave me a headache so I turned around and looked up the road for a change. Isn't the life of a private eye exciting? But then, at seventeen minutes past eight exactly, I got fed up. I shrugged deeper into my leather jacket, splished across the street and rang his bell. I'd do my Jehovah's Witness impression. No one in their right mind would ask you for proof that you really are a Jehovah's Witness. Byers' accommodation was on the first floor. There was no intercom so he'd have to come down or open a window to see who I was. Or preferably his girlfriend telling me he'd gone off to work and no thanks, they were fine for monotheistic religions at the moment.

Nothing. No answer. I rang again, for the heck of it. And then, just as I was turning away, the door did open and an elderly man let himself out. He was wearing a coat of a colour so depressing

that if you had mixed it by accident you would quickly scrape
it into the bin with a shudder. He raised his eyebrows, which I
took for an invitation. 'I was looking for Martin.' I pointed at
the bell button. 'Martin Byers.'

'Oh, he'll be at work now.' He pointedly pulled the door shut
behind him as he looked me up and down. Long wet hair and
ancient leather jackets do not inspire confidence in the elderly.

'Will his girlfriend be at work, too?' I tried.

'I wouldn't know, I'm sure. I don't know that he has a girlfriend.' He shook his head at my presumptuousness, opened his
black umbrella and walked off.

'What time does he normally get in?' I called after him but
he ignored me, just stiffened his gait a little and sped around the
corner. I stepped back into the road and looked up at Martin
Byers' window. That gave nothing away either. So far my breakfasts in bed looked safe.

On my way to Batcombe I swung past Byers' place of employment. It was housed in a converted warehouse by the river, with
plate-glass doors and a steel plaque so tiny you'd have to press
your nose against it to decipher the name: Mantis IT Solutions.
It looked like the kind of place where a lot of money was being
made quietly, almost anonymously. One look at the adjacent car
park, however, revealed that, privately at least, one was quite
happy to advertise one's success: sparkling 4x4s, BMW 5 and 7
series and Mercedes, all in the latest colours. Even the few
motorcycles here looked new and expensive. I had no idea what
car Byers drove – forgot to ask – but I would try and be here
when the Mantis factory hooter went. I'd been given a tiny colour
passport photo of him to make sure I'd recognize him.

By the time I arrived at Batcombe House the rain had stopped,
though thick grey cloud still hung low over the hillside like a
wet floorcloth. While I'd been waiting outside Byers' place my
boots had soaked through; my hair was still wet and breakfast
seemed ages ago. I went to the staff room to make myself a
coffee.

The staff room on the ground floor was pleasantly clapped-
out, and on colder days usually had a cheering fire going. There
was a magazine- and book-covered table with six rickety chairs,
a couple of sofas hiding their threadbareness under colourful
throws, and a battered sideboard with a tea- and coffee-making

facility colloquially known as 'the kettle'. Everyone was here and the mood was rebellious. Dan, the ceramics tutor, Kroog and Catherine Stott were flounced on the sofas with their mugs, Claire Kilburn was standing by the kettle, waiting for it to boil.

'Morning, Honeysett,' said Kroog as I steered a course towards the kettle. 'Hope you've got enough cash on you if you're thinking of making coffee.'

'Cash?' I said vaguely. I'm usually pretty vague about money.

'Oh yes,' confirmed Catherine, who didn't often agree with Kroog. 'The kettle has been privatized.'

'No more buying tea and coffee from the petty cash,' Dan explained.

'No more petty cash, full stop,' said Claire as she poured hot water into her mug. 'Here.' She pushed the kettle towards me. 'You'll have to fill it again. But better read the new instructions for tea-making first,' she said, eyes wide in mock astonishment.

A 'staff notice' had appeared above the kettle, printed in a stark totalitarian font. I read:

STAFF NOTICE

AS FROM TODAY TEA AND COFFEE
WILL NO LONGER BE FINANCED BY THE COLLEGE
VIA PETTY CASH. TEA, COFFEE, SUGAR AND MILK AS WELL AS
THE ELECTRICITY TO POWER THE KETTLE
MUST BE PAID FOR.
THERE IS NOW A CHARGE OF 50 PENCE PER MUG.
PLEASE BOIL ONLY AS MUCH WATER AS YOU REQUIRE.

'And look,' Claire said. 'She took away our Assam tea bags and Rich Columbian Blend and replaced it with supermarket own-brand stuff. The milk is UHT.'

'Shocking. What next? Powdered water, I expect.' I went to fill the kettle in the nearest staff toilet.

'Only one *mugful*, mind!' called Catherine, who had found fresh fuel to keep her pot of resentment seething.

I boiled my solitary cup of water to make supermarket instant, dropped fifty pence into the tin piggy bank, thoughtfully provided by the management, and joined the others on the sofa closest to the fireplace. There was no fire. The log basket had disappeared.

'An unnecessary luxury,' Catherine explained.

'I saw her carry the basket upstairs to John's rooms,' said Dan. 'I suppose that's where our Assam tea now resides too.'

'She wants me to do a complete audit of the place. And an inventory,' Claire said gloomily.

'I knew she would turn out to be a bean counter,' Kroog rumbled bronchially. 'Mark my words, there'll be price tags appearing on all sorts of things soon.'

I changed the subject. 'I went drawing in the wood yesterday, setting a good example to the students and all that. On the way back I saw what I think was a naked man running through the forest. Wild of hair and fleet of foot.'

Kroog pulled down the corners of her mouth. 'You didn't recognize him?'

'I saw him only through several layers of foliage and it was gloomy and raining at the time. Not a common occurrence then, naked men in the woods?'

'Well . . .' Kroog shrugged. 'They're not usually running, no. I mean, students get up to all sorts in that wood in summer. Sometimes I think we ought to install a condom machine in there.'

Catherine pretended to flinch. 'Elisabeth, really.'

'Oh, join the real world, Stottie,' Kroog said.

'I thought he might be an escaped life model,' I suggested. 'Gone feral, living off nuts and berries.'

'At the rate we're paying them, that's quite possible,' Kroog said.

I left behind the gloom of the staff room, safe in the knowledge that my tenure under the new-broom management of Anne Birtwhistle was purely temporary. I hadn't even seen a contract yet so I could, in theory, walk out any time I liked, though for the moment I was still quite enjoying the change. But when I looked at the drawing I had produced yesterday, my heart sank. It seemed lifeless to me now and the sense of achievement I had felt the day before had evaporated. Yet I did tell myself that I had learnt more about my subject and that it took my painting a little bit further. I worked on my large canvas until lunchtime. If you were not a painter and you had been watching me through the French windows, like some of the students did, you could have been forgiven for thinking that I achieved very little that morning. If you *were* a painter, of course, you'd have come to the same conclusion. I was glad when I had an excuse to go down to the refectory and eat a huge plate of fish and chips.

When I eventually made it back to Studio One, I found I had company.

ELEVEN

'Come to check it out?' I asked.

Dawn Fowling looked just as hungover as she had when I'd last seen her, which made me wonder whether hangovers were a permanent *ante meridiem* feature in her life or whether perhaps she always looked like that. 'Kind of,' she said. 'Any chance of a coffee?'

I nipped back into the staff room and procured a mug of the new supermarket's own for her. Dawn rolled herself a ridiculously thin cigarette and inhaled deeply. I waited. 'Sorry,' she said at length, shaking her head as though her thoughts had been far away. 'Not awake yet. Erm, did you say John would have been happy for us to work here? I see you've made a start. Of sorts.'

'Yes, I have. Yes, he thought it would be educational. You're thinking about it?'

'I need to leave my studio by tomorrow.'

'I thought you had longer than that?'

'They offered me some money to move out sooner. I took it. Couldn't afford not to.'

'In that case come and work up here. It's only until the show, but it'll give you a small breathing space. I must warn you though, people do press their noses against the windows and they might ask you a lot of daft questions. And you'll have to answer them, that's the deal.'

'That's fine, I don't mind an audience. Might have to take up pavement painting anyway, the way things are now. I have looked all over town for a studio – what am I saying, a studio "space".' She pulled a face and I knew what it meant: tiny clapboard compartments without heating, let out at astonishing rates. 'And you know what the bizarre thing is? Half of them are rented by amateurs who only use them at the weekends anyway.' We spent a healthy fifteen minutes having an ain't-it-awful session, drinking supermarket coffee and filling the air with tobacco smoke. 'I may have to find another job. But it doesn't mix well with painting. I blame Van Gogh. All that suffering-for-your-art crap. Romantic clap-trap.'

'Van Gogh was quite well off. His brother had a job at a gallery and kept him in funds, canvas and paints. He had the equivalent of eight grand a year and back then a meal with wine cost a few pence.'

'Get me a time machine. Hey, look! Out there! Well, if it isn't . . .'

I followed the direction of her outstretched arm and saw Rachel Eade, the conceptual sculptor John had invited to show, walking slowly across the lawn in the direction of the pond. She was dressed as smartly as when I had last seen her, looking almost *haute couture* in this environment.

'She always was a posh cow,' Dawn assured me. 'She's married to a *lawyer*.'

'That's a bad thing, is it?'

'I'm sure she has a little man to make her so-called art for her now. What's she doing out there?'

Rachel was standing on the grass near a confused heap of a sculpture, taking pictures of the college grounds on her mobile. Then all of a sudden she took a few quick steps forward and ducked low behind the sculpture, putting it between herself and the sculpture sheds.

'Looks like she's hiding from someone.' It soon became clear from whom. Kroog and her shadowing angel, now without her wings, were coming up towards the house, wreathed in smoke and deep in conversation.

'Ha.' Dawn was delighted. 'When Kroog was ill Rachel stood in for her. As soon as Kroog felt better she told Rachel that her so-called sculpture was a lazy con-trick or something equally pithy and that she deserved to be kicked up the arse for subjecting her students to it. Come on, let's blow her cover!' She opened the French doors wide and walked out on to the lawn where Rachel was slowly circling the rusty sculpture in a crouch, keeping it between her and Kroog. 'Hey, Rache, what are you doing? Step back a bit, it looks better from a distance.'

Rachel stood up as though electrified. Kroog turned to see who Dawn was hollering at, spotted Rachel and said something to Alexandra. They walked away laughing.

But Rachel hadn't escaped yet. Before we could close the distance between us, Anne Birtwhistle appeared in our field of vision. She must have espied Rachel's attempt at hiding from the house and now came storming across the green, clipboard in one hand, biro in the other. 'Hey, you there! What do you think you are doing? Who are you?'

We all reached the sculpture together. Anne gave it a respect-fully wide berth as though she now expected all sculptures to start chasing her. 'I'm Rachel Eade. *The sculptor,*' she added pointedly. 'Who are *you?*'

'*I,*' Anne said with equal emphasis, 'am Anne Birtwhistle. The *owner* of this madhouse.'

'Hi Rache,' said Dawn sweetly, waggling her fingers at her.

Anne rounded on her as though seeing yet another stranger was the absolute last straw. 'And who on earth are you?'

'Dawn Fowling. I'm in the show, too. I'll be working up here for a bit.' She hooked a thumb back towards the house.

'Right, that's it. The security in this place is appalling. Anyone could simply walk in and no one would know who they were and what they were up to. It's got to stop. From now on the gates will be closed and security passes will be issued. We'll need passport photos from everyone. And that includes you lot. I'll get Claire on to it straight away.' She turned and marched off towards the building.

Dawn watched her disappear. 'Blimey, things have changed around here.'

'You certainly haven't,' Rachel said. 'I knew you were here when I saw that clapped-out van of yours parked back there. I can't believe it's still going.'

'Well, unlike you I was always good with my hands.'

'I'm sure you were popular at school,' Rachel said distractedly. She swept her arm in a gesture that embraced the entire lawn. 'I decided to utilize the grounds in my piece. I've done some research and the original owners of Batcombe, it seems, made a lot of money from the wool trade, so . . .'

Dawn cut across her. 'Don't tell me, it's a dead sheep in formaldehyde. It's been done.'

Rachel ignored the remark. 'I will arrange for the delivery of a couple of sheep that will be allowed to graze predetermined patterns into the lawn, signifying the exploitation of the countryside in the pre-industrial era. Or do I mean post-industrial? I was thinking of treating some of the grass with chemicals so that the sheep would eventually die from pollution, but I don't think it'll be right for an art school setting.' She turned around to give Dawn a look of utter contempt. 'And you will paint pretty swirls of cloud, as always, I expect.'

'Absolutely. People prefer paintings to sheep dip.'

'It doesn't look like they've been voting with their wallets though, does it?' She turned to me. 'I'll reserve judgement on your stuff. I've not come across any of it yet. I'll be seeing you then.'

'Don't let Kroog catch you,' Dawn said to her back. 'You know what she thinks of your *stuff.*'

Rachel kept walking but I imagined I saw her gait quicken a little. 'Lizzie Kroog is a dinosaur,' she said over her shoulder. 'And we know what happened to them.'

'I don't know,' said Dawn as she stared at Rachel's retreating form. 'I'm with Ad Reinhardt when it comes to sculpture. Sculpture is what you bump into when you step back to admire a painting.'

'I thought it was Baudelaire who said that.'

'You're both wrong,' said a voice behind us. It came from Alexandra, making her way back towards the sculpture sheds. 'It was Barnett Newman. Another idiot who painted with a roller.'

'Kroog taught that one well,' I said when Alex had disappeared. 'What was it like when you worked here?' I asked.

'I told you. In retrospect it was bliss. Cushy. Hufnagel was teaching painting; I taught drawing and art history, Stottie did graphics and a bit of photography. Then Hufnagel got fired and I thought I'd got my chance but John hired Landacker instead. He was quite a pedestrian painter still. Someone must have dropped a tab of acid in his Horlicks because it changed so dramatically. As in *really good.* Is it OK if I move my stuff in then? It's all in the van.'

'I'll give you a hand. And then we'd better get some passport pictures done.'

Dawn groaned. 'Is that woman really in charge? It's hard to believe.'

We walked out to Dawn's van. It was an old-fashioned Transit van that had been knitted from three different vehicles, judging by the various colours of its doors and panels. 'But it works,' said her owner. 'And I'd be sunk without it.' Her entire studio was crammed into the back of it. We carried boxes of paints, armfuls of stretcher pieces, crates of oils and solvents, buckets of brushes, a couple of toolboxes and a roll of canvas into Studio One. When we dropped the last load I noticed that several red-and-white NO SMOKING signs had appeared on the walls; one had been stuck right next to my work area and the old sardine tin I used as an ashtray had disappeared. 'Damn,' I said. 'I was fond of that tin.'

By the time Dawn had established herself in a corner amid much grumbling about how she was going to miss the skylights of her studio, and I had managed to do a modest amount of work, the afternoon had turned to early evening. It was far too late to catch Martin Byers leaving work to see if he bought two of everything at the supermarket. Ah, what a shame. I'd have to do it some other time.

The next day I vowed to keep an eye on the time and slip away much earlier, but the truth was that between the demands of my freshly motivated students, drawing and painting for the exhibition and listening to Dawn – who had a different studio etiquette to the one I was used to – I forgot all about Martin Byers.

'You love it really, teaching up there,' Annis said when I complained about it. 'You haven't stopped talking about the place since you started.'

'Couldn't do it for long. And the place is changing. John's daughter wants to run the school like an army barracks. Which reminds me, I'll need a passport photograph. Haven't I still got a couple from when I had my passport renewed?'

'That was seven years ago.'

How does she remember this stuff? 'I haven't changed much since then, have I?'

'But of course not, what was I thinking? Pass me another croissant, old bean.'

With a quartet of fresh passport photographs drying in my pocket, I drove up to Batcombe House and handed them to Claire who gave two back to me. 'We're keeping one for the files. In case you run away.' She held my pictures at arm's length. 'You're planning on keeping the ringlet hair, stubbly beard and eye-patch look then? Very fetching. Anne will love it. I think she is personally laminating everyone's IDs.'

'She probably got a machine for Christmas.'

'Probably asked for one, too. Absolutely everyone needs a security pass now, including the canteen staff and Stottie's, sorry, Ms Stott's chauffeur.'

'She has a chauffeur? Just how much *is* the pay in this place?'

'Her boyfriend. Matthew, I think? Ms Stott lost her licence.' Claire waggled a hand in front of her mouth, signalling drink. 'Drops her off and picks her up.'

'How kind.'

When I stepped into Studio One the French doors were wide open. There was no sign of Dawn. It was a warm, sunny day again so I didn't mind the doors being open but it made me feel as though I might have 'privacy issues' after all. Security issues hadn't at that point entered my mind yet. I stood in the doorway for a moment, ready to close it, when I saw Dawn. She was lying motionless on the grass, twenty paces from me, face up, her eyes wide open, unblinking. For a moment I stood transfixed, staring at her eyes, willing them to blink, but the only thing that moved were loose strands of her frizzy hair in the quiet breeze.

I ran to her. 'Dawn! Dawn!'

She shot upright. 'Ahh! What? You scared the hell out of me! What's happened?'

'Nothing, nothing,' I said, feeling more than half-stupid. 'I just couldn't see you moving and with your eyes open . . .'

'I was observing the clouds, I paint skyscapes, remember?'

'Course you do. Right. Good. Leave you to it then.'

'Don't worry, you're only the third person this morning to come and see if I'm dead. I think I'll have a sign made: *Not dead yet, just looking, thanks.*' She flopped back down on the grass.

'Good idea. Get Anne to laminate it for you. In case of rain.'

My students had without exception gone and produced drawings of a place no more than half a mile from the college, as I had asked. True, some of them had produced sketches that looked like they had spent five minutes on them, and some had obviously been so horrified by the prospect of having to lug their paints there that they had chosen a view less than a hundred paces away.

I had them all crammed into Studio Two when I delivered my second challenge. 'You've all done extremely well so far. This project comes in four parts. That was part one. Here comes part two: I want you to go out there again and paint the same view, any size, on anything you like, with three colours only. Ultramarine, Raw Umber and Raw Sienna.' Murmurs that could mean anything from excitement to mutiny. 'No white?' asked Phoebe.

'You're allowed white,' I conceded, 'but you'll get Brownie points for not using it.' I saw Hiroshi nod wisely at this. As they trooped out some of them looked like they relished the challenge, while some obviously hated the whole idea. I didn't care; I had my own challenges to face.

Now, as I looked at the drawing I had produced with a pencil stump and no sharpener in the wood, it looked useless to further my ambitious forest scene. I would have to refresh my memory, and this time I took several pencils, two sketchbooks, an eraser, craft knife and sandpaper for sharpening. I had also brought something to carry it in, a crafty present from Annis, a packsack that turned into a folding stool. This time, of course, I would have an easier time finding the place since I had left little stone cairns for myself and arrows fashioned from fallen twigs that indicated the direction to take.

I got lost. I found one of the cairns, but of course I had no idea which way I should walk from there. I blundered through the undergrowth, got snared in brambles, found places I definitely hadn't seen before, and retraced my steps. At last I came by chance across one of my arrows and marched on more confidently in the direction it indicated. Then a second one confirmed that at last I was on the right track. Before long I fetched up at a complete dead end in front of a damp, bramble-choked ditch; I had completely missed the clearing with the kiln. But how? The last arrow had only been forty paces back. I stood irresolute and annoyed with myself. How could a grown man get lost in a wood after ten minutes walking?

Then I saw him. On the other side of the ditch, through the brambles at the top of the bank, I could see the outline of my wild man of the woods, standing very still. I thought he had his back to me, or else was densely bearded, but I saw no eyes and no movement, even when I called 'Hey, you!' I nearly added something stupid like 'who are you?' or 'what are you doing?', none of which was really my business. I squelched down the soft bank into the damp ditch choked with mouldering leaves and climbed up at an oblique angle along a fallen tree limb to where the brambles grew sparser, but even as I clambered up the other side I could hear fast-receding footfall. When I got to the top there was no one in sight. My phantom had either run very fast indeed or found a hollow tree to hide in. Someone had obviously tampered with my markers to make me get lost in this place and I imagined him hiding somewhere near, watching me. 'Yes, very funny,' I said loudly for the benefit of anyone who might be listening, and walked back, kicking the false arrows in to the weeds and knocking over the cairns as I went.

Eventually I did stumble across the clearing by sheer luck and set up shop, unpacked my drawing materials and made myself comfortable on the packsack that turned into a stool. Once I started work I found concentrating on my drawing, something that usually came so naturally to me, hard to do. It would have been easy to dismiss the changing of the arrows as a student prank. Which it probably was. Yet in order for someone to change them they would have to have known about them in the first place, and that meant someone had been watching me. Even now, as I tried to render the contrast between the dry appearance of oak bark and a fleshy hart's tongue fern in the shadow of the kiln, I kept feeling that I was being stared at and kept looking around at every little woodland noise. And who was the naked, wild-haired figure running about? A student? A local? And should I be worrying about any of this?

Having finished my drawing, I packed up and walked back slowly. Every so often I looked back over my shoulder to commit the view to memory so that I would find it again without the aid of artificial landmarks. Hansel and Gretel, of course, had dropped pebbles to find their way back, which had long convinced me that the brothers Grimm had never actually seen a forest, let alone been inside one.

Back in Studio One I found that Dawn's observation of the heavens had not only yielded fruit but she also had an audience in the form of Phoebe, who watched her every move as she produced delicate skeins of greys, blues and whites in a large, wetly bulging sketchbook. The cigarette in the corner of her mouth had gone out; the no-smoking signs had mysteriously disappeared. Both Dawn and Phoebe were displaying their laminated picture IDs on their chests. 'There's yours on the stool. Wear it *visibly at all times*,' Dawn said, mimicking Anne's voice, 'or Anne will come and rugby tackle you.'

I stuck mine to my jumper upside down, feeling more like a rebellious schoolboy than a tutor. I worked on my painting for a couple of hours, distracted by thinking about getting lost in the wood, irritated by Dawn and Phoebe's chat and aware that I ought to go and find out who it was that could look forward to breakfast in bed for a month. And just like a schoolboy I was almost glad when it was time to leave.

Martin Byers looked awful in the passport photo his wife had furnished me with, but marginally better in real life. I was ready to hate him anyway if he was cheating on his pink family in Southampton. There was nothing pink about Martin, however. His hair was a glossy black; he had a five o'clock shadow that was perfectly on time and he wore what his employer probably called 'smart casual': black trousers and shoes, a dark blue shirt, no tie and a black jacket he was now zipping up, for it was getting noticeably cooler in the evenings now. He left the Mantis building in tandem with another man, similarly dressed but taller and fairer. I was stuck in my car a hundred yards down the road, with two wheels on a double yellow and the other on the pavement, watching them through binoculars as they walked side by side into the car park. I had hoped to find out what kind of car Martin Byers drove but was disappointed; he dropped into the passenger seat of his companion's Audi. They sat for an annoying five minutes while the driver talked on his mobile and a traffic warden made his eager way towards me from the other side of the road. The Audi moved just in time to disappoint the traffic warden. I started the engine and followed. The blue Audi joined the processional traffic up towards Bear Flat, with me a few car lengths behind. There is always a danger of losing your prey in slow-moving traffic if the car in front decides to turn off and it takes you several minutes to reach the same side street, but things eased up once we had passed The Bear pub. Here the Audi turned immediately off into Bloomfield, slowed and then turned left into St Luke's Road. I crept up to the turn-off and could see they were getting ready to park. I got out to walk to the opposite corner, where I hid in the entrance to the grounds of St Luke's church. St Luke's Road was quiet and leafy, residents' parking only. Byers and his driver walked to a Victorian semi with sugar-icing gables and a yellow tricycle on the front lawn. The door was opened by a dark-haired woman in a green apron before they even reached it and they disappeared inside. Byers, presumably, was staying for supper at a colleague's. I had got no further and would have to do it all again tomorrow. Or perhaps some other time.

TWELVE

'Pilfering?' Kroog dismissed it with a wave of her unlit pipe. 'We get that from time to time.'

I always found that a couple of croissants in the morning wear off quickly, which is why I found myself in the refectory this morning, loading my tray with jam, a boiled egg and coffee and popping some bread into the big toaster.

Mrs Washbrook was insistent. 'I know, but recently it's been worse. It happens nearly every day. Or night, I should say.'

'Are they walking off with legs of lamb?' Kroog asked.

'Not yet. It's bread, cheese, slices of ham. And leftovers,' she admitted.

'Leftovers?'

'Leftovers.'

'That suggests it's an admirer of your cooking. You should feel flattered.'

'Well, I don't. I never really minded before: kids get hungry late at night and they have no morals, so they climb through a window into the house and pilfer. But I have a budget and Anne Birtwhistle is demanding I balance it. That I keep accounts. And pilfering doesn't help.'

'Ah, that's where the trouble lies.'

'Oh, yes, and more is to come, I am sure. Until now I was given money and spent it as I saw fit. I'm here to feed the college, you know? Not to run a business or make a profit, after all. But Miss Birtwhistle has other ideas, I'm afraid.' She turned to me. 'You're a private detective, I'm told. Why don't you do something and try and find out who sneaks in here each night to make sandwiches?'

Here we go again. This never happens to anyone else. If you're a structural engineer, no one will ask you to design a bridge while you wait for your toast to pop, but if you're a private detective, nowhere is safe. 'Can't you make the place more secure?' I asked. 'How do they get in?'

'Same way you did. They walked in. There's no door, you just come down the stairs and there you are, help yourself. I can't throw chains around everything, it's ridiculous.' Fortunately this is when my toast popped up and Mrs Washbrook was wanted elsewhere.

When I got into the studio the no-smoking signs had reappeared. 'Super-glued straight to the wall,' Dawn said. 'Unmovable.' She was busy painting over the one on the wall beside her easel. It was a study of dark clouds.

'I'm reliably informed that only idiots smoke,' I said with a sigh, realizing that I'd have to go through all the irritating business of giving up again. 'Oh, look, Rachel is back. And you were right, she did bring a little man with her to carry her things. No, I lie, two little men.' Dawn stopped what she was doing and together we stood by the window and watched Rachel leading the way as two rural types, flat-capped father and bare-headed son by the looks of it, carried what appeared to be giant jigsaw pieces cut from plywood. They dumped their load on the lawn, walked off and soon returned with more things to drop on the grass. Rachel set them to work, directing them here and there, flapping her arms, an iPad in one hand, her mobile in the other.

'She brought her masterplan,' commented Dawn. 'Cobbled together on her iPad over breakfast with a "conceptual sculpture app" no doubt. I bet she didn't spend more time on it than it took to eat her organic muesli. Let's see what the airhead is up to. Should be good for a laugh.' She opened the French windows and strolled out. 'Lovely to see a sculptor with a hands-on approach!' she called as she strutted over. 'Are your servants part of the exhibit?' Rachel chose to ignore her but the older one of her helpers stopped to look at us, pushed his flat cap back on his head and scratched his scalp with a thumbnail. 'Have you decided not to use sheep but serfs instead?'

'Don't mind her,' Rachel said airily to her helpers. 'It's only one of the resident nutters and her retinue.' I looked over my shoulder and saw that Phoebe had followed us out. 'Have another look at the image,' Rachel said to the man in the flat cap in a voice that implied she thought he was dim-witted. She held her iPad up for him to see. It had a shakily drawn diagram on it.

'Still can't draw a straight line, I see,' Dawn said. She turned to me. 'I'm sure there's an app to improve useless drawings.'

'There is,' I chipped in. 'It's a free app, too. It's called "practice".' I hadn't really planned to get drawn in to this spat but it simply slipped out.

What the two men were in fact installing, once the large plywood shapes had gone on to the grass, was an electrified sheep pen in the shape of a five-pointed star, consisting of nothing more than a few stakes in the ground supporting three strands of wire that were connected to an energizer and a twelve-volt battery. There was a small solar panel to keep the battery topped up.

Even Dawn got bored watching it being set up and, having temporarily run out of bitchy comments, turned to go back to her painting.

That was the moment Rachel had been waiting for. 'Oh, yes,' she said distractedly. 'By *sheer* coincidence it seems that we are now renting the garage you used to try and paint in. My husband's offices are just around the corner, you see, and he really didn't like leaving his Lexus parked in the street, so close to the council flats. Small world, isn't it?'

'Isn't it just? And so *crowded*,' Dawn managed, but I could tell it had hit home. Back in the studio she was subdued and for a while stood staring blankly at her canvas. Phoebe had followed us back inside but, perhaps intimidated by Dawn's mood, hung around by the French windows.

'Don't you have a project you could be getting on with?' I asked her. She squeezed out of the door without a word. Outside, the finishing touches were being put to Rachel's pen by the younger man. A few minutes later the older man arrived with two fluffy sheep, led reluctantly on a rope. 'The sheep are here,' I said. 'And they look freshly laundered.'

Dawn turned around and stood by her canvas, arms folded in front of her chest. She was staring down at the floorboards. 'A *Lexus*. Only a complete non-entity would buy a *Lexus* anyway.'

'Let it go, Dawn. It's just an unfortunate coincidence.'

'I don't think so. I think it's karma.'

After many years of living in the valley I knew what sheep normally looked like and the two Rachel had bought, borrowed or rented for her 'piece' had definitely been washed, bleached, clipped and fluffed. Sheep only ever looked like that five minutes before they were to be judged at an agricultural show. They were duly shut up in the electrified star so they could munch a deeply significant pattern into the grass. Rachel took several pictures on her mobile, then wafted off towards the car park.

'How about I make us some coffees?' I suggested. Dawn grunted. 'I'll take that as a yes, then.'

Only Catherine ever called it the Senior Common Room; to the rest it was the staff room. I found her in a foul mood at the kettle. 'First this fifty pence a mug business, now someone's pinched the entire packet of biscuits I put out there not an hour ago. Gone, disappeared, not a crumb left behind.'

'Nice biscuits?'

'Chocolate chip.'

'Tragic.'

Dawn's mood remained dark. The next morning she looked gloomy and tired, as though after a heavy night's drinking, and her chatter had been replaced by monosyllabic answers and grunts. If her easy chatter had been distracting me before, her brooding depression in the corner was even more off-putting. When just after lunch Rachel came to inspect the progress of her sheepish piece, Dawn stood like Nosferatu by the window, staring out at her, snorting and wreathing herself in smoke. There was no way I'd ever give up smoking while this went on, with Kroog and Alex in a permanent tobacco cloud and Dawn lighting up twice an hour, more often if she was agitated. With the typical self-delusion of the addict I was now smoking Extra Lights, so at least I could claim not to be enjoying it, once the inevitable confrontation with Anne arrived. That Anne had so far avoided having a major anti-smoking confrontation with Kroog, who I'm sure even puffed her pipe in the bath, made me think that Kroog continued to successfully give her the slip.

But I was wrong. I was taking a stroll in the warm sun after lunch when I bumped into Kroog as she exited the ceramics department via the conservatory, closely shadowed by her guardian angel. She was fuming, and this time she needed no tobacco. 'As though it isn't enough that this airhead Rachel gets invited to do her art charade here' – at this she pointed the stem of her pipe at me as though it was all my doing – 'now I have to listen to John's demented daughter, telling me *that*,' she stabbed her pipe in the direction of the sheep pen, 'is the kind of sculpture we should be teaching at this college! And while I'm telling her in no uncertain terms that *that* has nothing to do with sculpture, or even art, but is merely an illustration of shoddy thinking and a pile of sheep dip . . .' Kroog needed the rest of her breath for a grumbling cough that seemed to last for an awfully long time. Alex produced a wad of tissues from her jacket pocket, which Kroog accepted with a nod. When finally she had recovered she looked into the black bowl of her pipe, nodded and stuffed the thing into the pocket of her waistcoat. 'That's when I found out why she liked that sort of thing. *Because it's cheap.* That's what she said. She's been looking at the bills and she thinks we're using *too much electricity* in the sculpture department.' Kroog gave me a heaven-help-us look. 'Presumably we're to make sculpture from egg cartons and loo roll cores now.' She stormed off towards the sculpture sheds. 'I'll show her "too much electricity"!' Alex hesitated for a moment, as if wanting to say something to me, but changed her mind and rushed after her mentor.

That explained the note by the kettle, then; Anne was on a drive to make savings around the place, and sculpture, at least the kind of which Lizzie Kroog approved, used cosmic amounts of energy, mostly through the use of power tools. So did kilns and kettles. Painting, for the moment, looked safe.

Appropriately, the sun had gone in and a cool wind had sprung up. I walked on, past the conservatory, where I could see Dan was giving a demonstration that looked more like chemistry than pottery. Among the rapt students was Abbi, the pottering girl I had met on my first day. She looked up as I passed and gave a small wave. My mobile chimed: it was Annis.

'Where are you, hon?'

'At work, why?' It felt strange even to say it, let alone do it.

'I just had a weird phone call. From Hufnagel. He was in a phone box somewhere and wanted to talk to you. Something's happened but he ran out of money almost immediately and the

pips went. He sounded pretty desperate and wants you to go out
there. Round his place. Can you do it? He sounded like he was
in a right state.'

'Drunk?'

'He didn't sound drunk to me. Just upset.'

As I drove out towards Stanton Drew I contemplated what
miserable specimens most oil painters really were. Perhaps it
was breathing all those turpentine fumes; watercolourists seemed
to be a much sunnier bunch on the whole. For a start they didn't
have to lug seven tons of equipment across their lives. And who
had ever heard of a *tortured* watercolour artist?

While I certainly didn't wish Hufnagel ill, I still sincerely
hoped that this emergency was more than just having run out of
coffee and bin liners. When I parked at Honeysuckle House I
could see that his car was there but had a crack in the windscreen.
He had better not have called me out here for that, either. When
I squeaked open the little wooden gate I could see that the rubbish
was still around but had been rationalized into black bin liners,
which had already been savaged again by the wildlife. I stepped
over the escaped bits of gunk and walked towards the back door.
It was wide open. I could immediately see that some sort of
emergency was indeed in progress The budgie cage was lying
on its side in the corridor and looked as though it had been
kicked. I briefly wondered whether whoever had kicked it had
known the budgie inside was fake. There was other debris lying
about and it seemed to get worse further along. I was just about
to step inside when I heard a subdued call from the back of the
house.

I found Hufnagel in the garden. He was in his shirtsleeves,
perched like a bird on one of the two broken fridge freezers, his
arms wrapped around his knees, staring at the ground. His hair
was even wilder than usual; his hands were covered in red paint.
He looked very much like a man who was suffering a breakdown.
I managed to resist the urge to put my arms around him, but I
stood close, looked into his eyes. He had been crying.

'It's all smashed. The whole place. The studio. And Sophie.'
He nodded his head towards the studio annex. 'They attacked
Sophie,' Kurt said with a voice that sounded like he had been
hollowed out.

I suddenly felt more than just uneasy. 'Where is she?'

'She's inside.'

I left him perched there and rushed to the house. The kitchen was a complete shambles, but that was normal. Past the kitchen door, however, the debris on the floor was of broken crockery mixed with torn books and papers. I kicked a dented lampshade out of the way. It got worse near the studio, and when I stepped through the wide-open studio door I saw that he had been only too right; it was indeed all smashed up. Someone had gone to town on it. Everything that could be broken lay broken on the floor: glass vases, ceramic jugs, decorative boxes, stools, plant stands and plant pots had been smashed on the floor or thrown against the walls. Even the plants had been mangled. The easels lay splintered. The sofa slashed, the hangings shredded. Every single painting in the room had been cut to ribbons with a knife.

Then I saw a limb where there wasn't supposed to be one. A pale arm protruded from behind the sofa at an unnatural, twisted angle. I took a deep breath and rushed to it.

She was completely naked. Someone had indeed got to Sophie and by the looks of it with a meat cleaver. It took me a moment to get my bearings before I realized that while Sophie looked exceedingly dead, she had never been alive in the first place. I touched a lifeless arm. It looked real and it felt real. What I had seen when I first came to the studio had not been a real woman. No wonder Kurt had been reluctant to make tea for her.

Her arms and chest had been hacked and slashed but her face was unharmed and showed the same neutral expression I remembered from when she had 'posed' for Kurt. She looked more real than any waxwork I had ever seen and the revulsion I felt at looking at her smashed body felt ridiculously real too. I moved the arm; it bent at the elbow and remained in the position I put her in. I played with her fingers. She was completely articulated. The perfect model. Now sadly broken and bent.

I straightened up. Hufnagel was standing in the door. 'I've had her for five years,' he said flatly. 'A friend left her to me when he went back to America.'

'What is it? It looks very real.'

'It's sculpture, I forget the name of the guy who makes them. You can put them in any position you want.'

'The perfect model.'

'The perfect model. And you don't have to pay them.'

'Or make them cups of tea.'

'Or keep the blowheaters going to keep them warm.'

'Or make appointments.'

'Don't have to keep them entertained.'

'With a choice of hair, I presume.' On the wall next to the door was a rectangular patch of glistening black oil paint that had been painted, not splashed on. 'Did they paint that black rectangle, too?'

Hufnagel wrinkled his nose in distaste. 'No, I painted over something they did. It was obscene.'

'Who did this?'

'I haven't the foggiest. Or why. That's the second break-in. Presumably that's what they wanted to do in the first place.'

'Kurt, do you owe money?'

'Yes, but HSBC aren't the type.'

'You're not in a dispute with anyone? About the house or anything?'

'You're talking like a detective now. No, I'm just quietly painting, going a bit mad from time to time, but minding my own business. Me, Sophie and Tweetie.'

'Tweetie?'

'The budgie.'

'Where were you when it happened?'

'Visiting my mother. She's in a home. Dementia. Doesn't know who I am half of the time. And I might be deluding myself about the other half.'

'Called the police?'

'Before I called you.'

'Have they been?'

'Are you kidding? They wanted to know if the intruder was still on the premises. When I said they weren't, they lost interest. They gave me a 'crime number' and that was that. Someone will come round eventually. I told them what they could do with their crime number.' Hufnagel sighed, his hands buried deep in his trouser pockets, looking about. 'It's all completely smashed. I mean *everything*. I'm finished.'

'Rubbish.'

'Look at it; it's all been hacked to pieces. Someone wanted to destroy me and they've done a pretty good job.'

I had to admit, it looked bad. It looked like a typhoon had been through it. It looked daunting. I gave the mess on the floor an experimental stir, uncovered a tube of paint – Indian yellow. I picked it up; it was unharmed. I lobbed it towards Hufnagel. 'For your yellow period. Catch.' He did. I found some more tubes. They were all intact. A bottle of turps, half full. A scattered bouquet of brushes, all unharmed. His painting table on which he mixed his colours, once turned the right way up, was intact. 'They didn't bother to destroy everything. They left you the means of production. Well, some of them,' I said, stepping over the splintered easels and taking another look at the mangled Sophie. 'You'll need a new model.'

Hufnagel shivered. That's when I noticed for the first time that the skylight had a big hole in it. 'I can't work in here. And I can't afford a new model. Real or otherwise.'

'Then you have no choice, you'll have to work up at the college. If you need props, they have thirty years' worth of stuff cluttering up the place.'

'What will I do for a model?'

'There's a model I'm sure you can borrow. She's very nice too, you'll like her.'

I called Annis, told her Hufnagel was OK but we could do with her Landy for moving another painter up to Batcombe.

'What's wrong with your car?' she demanded. 'Or his?'

'His rear suspension is gone and my car is pristine. I don't want to get paint on it and I don't want it to smell of turps.'

'And my Landy doesn't matter, I suppose.'

'You're happy to put Rick's sheep in the back.'

'Not sure about "happy".'

'Anyway, I thought you wanted to see Batcombe House.'

Kurt was just like me when it came to studio equipment, he couldn't do without this and couldn't work without that. We had just finished shovelling everything salvageable into boxes and piles when Annis arrived. 'Taxi for Hufnagel?' She was not in a shovelling mood and picked her way cautiously through the hall.

'Hi, I'm Kurt,' said Kurt.

'Are you hiring yourself out as landfill?' she asked tactfully. 'There's garbage outside and garbage inside.'

'Do you mind? This *was* my studio.'

'Then what *was* that outside?'

'That was always garbage,' Kurt said.

'I'm glad to hear it.'

'I just knew you two would get on,' I said happily.

Annis looked around wide-eyed. 'This looks like you upset someone. Your cleaner, perhaps?'

'Look, I'm grateful for the lift but I could do without the witticisms right now.'

'They killed Sophie,' I explained. I showed her the butchered model behind the couch. We had covered her with a sheet and I lifted it like an attendant at the morgue.

'Yup, it's her, inspector.' She turned to Hufnagel. 'Looks like you either upset a male psychopath or you upset a normal woman. Either way, I'd be very careful. I'll be outside.'

We stuffed the Land Rover to the gunnels with what remained of Kurt's studio, then Kurt took a few minutes to find his jacket, a few minutes to find his car keys, and quite a while to find first gear, after which our three cars trundled in convoy back towards Bath and then out to Batcombe House to add another artist to the collection of nutters.

'The more the merrier,' said Dawn without moving a facial muscle. Or any other. Annis was also not inclined to get paint on her dress by carrying the remnants of Kurt's painting life into Studio One. Her *dress*?

'Why are you wearing a dress?'

'I'm meeting Tim. We're going to see the new whatsisname film and grab a bite afterwards.'

'Right. Enjoy.'

'I will.'

I didn't even know she liked whatsisname. A strange pang of jealousy tried to nest under my naval. I dismissed it. Annis spent most of her time at Mill House not six feet away from me. Why should I feel jealous about her having a night out with Tim? Especially since I hated cinemas. Surely it was the nights in that counted? Don't ask. Just don't ask; she hates it when you ask. 'Coming back tonight?' Couldn't stop myself.

'Maybe, maybe not. Hard to tell from here. Get on with clearing the stuff out, I want to do some shopping before the cinema.'

When Kurt and I came back to the car to get the last few boxes, Annis was in deep conversation with Kroog. Lizzie turned to me. 'You didn't tell me you knew Annis Jordan. I saw her last show, it's fabulous work. That's the kind of painting I approve of.' She turned back to Annis. 'You must come and give a talk to our students about your work.'

Annis knitted her forehead. 'Tell you the truth, I hate talking about my work.'

Lizzie linked arms with her and gently dragged her away. 'Let's give the boys some room. *Of course* you hate talking about your work, love, only complete idiots *enjoy* it, but you owe the next generation . . .'

'Kroog,' said Hufnagel as the two strolled off across the lawn. 'As scary as ever. Luckily she completely ignores me.'

So did Dawn. Her mood was still as dark as it had been ever since her last encounter with Rachel and the mood of her painting had changed accordingly. Gone were the delicate pinks and yellows of her colour studies; dark clouds advanced across her canvas now, harbingers of a storm that would surely be breaking soon. I heard Annis's Land Rover grind away outside, pretty sure that Kroog had successfully twisted her arm about giving a talk to the students.

Now there were three of us in here. Kurt wrenched the screw top off a bottle of supermarket red, took a long draught from the neck and began noisily to arrange his new studio. I tried to concentrate but as soon as Kurt had set everything up he started stapling a canvas to his stretcher. Our student days lay a long way in the past and we were no longer used to sharing studios and cramming ourselves into small places, which meant that between the three of us we had managed to take over the entire available space.

'If Landacker turns up as well he'll have a bit of a struggle fitting himself in,' Kurt said.

'I wonder if he'll bring his Persian rugs,' I added.

'Persian rugs?' the other two said in near unison.

Soon I wished I hadn't mentioned it. The light had gone and I was not in the mood for drinking plonk and playing 'ain't-it-awful', so I called it a day and drove back home.

THIRTEEN

Annis did not come home and hadn't returned when I grumbled into the kitchen in the morning. An excellent opportunity to cook a full English breakfast, I told myself; something Annis didn't go near and loathed the smell of. I checked the egg basket, I opened cupboards, I studied the fridge. Normally there is at least one constituent missing but this was a morning of miracles: every single ingredient was there. The two secrets of a good full English are, firstly, use three frying pans and your grill. The only excuse for cooking it all in one pan is being stuck up a mountain in a tent, otherwise it's three frying pans, no arguments. Sausages go in one pan, bacon under the grill, mushrooms get to roll around by themselves in a fiercely hot skillet, which they can't do if you have eggs stuck in there too, which is why they go in pan number three, and baked beans heat gently in a pot on the back of the stove. Secret number two is timing. It all has to come together beautifully at the end, even though they all take different lengths of time to cook, so it's absolutely essential that the phone doesn't ring persistently in your office and you feel so guilty about never answering it that you run all the way upstairs and snatch up the receiver.

'Aqua Investigations.'

It was Susan Byers. Had I made any progress? Was there any news at all?

'So far I have found no evidence to support your theory, you'll be glad to learn. He visited a male colleague's place after work, presumably for supper, and an early-morning call at his Circus Mews flat seemed to suggest there was no one but him staying there overnight. It's too early to say for sure but so far it looks good.'

'Keep watching,' she said. It sounded to me as though she wanted the guy to be guilty. The whole conversation couldn't have taken more than three minutes – well five at the most, surely – but the sausages were black on one side, raw on the other, the baked beans had boiled dry, the mushrooms shrunk to tiny marbles and the bacon was on fire.

I went off the full English idea, chucked the lot in the bin and drove towards Batcombe. I was a bit late for breakfast but I would throw myself on Mrs Washbrook's mercy.

'What have you done about the pilfering?' she demanded to know.

'Investigations are ongoing,' I said, something I had never said before in my life but if it bought me some non-incinerated food, why not?

'They'd better be,' she said, not believing it, but she allowed me a late breakfast in the empty refectory nonetheless.

This emptiness continued upstairs. There was no sign of my fellow exhibitors. Had I seen their cars when I arrived or only imagined it? The studio's French windows were open. I nipped around the corner to check if my memory was playing tricks on me. No, both Hufnagel's scrapheap and Dawn's multicoloured van were in the car park. So was Anne Birtwhistle, a clipboard under one arm, hauling awkwardly at one leaf of the wrought-iron gates, trying to pull it shut. I turned away but she had spotted me. '*Mr* Honeysett. I really would appreciate some help.'

'Oh, sure.'

'They have stood idly open for so long they're refusing to shut.'

'And why are you shutting them?'

Anne looked at me as though I had asked a question about bears and woods. 'I'd have thought that was obvious. Gates are supposed to be closed, that is what they are for.'

'I thought that was walls,' I said as I pulled half-heartedly at the gate. 'I thought gates were for admitting people.'

'Of course. If they have the right ID. Put your back into it, won't you?'

Together we managed to pull both leaves of the protesting gate shut. They probably hadn't been closed for thirty years. 'It doesn't have a lock,' I felt moved to point out. 'I'm not sure this adds significantly to our security.'

'That is not a very constructive remark, Mr Honeysett. At least we now *appear* to have security and are no longer inviting all and sundry to just wander in whenever they feel like it.'

Right on cue a car arrived; three students in a tiny Renault. They were so surprised by the closed gate that they nearly crashed into it. Anne was already walking away. 'You let them in,' she said. 'But only if they have their passes. And they're late for this morning's lecture. I'm thinking of introducing fines for lateness. Make sure you close the gate after them, Mr Honeysett.'

One of the students got out of the car when he saw me struggle with the gate but left me to shut it by myself. My hands were covered in rust and I had broken into a sweat. It was already a very warm day again. For one of us it would soon get a lot warmer.

Back in the studio I was still alone. I scanned the lawns to see if Dawn was lying out there studying the sky, but I realized its fluffy white cloud would contribute little to the stormy painting she was working on and I didn't see her. Kurt, I noticed, had managed to prime his canvas and finish his bottle of wine before disappearing. That left Mr Honeysett with a patchy canvas and a couple of drawings in Studio One. It was too fine a day to be stuck inside, though everyone else appeared to be. I could faintly hear the lecture being delivered upstairs and thought I could discern the familiar rhythms of Kroog-speech, interrupted by coughing. Just look at that sunshine, I told myself, how many more days like this are we likely to enjoy this year? Get out there and draw. Or even just get out there. At that moment Rachel appeared on the lawn, in designer jeans and a black-and-silver top, come to inspect her sheep pen as she did every day – for nibbling progress, I assumed. OK, I'd wait until she was gone and in the meantime check that my drawing gear was packed. I was going for all-out effort: watercolours, inks, graphite, coloured pencils, the lot. It was all in place. Only not as I had left it. Someone had definitely been through it; the sketchbook was in the wrong place and shoved back inside with the spine facing down, something I never did. Ah well, the joys of a shared studio, I supposed. And after all, my sketchbook should be open to inspection for educational reasons alone. When I looked up I could see no sign of Rachel, so I shouldered my heavy little packsack and set off, feeling deliciously like I was skiving. I was halfway across the lawn, giving the giant spider a respectful berth, when I saw Rachel. She was lying on the ground inside the sheep pen. She was lying face down and she was not examining the grass.

I didn't run. Should I have run? I quickened my step, not taking my eyes off her, hoping she'd get up but the leaden feeling spreading from my stomach said she was not going to. I dropped my pack by the electric fence. 'Rachel,' I called. The sheep stood side by side in the furthest point of the star-shaped enclosure, staring. My stride just managed to clear the electric fence. On the other side I knelt down beside her; she looked unharmed but she also looked dead. I called 999 and asked for an ambulance. I felt for a pulse at her neck; there seemed to be the faintest flutter but I couldn't be sure that it wasn't my own. 'She's dead or unconscious. And send the police as well. No, I have no idea what the sodding postcode is.' Now what do you do? What had happened to her? There was no blood, no immediate sign of an injury, but I wasn't about to roll her about. Should I try CPR? Could I do CPR? What did CPR stand for? I couldn't think. Pull yourself together, Honeysett. I felt for a pulse again. There was definitely something. She looked very pale, despite the make-up.

I thought I'd best leave it to the professionals, vaguely wondering if I should get a jacket to keep her warm but deciding it was a warm enough day. So I stood around feeling helpless. Then I saw the piece of paper. It was lying on the ground, crumpled up, half-covered by Rachel's left hand. What the hell, when the police got here I was going to be in trouble anyway so I took out my mobile, took a picture of where it lay in relation to Rachel's body and then teased it out from under her hand.

'What are you doing?' It was Dawn, standing by one of the tall wood sculptures and screwing up her eyes, frowning at me.

'It's Rachel, something's happened to her. She's alive I think but unconscious.'

'Now what's the stupid cow done to herself?' she said but she looked more concerned than she sounded. I saw she was carrying a sketchbook. I could hear faint sirens.

'The gate is shut. Could you run and pull it open?'

'Why's the bloody gate shut? It's never shut,' she said but jogged towards it anyway.

First to arrive was a tiny police car and soon afterwards two uniformed officers walked towards me, with agonising slowness it appeared to me. They had only just reached me when the ambulance arrived.

'Right, can we have you out of there please,' said one of the officers. 'Let's make room for the ambulance. Is the victim alive?'

'I think so,' I said and climbed out.

'If you would come over here,' he said and led me aside. 'My colleague is a trained first-aider. In the meantime I'll need to take some details . . .'

Police love details. I gave him all of mine. Who I was and why I was where I was when I was, though I was distracted by the ambulance crew arriving. When I saw the oxygen mask go on to Rachel's face I felt relieved; they tend not to bother with dead people. The other police officer fiddled with the energizer and took down a section of the fencing. The sheep saw their chance and, despite a half-hearted 'shoo' by the officer, made a successful bid for freedom. While the paramedics lifted the unconscious Rachel up on to a stretcher, the sheep were pursued by police but they cleverly split up and the PC gave up. He came walking back. Then he stopped. 'Hey Colin?' He beckoned to the other officer. 'Over here a minute.'

'Stay here, please,' I was told. The two stood on the opposite side of the pen and squatted down, looked left and right, talked into their Airwave radios, then stood up and then both looked at me. Of course. And chatted among themselves a bit more. Then they both came up but one strode off towards the car park while the other took me gently but persuasively by the arm and led me further away into the shadow of the next sculpture, a rusty menacing slab of steel. I hate being gently led. 'We'll need to secure this area,' he explained. 'Now, I'd like you to go over the events again, but first, do you have any ID on you?' I showed him my laminated name badge. 'Not really sufficient but it'll do for the moment.'

The other officer came back and started fluttering caution tape spelling *Police Line Do Not Cross* all around the area, using the sculptures to fasten it on. Dawn, who had been standing and watching nearby, was no longer alone but was explaining to Claire, Anne and a gathering crowd of students whatever she knew.

'Can I just get my bag from where I left it?' I asked.

''Fraid not, nothing must be removed from the area.'

'It's just my drawing stuff in there.'

'Sorry. We have reason to believe this is a crime scene and it could be evidence.'

Crime scene? Evidence? But none of my questions were answered; instead I was cordially invited to go through it all again and was almost relieved when the familiar figure of

Superintendent Needham appeared on the lawn, the jacket of his suit flapping open and perspiration beading on his brow.

'Thank you, Constable, I'll take over from here,' he said to the officer, waving away his offer to fill him in about my 'details'. 'I'm familiar with this one.'

'Over-familiar,' I said as he grabbed me by the arm and led me even further away. I hate being led, did I mention that?

'Why am I not surprised to find you here?' he asked.

'Because you knew I was invited here by the late John Birtwhistle?'

'I mean next to a crime scene. Now stand there, say nothing and touch nothing until I get back.'

I was slowly beginning to get narked off. Stand here, stand there, tell me all, say nothing, don't touch. The metal sculpture I stood next to was radiating heat, there was not a cloud in the sky, and I was wasting one of the last fine days of the year watching Avon & Somerset's finest moving very slowly. More and more of them arrived, too, including forensics who wandered about in moon suits and inspected everything, including my bag. This narked me off particularly, especially when they dropped the whole thing into a clear plastic bag, then labelled and sealed it. People were coming and going between the sculpture sheds and the pen. After an age Needham came back and I pretended to be asleep.

'Let's find some shade somewhere,' he said. 'And some coffee. Lead the way.'

I did, past the crowds, towards the studio. Anne Birtwhistle rushed across to try and cut off our retreat. 'Inspector . . .'

'John's daughter, Anne,' I filled him in.

'Ah, Ms Birtwhistle,' he said genially without stopping. 'It's "superintendent", and I shall speak to you in a little while. Please don't leave the premises.' He closed the French doors of Studio One behind us.

'*Really*,' I could hear Anne say through the glass. I let Needham sniff around the paintings while I went and made two mugs of supermarket instant that in vileness rivalled any cop shop coffee I'd had inflicted on me at Manvers Street police station. Revenge is a cup best served not quite hot enough with brown bits floating on top.

Needham took one sip, then nearly spat it out. 'Jesus, Chris, what is this muck?'

'It's a crime, that's what. You can thank Anne Birtwhistle, the new management, when you interview her later. I want her charged for crimes against this and that. What do you think happened to Rachel?'

'Let me ask the questions. When you went down there, what were you looking for?'

'A quiet place to draw in the forest.'

'But you saw the woman lying in there with the sheep.'

'Yes.'

'So you went to have a look. You climbed inside? How did you do that?'

'I pole-vaulted. How do you think? The fence is three foot tall and I'm no midget.'

'You didn't touch the wire?'

'Why would I? It's an electric fence, Mike.'

'Well that's good, because a minute earlier it had two hundred and forty volts running through it.'

Involuntarily I crossed my legs when I remembered how I had blithely stepped across it. 'Blimey. That can kill, you know.'

'No shit, Sherlock. We think it was meant to. Someone ran a cable from the nearest sculpture shed through the long grass to the pen. So who is this woman?'

I explained about the anniversary exhibition and about the 'site-specific' installation Rachel had planned.

'Someone here disliked her enough to want to frazzle her. Who?'

Who didn't? Kroog loathed her and her work and had probably infected her students with it too; Alex came to mind. Dawn obviously resented her for all sorts of reasons. 'I couldn't say off-hand,' I lied.

'The next question is: how did they know she would climb inside? I mean, did she always do that? She must have turned off the current at the battery thing . . .'

'Energizer,' I supplied.

'Then climbed into the enclosure. Someone observing her, probably from the sculpture shed, then kindly plugged the fence into a high-voltage socket meant for running beefy stone drills. When she climbed out and held on to the wire to swing her legs across, she had two hundred and forty volts pass through her body. Someone must have seen her do it like that before and got an idea of how to get rid of her.'

'Perhaps.' I was pretty certain I knew why she climbed inside; a crumpled piece of paper was trying to burn a hole in my pocket but I wasn't going to mention it until I'd had a chance to see what, if anything, was written on it.

Needham looked unhappy. "'Don't know, couldn't say, not the foggiest and *perhaps*"? You're being very unforthcoming and that usually means you have something on your mind. Something you ought to share with your friendly neighbourhood bobby.'

It was hard to imagine anyone less likely to be recognized when described as a 'friendly neighbourhood bobby' than Mike. Superintendent Needham looked slow and needed to lose a few stone but he had the temperament of a grizzly bear – attracted to chocolate bars but not at all cuddly.

'No, honestly, I'm as baffled as you are.'

'Speak for yourself; I've never been baffled in my life.'

'Really? I often read in the paper that "police are baffled".'

'That's media revenge for when we refuse to tell them anything so they can't blurt it all over the front page.' The sand-coloured figure of Needham's sidekick appeared at the French windows: DI Reid, an Airedale terrier in a suit. 'Enough chat. I'll see if Reid has rounded up someone *useful* for me to interview.' He opened the French windows and nodded at Reid. To me he said: 'I might want to chat with you again before the day is done, so don't go anywhere.'

'Sure,' I said and wondered if the heart of Summerlee Wood counted as 'anywhere'. Then I took out the crumpled note I had found next to Rachel and smoothed it out.

FOURTEEN

It was handwritten and in French and since it wasn't a menu I had no idea what it meant, even though I could read and pronounce it. Yet there was a clue: it was dated 1793 and the name Marat was prominent and underlined. I took out my mobile, called my in-house translator and read it to her.

'It's very formal, old-fashioned French and it more or less says "My unhappiness is enough for you to owe me kindness"

or some such drivel. The death of Marat. It's the note from
the woman who stabbed him. In the painting he's lying dead
in the tub, holding it. Don't be cryptic, Chris, why do you
want to know?'

'Rachel, one of the exhibitors, got electrocuted, the one with
the sheep pen. Someone connected her to the national grid.'

'Nasty. Is she dead?'

'She was alive when I found her but unconscious and she had
this crumpled note.'

'Mysterious.'

'Not really. At the funeral party someone came as Marat,
bathtub and all. Rachel probably saw the bit of paper had blown
into the sheep pen and climbed in to pick it up. Grabbed the
wire and zap.'

'And the electric fence had high voltage going through it?
Could that have been an accident?'

'No way.'

'Someone deliberately tried to electrocute her? Your Mrs
Kroog talked me into giving a spiel on my work up there but
I've gone right off that place. It's creepy and crumbling and
right by the forest. I bet the trees move by themselves. And I
don't like the sound of your wild man of the woods, either. Be
careful up there, hon.'

'Don't worry, I'm a painter. What could possibly go wrong?
Anyway, the place is crawling with police. Needham is here.
Already grilled me a bit. But I'm only half done, apparently.'

'Do they suspect anyone?'

'Everyone.'

'Do you have any suspicions?'

'Loads but nothing concrete. I'll give you a hundred to one,
though, that I'm the only one without an alibi for when it happened.'

'We already have a bet running, don't forget. I'm looking
forward to a month of luxurious breakfasts in bed. I've already
written a list of what I want.'

'A list? You mean you want different stuff each day?'

'What do you think? And there's no cornflakes on that list.'

'Thought not. Oh and guess what? Forensics confiscated my
drawing gear; I'd dropped the bag by the sheep pen. There's tons
of drawing material around though so it doesn't really matter, I
suppose.'

Just how wrong can a man be? Stick around and find out.

But until then I would go and find Kroog and see if she had any ideas or suspicions. I found her in the staff room, along with everyone else. Kroog, Claire, Dawn and Dan the potter were on the sofa, Petronela the model was stirring pot noodle at the kettle, Hufnagel was sitting at the table flicking through a magazine and Stottie, as everyone called Catherine Stott behind her back, was perched at the other end, looking peeved, which, I decided, was her normal expression. This was not the moment for confidential talks. The only person not there was Anne.

'Helping the police with their enquiries,' said Kroog. 'Was it you who found her?'

'Yes. Looks like it was done deliberately. Someone must have been watching Rachel from the sculpture sheds and thrown the switch at the right moment.'

Stottie made a contemptuous noise. 'And the police would like us all to "remain on the premises". Students, too. Presumably we're all under suspicion. It's preposterous; I was barely acquainted with the woman.'

'A little goes a long way with Rachel,' Dawn said.

'But why would we want to kill her?' Hufnagel said, slurping instant coffee. His eyes were following Petronela around the room; I suspected they were actually following her pot noodle. 'I can't be a suspect anyway, I've never met her.'

'I think is very scaredy,' said Petronela, staring wide-eyed into her instant snack. 'Big house with mad electrocutioner on the loos.' She gave a theatrical shiver.

'I was downstairs stocktaking when it happened,' said Dan. 'We'll need to order more clay soon.'

'Ah, but can anyone confirm that?' said Claire, who seemed to quite enjoy the intrigue.

'Can, as it happens; I had a student with me, Abbi. She was chatting to me about her latest ideas for ceramic sculpture.'

Kroog chewed on her unlit pipe. 'Hurrah, one convert,' she said.

The door opened and Anne walked in, looking grave and businesslike. Behind her followed Needham with DI Reid, who closed the door behind him and stood as though guarding it against a mass break-out. Needham gave me a critical look, as though he'd rather I wasn't there.

'We've been concocting our alibis,' I said, perhaps too cheer-fully. 'How is Rachel?' I added quickly. 'Any news?'

'She remains in a serious condition in hospital,' said Needham. 'She's still unconscious,' said Anne.

'I'm glad you all gave some thought to where you were when the incident occurred,' said Needham. 'Mr Honeysett called the emergency services at ten fifteen precisely and says he saw Rachel Eade walk towards the pen perhaps ten minutes earlier, fifteen on the outside. This could, of course, be a student prank that went too far. Perpetrated by someone who had no idea what damage high voltage can do.'

Reid's phone rang and he went outside to answer it.

Kroog spoke up. 'All my students would know exactly what electricity can do; we have safety talks each year.'

'And where were all the students at the time, do we know that?' he asked.

'I was giving a lecture,' Kroog said, pointing at the ceiling.

'And all the students were there?'

'Quite a few of them.'

'Can you give me a list of who was and who wasn't at the lecture, please?' Needham said.

'No, I can't.'

'Oh? Don't you know?'

'I haven't the foggiest, Inspector.'

'How come? And it's Superintendent, by the way.'

'But,' Anne blustered, 'surely all you have to do is consult the register.'

Kroog wasn't the only one to smile at this. 'This isn't a primary school, miss,' she said. 'Not only do we not keep a register, but students walk in and out of lectures for all sorts of reasons – to go to the loo, because they're bored or because they're gasping for a fag.' She slapped the bowl of her pipe into her palm.

'Can you remember if anyone left and who?' Needham wanted to know.

'I was giving a good old-fashioned slide talk. With the lights out,' she added. 'And I have never been interested in the students who walk out, only in the ones who stay.'

'Well, from now on all tutors will keep a register,' said Anne. 'We need to know where everybody is at all times.'

'What would be the point in that?' Stottie asked.

'That's perfectly obvious, isn't it?' Anne said. 'We wouldn't be having this discussion at all if proper attendance sheets were kept. Claire, I want you to devise an attendance sheet, make copies of it and distribute them to all the tutors.'

DI Reid came back into the room, holding his mobile out to Needham. The superintendent took it and said: 'DSI Needham . . . yes . . . I see . . . will do . . . thank you.' He handed the phone back to Reid, then drew himself up and took a deep breath. 'Rachel Eade has died in hospital. They suspect she may have had a weak heart.'

Everyone expressed surprise and regret in some way, except Dawn. 'I'm surprised she had one at all,' she murmured next to me.

'This is now a murder inquiry,' Needham continued, 'and that changes everything.'

Suddenly everyone was falling over themselves to volunteer their whereabouts at the time of the attack. 'I was out for a walk with my sketchbook,' Dawn said.

'And what were you sketching?' Reid wanted to know.

'Clouds,' Dawn said.

'And why would you go for a walk to sketch clouds?' Reid asked. 'Surely clouds look the same from outside your door as from anywhere else you could walk to?'

Dawn spoke as to a child who had annoyed her. 'It's not about what clouds look like, but how I experience them. Otherwise I would use a camera and be done with it.'

Hufnagel said he had been looking for props in cluttered store rooms and all over the building.

'What kind of props? What do you mean?' Reid asked.

'For my next painting. I'll be painting it in Studio One, as an educational demonstration to interested students.'

'I am in Hufnagel's painting,' said Petronela proudly. 'I will be angel. Educational angel for students to look.'

Reid's eyebrows flickered.

Dan repeated his assertion that he had been in the basement with his student, Abbi. I, having no witness and having found the victim, was of course highly suspect. If Needham hadn't known me so well I would have been top of his list, since, in a surprising number of cases, the person saying they had found the murder victim did in fact commit the murder. Claire had been in the admin office, with no witnesses. Stottie had been alone upstairs, 'sorting out the shambolic print room'. Good – at least I wasn't the only one without an alibi.

'We will need to set up an incident room,' Needham said to Anne.

'What about it?' asked Anne irritably.

'Preferably on these premises where we can speak to students and staff without having to invite them all to the station. I think that would be preferable, don't you agree?'

'I see. Well, you can use this room, can't you? I'll be upstairs in my quarters, if you need me. But I feel I want to lie down for a while; this has given me a headache.' Reid held the door open for her as she swept out of the room.

Needham turned to Claire. 'I believe you do the admin around here.' Claire nodded. 'I will need a list of all persons likely to have access to the college, students, staff, regular visitors and so on.'

Reid was speaking into his mobile, no doubt ordering up an armful of recording equipment and a bevy of supporting officers. Murder, even suspected murder, provides a lot of work to a lot of people. While he talked he held the door open for us so we could vacate what had now become police premises. I was the last to leave, carrying the kettle, coffee and milk.

'Leave the kettle,' he said as I walked past him.

'Dream on, Reid.'

'Oh, and bring up a kettle if you can,' he said into his phone.

'Tell them to bring their own electricity, too,' I advised him. 'Strict rules about that here.'

Hufnagel greeted the arrival of the kettle in Studio One with delight. 'Shame you couldn't have savaged the sofa as well,' he added.

'Savaged?'

'Did I say that? I meant "salvaged". I never understood why art school studios have to be so bloody uncomfortable.'

Someone who knew all about the uncomfortable life in painting studios was Petronela. Hufnagel had posed her among a pile of clutter he had found in the store room. He had dragged a broken barrel, several tea chests, wooden exhibition plinths and armfuls of dustsheets into the studio and created a bit of rocky landscape for Petronela to stand in. A couple of blow heaters were humming.

She was naked to the waist, the rest of her wrapped in a paint-stained sheet. Her hair was down and she was posed with a bow and arrow which she was pointing at the window. 'Cupid?' I asked.

'Anteros,' Hufnagel enlightened me. 'Goddess of requited love.'

'I'm sure he was a chap,' Dawn objected.

'Antera, then. Artistic licence.'

'I hope yours is current,' I warned. 'Anne will be making the rounds, checking all artistic licences.'

With my drawing gear still impounded by the SOCO team I stapled several loose sheets of paper to a piece of thick card, borrowed a pencil and sharpener from Dawn and stepped outside to resume my sketching in Summerlee Wood. And I stopped right there on the threshold. The place was teeming with police, both uniformed and plain-clothed, forensic technicians and assorted others. It was a textbook demonstration of how murder is in a class of its own when it comes to police effort. If you come home and find your house has been emptied by burglars, there's a twelve per cent chance the police will catch them. If, however, you find one day that you have been murdered, you can rest in peace in the knowledge that there's a ninety per cent chance your murderer will be caught.

At Batcombe House it looked as though no stone was being left unturned by forensics people, no bush unbeaten by constables bearing sticks, no shed unrummaged by gloved officers and no nook or cranny left unphotographed. There was now a cameraman taking long, sweeping shots with a shoulder-held video camera and officers were herding gaggles of students from here to there in order to quiz them about their whereabouts at the time of the murder. I crossed the lawn at an oblique angle, trying to avoid getting entangled with the police effort, but I failed. As I passed the rusting hulk of a sheet steel sculpture I could hear banging and cursing – someone had squeezed inside to inspect it – and when the author of the blasphemy emerged streaked with rust he was in a foul mood. 'Hey, you!' He waved me over. 'Sir!' he added belatedly. 'Who are you and where do you think you are going?' I stopped and since I made no move towards him he walked up to me, still brushing dirt from his uniform. 'Well?'

I opened my jacket to reveal the ID tag on my jumper and pointed at it.

'That's upside down, sir,' he objected.

'Yes, I do a lot of yoga. It says "Chris Honeysett". I'm a tutor here. I have had a long chat with your DSI and am now going into the woods to do some drawing. If you have no objections, that is.'

He considered this for a moment. 'No, that will be fine, as long as you stay away from the taped-off areas.' Half a mile of blue-and-white caution tape was fluttering from tree to tree and sculpture to sculpture in the autumnal breeze. 'I'll just make a note of it.' He tilted his head in an effort to copy my upside-down name into his notebook.

I walked away. 'Honey followed by a sett. Two Ts.

'Got it.'

I couldn't help it, all this was bringing out the schoolboy in me – Anne's primary-school style of trying to take charge, police trying to control our movements and questioning our motives.

An unfriendly wind was sweeping the hillside now and Summerlee Wood had become an unquiet place. The breeze was noisy in the trees and looking up I could see the first leaves had begun to turn. It suddenly felt much cooler, too. I zipped up my leather jacket and crunched over freshly snapped twigs to the scene of my painting. I sat down on a mossy log and began covering the first sheet of cartridge paper with pencil marks, greedy for information for my painting. The gusty wind snatched at my paper and I fought the flapping corners. I was determined to get down enough in this session to keep my painting going for a few days. Next sheet. My eyes jumped to the tree trunk that would form the right edge of my painting and my pencil probed the folds and furrows of the bark. Then I stopped. The light was getting worse, now there were dark clouds riding on the wind. I squinted at the tree trunk. There it was. I got up and looked closely at it. Someone had carved something into the bark, a simple design I had seen once before elsewhere: I><I

I ran my finger over it. It had scabbed over and did not look fresh to me, yet I imagined I would have noticed it had it been there before. It was the same stylized butterfly design I had seen carved violently into Landacker's gate, though it could of course be something else or it could mean nothing at all, just one of those mindless tags vandals left everywhere. Whatever it meant, it looked like there was a connection between Landacker, the school, and whoever carved these tags. I copied the tag's design on to a sheet of paper – just a flattened X, really – and put my pencil away. There was too much to think about to allow me to concentrate on drawing.

There had been three incidents now: attacks on Landacker's studio and then Hufnagel's, and on Rachel herself. Rachel of course did not have a studio. Could the killing have been unintentional? Had the intention been to give her 'a nasty shock' and her death been an accident? Apparently no one had known about her weak heart.

I walked back a different way, skirted the swampy back end of Fiddler's Pond and passed the back of the sculpture sheds. Not that you could have got close to them from here – they had spawned a lagoon of metal and wood junk heaped there by generations of students. And if even sculpture students thought it was useless junk then it definitely was. A forest of nettles grew through it all. I hoped for their sakes that the police weren't intending to search this lot.

My stalking through the undergrowth meant I was keeping out of sight and therefore out of Needham's clutches while managing to approach Kroog's cottage from behind. The rotten remnants of a wooden fence barely required me to lift my feet to step over it and into what had once been a sizable garden. It had been allowed to revert almost completely to nature and had it not been for the remnants of the rotted fence it would have been impossible to say where garden and wilderness met. There were however a few tomato plants in pots close to the back door. The windows had almost disappeared under tall weeds that would have been easy to chop down, which meant that Kroog probably liked it that way. Looking back I could see a corner of the pond and remembered that the windows of the kitchen faced this way. The snooping part of my PI brain has never found it too hard to subdue my polite upbringing, and I made a careful foray into the weeds until I could peer in through the window. Not that I harboured any particular suspicions about the elderly tutor; I'm just made that way.

I was looking into what was indeed the kitchen where I had drunk coffee a few days ago. Kroog was there, sitting still at the table with her pipe in her hand and her skull cap lying beside a cup of tea or coffee. She was looking straight ahead through a cloud of tobacco smoke. Behind her stood Alex, also looking silently at nothing, smoking a cigarette while stroking Kroog's sparse hair, almost absentmindedly, like one would pet a cat while thinking of something else. Carefully I extricated myself from the weeds and retreated. Then I walked to the back door and knocked.

After a long while it was Alex who opened the door, a couple of inches first to check who I was, then she opened it wide and stood wordlessly back to let me in, her eyes unblinkingly looking into mine as though trying to convey a message. If so, I could not decipher it.

Kroog was sitting at the table with her skullcap back in place. 'Hello, Honeypot. Coming round the back like a true local. Are you hiding from the hairy arm of the law? So are we. You are welcome to join us. Alexandra will make fresh coffee.'

And Alexandra did make coffee, fresh, strong and brewed in the kind of chipped enamelled coffee pot that you can safely leave on the back of the stove to keep hot. There was already enough smoke in the room to fulfil all my nicotine requirements just by breathing but eventually we all three lit up again, purely from habit. 'Don't let DSI Needham find out Alex makes good coffee or he'll find excuses to come and sit in your kitchen,' I warned them.

Kroog smiled at Alex, endorsing the compliment, but it looked like the smile took some effort. Then she narrowed her eyes at me. 'It was murder, of course.' She paused and shook her head. 'I'm sounding like Miss Marple, have to watch that. And the police think it's one of us who did the silly woman in.'

'I'm sure they do. And I'm sure they're right. Someone set a trap for her. They probably saw her climbing across before, touching the wire. That gave them the idea to connect the fence to the mains. All they had to do was watch and wait. Needham and his lot will question everyone who was here as to where they were and who else they saw or were with. Then they'll draw up the diagram from hell to see who gives whom an alibi and if there are gaps or contradictions. Then they'll pounce.' If, on the other hand, they come away empty-handed, they will of course pounce on me as statistically the most likely suspect. But I kept that thought to myself.

'And they'll be completely wasting their time,' Alex said while exhaling smoke towards the ceiling.

'How so?'

'Whoever did it could have connected the current any time and then gone to the lecture or whatever. They didn't have to be there. She could have climbed in without touching the wire, but did touch it on the way out. That's probably why she was found inside. No need for someone to turn it on in between the two actions.'

'Then why didn't we have two dead sheep in the pen as well?'

'You don't know much about sheep, Chris,' said Kroog. 'Put them in an electrified enclosure and they'll get themselves zapped at the fence once, but after that they'll never go near it again. That wire could have been connected to the grid all morning without anyone noticing.'

'Ah,' I said while the implication sunk in. Not only did this mean the alibi question was useless, it also meant that the fence could have still been connected when I climbed across it. Twice. 'But it was turned off when the police found the connection.'

'Apparently.'

'So someone did turn it off after they had achieved their aim.'

Kroog wagged her pipe stem at me. 'Yes. But until then anyone could have touched the wire, which means they didn't give a lot of thought to who else they might have killed.'

'So whoever killed Rachel hated her enough to allow for some collateral damage.'

'Quite possibly,' said Alex. 'Let's hope Rachel is the only one the killer took exception to. Or we can expect more booby traps around the place.'

FIFTEEN

There are traps enough for the unwary in even the most ordinary lives, but some of the more painful ones are surely those we set for ourselves. At times my own life appears to be strewn with booby traps that, on closer inspection, were built by myself, often long ago. As I was driving towards the offices of Mantis IT Solutions – by special dispensation from the superintendent himself – I was not yet thinking of booby traps but did think I had made a mistake in agreeing to Mrs Pink's request to check over her husband. I felt too restless, too busy to sit in the car and wait for hours for Martin Byers to do something even remotely suspicious. Or even remarkable. But then again, what better opportunity to think things over than when you have to sit still and stare at nothing much anyway? There was my new painting, something that is often enough to preoccupy me; the way it looked so far was hardly a showcase for artistic brilliance that students could aspire to. There was the teaching, which was an odd thing to be doing if you hated teaching. Was I doing it justice or was I even worse than the last tutor they'd had? To top it all there were the strange goings on in Hufnagel and Landacker's studios and now Rachel's death. I was still not calling it murder in my mind: there was still the possibility that it was a prank gone wrong. I was reserving judgement. Unexplained death. Or let's split the difference: manslaughter. I was surprised it had not been renamed 'personslaughter' yet, surely an oversight soon to be remedied.

In the event I didn't have long to wait. There was Martin Byers, leaving the building with the same man, going into the car park and getting into the passenger side of the same car. I was beginning to have a bad feeling about this: I was letting Mrs Byers down by not taking this seriously enough. The woman was pregnant and needed an answer. But what if it wasn't another woman? What if it was another man? Although there were no signs in the men's body language to suggest even for a minute that they were anything other than work colleagues. My bad feelings were confirmed when I followed the Audi uphill again and the car turned into the same road, stopped in front of the same house and the same woman welcomed them in: Martin was being treated to supper again and I was ready for mine. I put a reminder into my phone to ask Mrs Byers what car, if any, her husband drove, then I set a course for home. Remember those booby traps I mentioned?

All I could think of when I got to Mill House was a shower, a change of clothes and some supper, preferably something involving the smoked salmon I knew was sitting in the fridge. The Landy was in the yard and I could see the door to the studio was open, so I knew Annis was around somewhere. I would make us some supper and then we could mull over today's strange happenings. Talking to Annis often made things much clearer, always depending on the amount of wine we consumed, of course. I skipped up the stairs, tapped on her door and walked in. I shouldn't have. Annis and Tim were in the middle of something. Nothing extraordinary, I was relieved to note, but nevertheless something I didn't expect them to be doing at Mill House. We had successfully shared Annis's favours for years now and there were unspoken rules about things. I had thought.

I turned round on my heels mumbling something like 'sorry guys' but the longer I thought about it the less apologetic I felt. I had a very hot shower, though a cold one would perhaps have served me better, then stomped downstairs and cluttered around in the kitchen, tearing salad leaves and slicing cucumbers with more gusto than was strictly necessary. It was Tim who came downstairs first.

He stood in the door and watched my performance for a minute. 'Sorry, mate, Annis thought you'd be ages yet.'

I kept chopping. 'Why is your bloody car not out there?'

'At the menders.'

'What's wrong with the damn thing?'

'Electrical fault.'

'Right.' I know diddly-squat about cars and we both hate football so that was all safe topics exhausted. Except one.

'Someone's been killed up at the art school?' Tim asked, coming closer but staying safely out of slicing radius.

'Electrocuted. Could be a bad prank or could be murder. I need you to do me a favour.'

'Sure, anything,' Tim said with unusual eagerness.

'I'll give you a list of people in a minute, find out as much as you can about them. Also I'm supposed to be following this guy who's meant to be a philanderer and all he ever does is go for dinner at a colleague's house. See if you can find any dirt on the man. I'm grasping at straws here.'

'Sure, mail me the stuff.'

'I'll write it down for you after supper. Nearly done.'

'Oh. Right.'

Annis came rattling down the stairs with her hair wet from the shower, ran her hand up my back and kissed my neck. 'Hi, hon, thought you'd be ages yet. You said.'

'Needham let me go early.'

'Oh, right. Smoked salmon, yum. I'll open some wine, shall I?'
And that's all there was to it.

Next morning an unusually eager Annis made breakfast while
I showered, and I sat down to hot poppy seed bagels, cream
cheese with freshly chopped chives, a perfectly timed boiled egg
and a cafetière of Blue Mountain. Ah, guilt. Long may it last.

'I was quite serious last night,' Annis said. 'Be careful up
there. Batcombe, the name says it all.'

'Means valley of bats. Not that I've seen any yet.'

'If that electro-shock thing was meant to be a prank then
someone up there has bats in their belfry. Ditto if it was murder,
of course. Hurry up with that bagel, hon.'

'Why?'

'There's one of those nondescript grey cars coming down the
track, can't see who's driving.'

'Not Needham again?' I asked through a hasty mouthful of
bagel. 'He must have smelled the coffee.'

'No, smaller car,' said Annis from the window. 'It's a Skoda
and it's Needham's Airdale terrier and some other guy.'

I stood by the window with my cup of coffee and watched. I
recognized bad news when I saw it; now it rolled into the yard
with that slightly exaggerated, arrogant speed of a DI on a mission.
DI Reid got out and strode towards the front door, followed
closely by a DS whose polyester suit I recognized from a previous
encounter.

'They look very sure of themselves,' Annis observed.

'Never more so than when they're barking up the wrong tree.'

'There's always the Norton in the sitting room. You could be
out the verandah doors and away over the fields before they've
found their running shoes.'

'Nah, Steve McQueen never made it either.'

The door knocker was being worked enthusiastically. I went
back to the breakfast table and attacked my boiled egg. It was
perfect; soft but not too runny. I could hear Annis stalling with
'I'll see if he's in, shall I?', but Reid was having none of it and
barged right through. He and his sergeant crowded into the
kitchen. When the DS had put on his styling mousse that morning
he had obviously overestimated the amount of hair he possessed;
it looked thin, greasy and rigid and showed his grey scalp through
the gunked-up strands. DI Reid was his usual beige-and-brown

self; I was always tempted to call him 'Sandy' but this morning I didn't get a chance.

'Christopher Honeysett, I'm arresting you on suspicion of murder. You don't have to say anything but . . .' He rattled down the whole caution.

Christopher! No one had called me polysyllabically since school. 'The condemned man ate a hearty breakfast,' I quoted and plunged the spoon into my egg.

'Cuff him,' Reid told his sergeant.

There was silence in the car on the way to Manvers Street nick; there's no point in arguing with them once they've arrested you. I sat quietly in the back while Reid drove and the sergeant used a crumbling tissue to wipe at the egg-yolk stains on his suit.

As soon as you get to a police station, time slows down. Everyone in there is horribly overworked, but since there are interminable regulations governing even the slightest activity, everyone acts as though they have all the time in the world. There are laws about wasting police time but none at all about wasting civilians' time. Being processed at Manvers Street police station makes the check-in for your El Al flight to Tel Aviv look casual. They also manage to be irritatingly evasive when answering simple questions like 'Where the hell is Needham?' or 'Are you out of your tiny mind?' By the time they parked me in Interview Room Two – that's the one with the unnerving stain on the wall – my breakfast had worn off and my patience thin.

'Calm down; it's all procedure,' Needham said when he eventually got round to showing up with a file, my drawing kit inside a huge evidence bag and the polyester sergeant by his side. I looked hungrily at the faded egg stains on his suit. 'Let's have three coffees here,' Needham said to the constable guarding the door.

'Aha, the torture begins,' I said.

'I think we can better *your* last effort; we have a snazzy new coffee machine. Right, enough beverage chat.' He went serious and scrabbled the plastic off a couple of new cassette tapes to load into the recorder.

'You're still using cassette tapes but you have a snazzy coffee maker. Wise use of resources.'

'Both for your benefit. No one can interfere with a tape recording; it would instantly show up. Nobody trusts digital stuff, it's too easily altered.' He pressed the record button, rattled down the date and time, his own name and that of the DS, I forget what it was. When the PC entered the room with our coffees he told the tape that as well; nothing if not thorough. He informed the tape that I had refused the aid of a duty solicitor – I was reserving judgement on whether to call on my 'own' solicitor since she charged by the second and I earned by the hour. Needham dumped UHT milk into his beaker, reached in his pocket for his sweetener and dropped a hailstorm into it, after which he tried to mix it all up with a little plastic stirrer that was two millimetres higher than the level of coffee in his beaker. 'You haven't asked me why you are here, so presumably you know.'

'Well, let me guess. I found the unconscious Rachel Eade and you somehow think I had something to do with her demise, though why I wouldn't have made sure of her before calling the ambulance must have given you pause for thought. Come on, Mike, you know I didn't do it. You *know* me.'

'While you are under caution it is Superintendent Needham. And yes, I have known you for a number of years, Mr Honeysett, but that has nothing at all to do with this line of questioning. If I thought it did, I would let someone else lead this investigation since you are the main suspect.'

'Rubbish. You don't believe for one minute I could have killed her.' His stony visage made me reach for the coffee. It wasn't real but drinkable.

'I am showing Mr Honeysett exhibit two, a black, cloth-bound book, size eight by eleven inches. Do you recognize this as yours?'

'Looks like mine.'

'It came from this bag, exhibit three.' He held up my sketch bag, still wrapped in plastic and labelled. 'Which, at the time when officers arrived at the scene of Rachel Eade's electrocution, you claimed to be yours.'

'What happened to exhibit one?' I asked, getting worried.

'I am now opening the sketchbook and showing Mr Honeysett some of the drawings inside. Drawings of trees and some kind of stone structure. Did you make these drawings?'

'I did. Can you get arrested for it? Your drawings are rubbish, ergo you must have killed Rachel Eade? You should have seen *her* drawings; they really *were* crap.' The DS scribbled something on his notepad as though I had just said something deeply significant.

'Yes, witnesses have mentioned your hostility towards Rachel Eade,' Needham continued.

'Hostility? Me? I hardly knew the woman. And what witnesses?'

'A Mr Howard and his son. They delivered the sheep and pen that Eade rented from them to Batcombe House. According to their statement, you and Dawn Fowling got into an argument with Mrs Eade.'

'I don't remember arguing with her. Dawn had a bit of a ding-dong with her. Rachel was quite scathing about Dawn's work.'

'Was she scathing about yours?'

'I don't think she knows my work.'

'You are being evasive. Was she scathing about your work? Did she say anything provocative about your painting? I hear you have recently changed styles.'

My, he was thorough. 'Yes, I have recently changed styles . . .'

'And are therefore a bit touchy about criticism of it.'

'She didn't criticise it. And even so. Running down another artist's work is hardly enough to make you feel murderous towards them. No one is that touchy. There wouldn't be an artist left alive.'

'I am now showing Mr Honeysett the chronologically most recent drawing in his sketchbook.' He turned the page and pushed the book towards me. 'Then how do you explain this?'

I had reached for my coffee but set it down again very slowly. The drawing on this page I had never seen before. It was very competent and showed part of the sheep pen. The sheep were standing huddled in one corner and in the foreground lay a figure that was clearly Rachel, competently drawn, easily recognizable. She was wearing a dress I recognized and she looked dead, her eyes wide open. Just visible at the edge of the drawing were the clips that had been attached to the wires, delivering the lethal current.

'How did that get into my sketchbook?'

'Like all the others did. You drew it.'

'I've never seen this drawing before. And look, Rachel wasn't wearing a dress. She was wearing that a couple of days earlier, though.'

'Are you trying to tell me you did not draw this?'

'Of course I didn't draw this. Do you think I found her body and stopped to do a drawing?'

'No,' said the polyester sergeant, 'we think you drew this the day before you say you found her unconscious. At least that's what the date suggests. It's there on the side of the wooden post. That's the day before Rachel's death.'

I turned the drawing sideways; he was right. 'Well that proves it's not my drawing. I never bother with the date.'

Needham took the book off me again. 'Nonsense, all your drawings are dated.' He turned back the pages and pointed out the dates, hidden on branches of trees or among the foliage of ferns, a date had been inserted, and the dates were correct.

I snatched the book from his hands and squinted at the numbers. 'It's not my handwriting. It's very close, it looks like mine, but it isn't. The drawing too is similar to my style. Someone's made an effort to make it look like it's mine. And put all the dates there in my handwriting.' Then I saw it. The butterfly symbol that had been carved into the tree I was drawing had also been drawn on to the tree I had drawn. If you follow me. 'Here, do you see that?' I turned the book round and tapped it. 'It's some kind of symbol I keep seeing and I did not draw that bit either. Someone added it to the tree recently and also added it to this drawing, which I made before the symbol appeared on the tree.'

'What is it?'

'It looks like a stylized butterfly to me. And I saw the same thing scratched into Landacker's gate at his house.' I now had to launch into a lengthy explanation on who Landacker was and what connected him to the college.

Needham took his time thinking it all over. 'How would this hypothetical person who did all that have gained access to your sketchbook?'

'Easily, it's in my bag, the bag is in the studio, the studio is always unlocked. Anyone could have taken it and drawn in it. Come to think of it, I did notice yesterday that it had been taken out and put back in upside down.'

The detective sergeant came to life again. '"Come to think of it"? Very convincing. And you didn't think anything of it at the time, naturally.'

'Who asked your opinion?' I was beginning to get angry

because I was beginning to get scared. Someone had done a convincing job on this sketchbook. 'Did you check this for fingerprints?' I asked Needham.

'We have. There were none on the cover, which is why I'm allowing you to handle it. There were only yours on any of the pages inside the book.'

'None on the cover? How do you explain that? Why wouldn't there be any on the cover?'

The sergeant looked dismissive. 'Because you spilled something on it and cleaned it? Who knows?'

Needham took the book from me and slid it back into the evidence bag. 'It had no fingerprints on it because it was cleaned and it was cleaned because whoever took your sketchbook was not wearing gloves when they took it and then realized they had left prints on it. It has been wiped with some sort of kitchen cleaner. Someone is trying to set you up, Chris, and making a pretty good job of it.'

'Then you do believe that I had nothing to do with it?'

'My sergeant here doesn't believe a word you say. Believe is neither here nor there. What I believe doesn't outweigh what we found in this sketchbook. I certainly can't tell the difference between the drawing of the murder victim and the rest of the drawings. They look like they are of one hand, Chris. Yes, I believe you, but that's not enough to get you off the suspect list.'

'The drawing at least proves one thing,' I said, breathing a little easier. 'The drawing was done before the event. Whoever drew it did it from memory and showed her in the dress she wore the last time she was up at Batcombe. In the drawing she is dead. So it was definitely planned. It was murder. And since I didn't do it, that means the murderer is still up there.'

And as Alex had pointed out in Kroog's kitchen: we didn't know if the killer's hatred confined itself to Rachel Eade.

The sun came out just in time to greet my exit from Manvers Street police station where I lit a cigarette, inhaled deeply and broke into a lung-emptying cough. I staggered out of the car park, dropped my cigarette and trod on it. Then I chucked the remaining pack into a nearby bin. There – I had stopped smoking.

All you need to stop smoking is to stop doing it.

I had been offered a lift home but I declined; one ride in a police car is much like any other and the air fresheners they use instead of opening the windows give me a headache. Quite apart from that I needed to replace all my drawing gear; it appeared it was safe to release me back into the community but my entire sketching equipment – sketchbook, pens, paints, the lot – remained in custody. Ah well, buying more art materials could hardly be described as hardship, the more the better. Since the stuff doesn't go off it makes sense to stock up – it's not going to get any cheaper. At Harris & Son in Green Street I explained my predicament to Ronny, a painter who sometimes moonlights as a shop assistant there. She found me a complete kit from all four corners of the shop. Half an hour later and I had remortgaged my house for a bijou watercolour kit with twelve colours, two retractable travel brushes to go with it, watercolour sketchbook, another sketchbook (can't have too many), dip pen, Indian ink, Chinese ink, a fistful of watercolour pencils, a selection of water-proof fine liners, assorted pencils of various grades, a craft knife and a collapsible water pot that looked like a Chinese lantern. Always wanted one of those.

Since Ronny had given me a ten per cent discount, I somehow imagined I had saved enough money to take a taxi home. 'There's me worrying about you languishing in a cell,' Annis said, 'and you take a taxi home via a paint warehouse. How much did that lot cost?'

'Let's just say my discount paid for the cab.'

'So that's what earning regular money does to you.'

No one had called from the college, so presumably no one was missing me yet. Plenty of time to have lunch then. It was after two o'clock by the time I rolled through the Batcombe House gates, which were wide open again, though Anne was there doing her best to shut them even as I drove past her. There were still police cars in front of the house.

'Mr Honeysett!' Anne summoned me. I wandered over, carrying my new sketching gear in an old shoulder bag, itching to get away into the woods. 'The police gave me a lecture on security yesterday and they are still here quizzing everybody, and these bloody gates are standing wide open and I can't get them shut. Kindly deal with them, will you? I have too many other things to do.' She stomped off, leaving me to 'deal with them'. I had no more luck than her: first one leaf, then the other failed to budge.

A student ambled past. 'I wouldn't bother if I were you,' she said.

'Yes, thank you for the advice.'

'Suit yourself. But rumour has it someone welded them solid.'

'Oh good, at least that makes me feel less of a wimp.'

At the studio a half-naked Petronela greeted me with a quick smile without disturbing her pose, Hufnagel greeted me with a grunt and Dawn greeted me with: 'A few students came in, wondering where you were.'

'Nice to be missed. I was going to talk to them about their assignments this morning but was held up. I'll try and round them up now.'

'They are all a bit jittery about Rachel's death. They're now saying it was murder. They had me in the staff room twice, going on about how I hated her. There's a difference between hating an arrogant dilettante and killing someone, I kept telling them. But that detective inspector has cloth ears. Do you think it was murder?'

Hufnagel spoke without taking his eye off his canvas. 'Yes, Honeysett, you're supposed to be a detective – give us your considered opinion. Was it murder and, if so, who dunnit?'

'I'm not sure. But whoever did it is pretty damn good at drawing.'

'What makes you say that?' asked Kurt, but I walked out, leaving the remark to hang there.

With us old folks hogging one painting studio (and the only life model), Studio Two was crammed with painters and the drawing studio had been invaded too. Neither pleased Ben Creeling, who cornered me as soon as I walked in. 'I have been working on a series of drawings of Petronela and had planned a painting of her, and now that Huffniggle is claiming her all for himself.'

'I know, the cheeky sod,' I said. This seemed to cheer Ben somewhat but I had not much else to offer him. 'You'll be kept quite busy with your next assignment and Mr Hufnagel will have finished with Petronela in a week or so.'

'A week!'

I left him steaming. I was pretty sure he had developed a more than purely artistic interest in the model and this was one lesson every painter has to learn early on: *you can't have everything you draw.*

'Right. You've all been drawing out there, on location, and some of your drawings were very good indeed. I now want you to go out there and paint the same locale. No paintings bigger than, say, twenty-two inches. Use your favourite medium and have a finished painting around this time the day after tomorrow.'

'The day after tomorrow!' came the chorus.

'When Van Gogh got going he produced at least one painting a day. Plus sketches and drawings. He also illustrated his letters and he didn't have a Mrs Washbrook to cook for him. So there's no reason why you can't paint a small canvas in two days. Of course those who didn't walk more than twenty paces from the college will be at a slight advantage, but I expect might soon wish they had drawn somewhere more interesting.'

'What if it rains?' came the question.

'Wear a hat.'

Naturally I was just putting it on. I had never painted in the rain in my life but I was determined to go out into the woods, whatever the weather, and do my drawings so that at last I could get properly going on my ambitious canvas. I realized, of course, that I had competent competition in Hiroshi, who was also painting a woodland scene, though minus the kiln, but I could catch up while he was busy with his assignment, I thought. When I'd finished my pep talk, Hiroshi came over.

'I have been busy drawing for my large canvas. I saw you too have been going into the woods. Is it permitted to see your sketchbook?'

'That's not possible at the moment.'

'You are keeping secrets, sensei?'

'No, the police have it. All my drawing gear.'

'What can the police want with your drawing things?'

'Nothing. It was just that I had dumped it at the scene of Rachel's murder and it got bagged up along with the rest.'

'And will the police study your sketchbook, do you think?'

'Why should they be interested in my sketchbook?'

'They have been looking at a lot of sketchbooks. All morning.'

'Have they? I wonder why.' If the police had been looking at students' sketchbooks then I had to hand it to Needham. Even while he had me arrested he was already working on the hypothesis that the drawing in my book wasn't by my hand, despite appearances to the contrary, and he had been looking for a candidate. My esteem of the man's brains was on the rise.

Back in Studio One all was quiet business – Dawn was sitting with her nose six inches away from the canvas like a short-sighted Monet, watching wispy skeins of pink paint dry. Pink? What had happened to the darkly stormy canvas, all greys and dirty purples, that Rachel's arrival had spawned? This, by comparison, looked like a celebration. Hufnagel – somehow he never became Kurt in my mind – was scrutinizing his composition while absentmindedly wiping a brush on his jacket. The only one who appeared to be working hard was the half-naked Petronela, standing in the middle of Hufnagel's arrangement, surrounded by humming blow heaters. 'Take a break, Petronela,' I said.

'Oh, good, I am for a desperate fag,' she said.

A flash of annoyance crossed Hufnagel's face as he looked up at me.

'This one's real, remember?' I tapped my watch. 'Breaks every thirty minutes, all right?' I picked up my second-edition sketch bag and filled a plastic bottle with water. 'If anyone wants me I am in the woods, drawing.'

'I can't believe you get paid for that,' Hufnagel said, throwing his brush on to his painting table in a gesture of mock disgust. 'You jammy bastard.'

I was beginning to think of him as Huffniggle too. But perhaps I *was* quite jammy, I thought, as I dodged the tobacco cloud around Petronela who was – fully covered up now – smoking just outside. As I passed the first big hulking sculpture, I found Ben Creeling behind it, trying to hide from me.

'Ben?'

'Yes?'

'You're really into drawing, aren't you?'

'Yes. It's important. Fundamental.'

'I agree. But I wonder if you have had enough opportunity to draw the male form. Do you think we should let Petronela go and instead hire a male model for the rest of the year?'

There was panic in his eyes. 'No.'

'Then stop creeping around her and get on with your assignment.'

By now I knew my way around the woods a little better and

found my spot without first having to get lost. I unpacked my virginal sketchbook, pencils and paints and began the process of recording the place all over again. Now the carved I><I motif seemed to glare at me from the bark of the tree and it did briefly occur to me that it could probably be taken for granted that anyone who carved symbols into tree bark was carrying a knife.

SIXTEEN

With only a few short days (or so it seemed) to go until the anniversary exhibition was to be hung, I was keen to get some painting done. There had been enough interruptions to throw the most dedicated painter. For starters there was the nagging feeling that I should be watching Martin Byers, to either nail him or exonerate him for his suspicious wife. Then there was the very real possibility that a killer was walking free up here in Batcombe House, not to mention the confiscation of my drawings. At least any doubts I'd had over Annis's commitment to the wobbly status quo of our relationship had been energetically dispelled by her last night, and my worries about failing my students had been diminished by seeing them all stagger around with canvases and paints and by Kroog growling 'You're doing fine, Honeysett' as she wheezed past me this morning (whilst helping to carry an 18-foot-long piece of inch-thick iron towards the sculpture sheds with her pipe in her mouth). I had now got into the habit of entering straight through the French windows of Studio One since they were always unlocked – I doubted there still existed keys for them – and thereby avoiding the front entrance all together. As I approached I could see that in fact one leaf of the door stood open; perhaps I was not alone in wanting an early start? Just as I was about to step through it, something in my peripheral vision caught my eye.

On the sandstone wall to the left of the French window, directly at my eye level, was the butterfly symbol. But this time it had not been carved, scratched, drawn or painted. The stone had darkened considerably over the many years since the house was first built and a bloom of grey-green algae was spreading up the side of the building. This time the I><I symbol had been made by cleaning off the grime of centuries, revealing the bright, pristine sandstone underneath. It had created a ghostly, fuzzy image that was hard to focus on but it was undoubtedly the same tag.

I stepped a little more warily across the threshold after this. The studio was empty. There was no sign of Dawn or Hufnagel. I dumped my bag, got out the kettle from where I hid it at night and filled it. I had brought my own coffee and a tiny cafetière to bring some much needed beverage culture to the proceedings. Coffee made, I sat in my chair, patted my pockets for cigarettes, remembered that I didn't smoke any more, and settled back to study the excruciatingly slow development of my canvas. It didn't look too bad this morning. I had made a bit more progress in fact than I remembered, and despite the pressure I was under, the quality of the brushwork had not suffered at all – in fact some of the last passages were very pleasing; it seemed to me that I was fast finding my feet in the world of figurative painting.

Dawn cluttered into the room, already talking. 'I can smell real coffee, please tell me there's a pot of the stuff somewhere.' I handed her the empty cafetière and my tin of Guatemalan coffee. She read the tin. 'You posh git.'

'I'm not posh, just a glutton.'

'Yeah, right.'

Coffee brewed, she stopped beside me to look at my canvas. 'I do like what you've done since last night. You must have started early this morning.'

'No, haven't done anything yet, just got here.'

'Really?' She stepped up to the canvas and peered at it from eight inches away as painters do. 'What about this passage here?' She pointed down the length of one tree trunk. 'You definitely hadn't painted that when you left yesterday, because I remember thinking that I'd be interested to watch how you'd render the lichen and moss on that.'

I nearly spilled my coffee leaping from my chair. I sniffed around the canvas, stared at my palette, scrutinized my brushes. And I came to an unusual conclusion: 'I didn't paint that.'

Dawn nearly drowned on a mouthful of hot coffee. 'You what?' she spluttered.

'You're right, I hadn't painted that bit when I left yesterday. I didn't paint it at all. Someone else did.'

Dawn stared at me, then the canvas, then me again. 'You're serious. How bizarre is that?'

'They did a bloody good job of it. There I was, admiring my own brushwork, and it was someone else's. Not that I'm incapable of admiring other people's work, but you don't expect to find it in your own painting.'

'But who could have done it?'

'Plenty of painters around, aren't there?'

'True, I don't mean *would* have but not all of them *could* have done it. That's good painting, it's a great passage and fits in completely with your style. I couldn't tell it was by someone else.'

'Yes. That's what worries me.'

'What do you mean? Ha! Perhaps they'll finish the whole painting for you.'

Until that moment Dawn had been high on my suspect list for Rachel's murder and for the drawing of her body in my sketchbook. But looking at her now and listening to her, I did what any unprofessional idiot would do. I changed my mind. She couldn't *possibly* be the one. Could she? So I sat down and told her all about the drawing in the sketchbook, the drawing I had, until five minutes ago, still suspected her of doing.

She hunched her shoulders and made herself small on her chair. 'That is *so* creepy, Chris. That would really have freaked me out. So not only do we have a murderer up here, they are also trying to frame you. I'd be careful if I were you.'

'I am being careful. But who? At least we know it's someone who can draw.'

'True. That knocks a few people off the suspect list, like Anne and Claire. And Mrs Washbrook. Unless they have suddenly developed artistic talent.'

'Even quite a few with talent are not good enough to have done the drawing in my sketchbook. As for this painting – there are even fewer.' I decided to tell Dawn the rest of it. I took her outside and showed her the I><I symbol on the wall.

'Oh, wait, I've seen that before somewhere. Somewhere around here, can't remember exactly where now.'

'I saw it on a tree near where I've been drawing and I saw it on Landacker's front gate, the gate to his property. He also had his place broken into.'

'I know, you said. This is beginning to get scary, you know. Of course, we don't know for sure that it's connected: Rachel's death and that x-motif everywhere.'

'If it was just around here I'd think nothing of it, just some idiot tag. But on Landacker's gate? Unless the idiot who does it lives in his village, of course. But my painting . . . I can't get over that.'

We went back inside and stared some more at my canvas. Dawn rolled herself a cigarette and when she wordlessly handed me her tobacco pouch I absentmindedly rolled myself one and lit it. Her black tobacco made me cough a bit at first but I soon got used to it.

All it takes to get back into a twenty-a-day habit is one cigarette.

Dawn scrutinized her own canvas but pronounced it untouched: 'One hundred per cent Dawn Fowling. No little helpers here.'

Outside a police officer walked past, carrying a box file – heartwarming to see they still had those; harder to lose than a USB stick, I supposed – while a student on a bicycle was practising her wheelies on the lawn and the sound of metal grinding and banging drifted across from the sculpture sheds. Another day at the Bath Arts Academy was under way. I had a go at cleaning my palette, which you have to do from time to time or your colours turn to mud. (Unless of course you are planning to paint mud, in which case you're already there.)

Half an hour later Hufnagel slouched through the door. Outside of his own shambolic house, he moved almost hesitantly and opened doors only just far enough to squeeze through the gap sideways. He acknowledged us with a friendly grunt and let himself fall into his painting chair. I was just about to tell him about my painting mystery when he shot out of his chair again and started swearing as though he had sat on a nail.

'What happened?' I asked when he ran out of breath.

'What ha— Are you *blind*? Is this some kind of joke? Is this a wind-up? Did you do this?'

'Do what?'

'That, *that*!' He pointed furiously at his canvas.

I looked. He was making good progress; the figure and imaginary landscape were taking shape. 'I can't see it.'

'Precisely! It's gone! The arrow is gone. Some bastard painted over it. If I find who has done this . . .' His hands were convulsing in a strangling motion.

In his painting, the bare-breasted Petronela was holding the bow in one hand, and her other hand was drawn back close to her cheek. But no arrow. 'Painted over it? Are you sure you put it in?'

'Are you taking the piss now? I know what I painted and what I didn't.' I quickly told him what had happened to my own painting. Hufnagel continued to fume. 'This is outrageous. Vandalism! Hooliganism! And at an art school! I don't care if they set fire to the principal's car, but at an art school paintings ought to be sacred.'

'Did they torch her car?'

'No, it's just a *suggestion*.'

I examined the surface of his canvas. 'It's amazingly well done though. There's not a hint that there has ever been an arrow.'

'I painted the arrow last thing. The paint was fresh.' He came closer and stared wide-eyed at what wasn't there. 'But you're right. If I had the merest doubt about the state of my memory I wouldn't now be sure if I had painted it at all. It's miraculously seamless. Couldn't have done it better myself. Had I bloody wanted to!' His anger exploded once more.

'You can paint it again,' Dawn said soothingly. 'It's not like they destroyed your painting.'

'Yes, shouldn't take you long,' I agreed.

'Shouldn't take me long? That's not the point! And you can talk; they *added* to your painting. It looks terrific. So you're all right. As ever.'

But was I really? I wondered about that as I walked to the little post office in the village where they kept a limited selection of cigarettes for idiots like me. Mmm, also shortbread, I noticed.

The mystery painter had added to my painting, and done it well, but could I simply let it stand? It was so much like what I imagined would have flown from my own brush (eventually) that it seemed idiotic to scrape it off and start over again.

When I made it back to the studio the place seemed crowded and noisy. Hiroshi was there, scrutinizing my painting; Ben was there pretending to look at it while stealing glances at Petronela; Dawn was having an animated conversation with Phoebe; Petronela in her paint-stained dressing gown looked bored as she watched Hufnagel and Anne argue. He was complaining to her about his disappeared arrow and she was giving him a piece of her mind about electricity use. She was hugging one of the blow heaters to herself.

'Don't talk to me about security,' she said. 'I've been trying to introduce some measures, like the picture ID I see you are not wearing, and everyone poo-poos my ideas. Someone has welded the front gates solid so now we are permanently open to all comers and I have had lectures from the police about it all. As if somehow I could have prevented Rachel from being killed.'

'Just lockable doors and windows would be a start,' Hufnagel bravely ventured.

'There don't seem to be keys to half the doors here, which would mean replacing the locks, and have you *any* idea what that would cost? Just putting window locks on the ground floor would cost an *absolute* fortune; I've never seen so many bloody windows and some of them don't even have a latch.'

'What I did at my place . . .'

But Anne didn't give him a chance to tell her how he had solved his own security problems with a mouthful of nails and a hammer. 'And may I remind you that you don't actually work here and are just allowed to splash paint around for a bit until that ridiculous anniversary exhibition is over. I should cancel it after what's happened out there, but the invitations have gone out, apparently. As for these blow heaters, one ought to be perfectly sufficient. The college can't subsidise nude painting at the rate of three kilowatts per hour, that's utterly ridiculous, you will have to admit. I'm taking this one away.' She marched past me out of the French windows and called over her shoulder: 'And now I'll go and confiscate whatever those sculptors used to ruin the front gate. It's sheer vandalism, that's what it is! Misuse of college property!'

I closed the door behind her. 'I'd like to see her try and take away Kroog's welding gear.' There was now a distinct chill in the air in every sense of the word. The sun had gone in, Hufnagel was fuming, Petronela was hugging herself and Dawn and Phoebe had fallen silent. Ben looked love-struck and Hiroshi stood by my painting, smiling serenely. Everyone was looking at me. Everyone thought they were there because of me. I remembered that at least three of these were my students. 'Let's all get on with some work, shall we? Hiroshi, Ben, Phoebe? You have assignments to finish. Kurt, stop whining about your arrow and paint another one. Petronela, wait until I've found you another heater. Dawn, could you make us all some tea?'

'Not coffee?'

'Tea. *Warming, calming* tea. No sugar for me, ta.' (*Exit left via the French window.*) I knew there used to be a cupboard full of heaters in the drawing studio; I hoped they were still sleeping there and hadn't been confiscated yet. A few yards further along, outside the conservatory, stood Dan the ceramics tutor, arms folded in front of his chest, staring straight ahead across the lawn at the fringe of Summerlee Wood. He looked stiff and furious.

'You all right, Dan?' I called.

He took a moment before he turned towards me. 'I don't know any more.'

That sounded serious, so I went over. 'Something the matter?'

He lifted his shoulders high, then let them fall and exhaled. 'It's this place. It used to be brilliant. Relaxed. Fun. And now . . . The police are still here. And even worse, I just had a visit from John's daughter.'

'Same here. Hang on a mo. Wait until I fetch a blow heater for the model, then come and join us for some tea and shortbread in Studio One.'

In the drawing studio I found the cupboard and opened it. There they all were, stacked willy-nilly, battered, clapped out, lovely paint-spattered blow heaters, six of them. They looked awfully familiar. I plugged one in – it rattled but it worked.

Back in our studio I furnished Dan with tea and shortbread. 'Welcome back to civilization. Now, let me guess: ceramics is too expensive?'

Dan practically exploded. 'The main kiln is using too much electricity. We are only allowed two firings now.'

'What's that, a week? A month?'

'A year! That's insane, you can't teach ceramics without using the kiln! Now I'm supposed to use the test kiln for demonstration purposes and allow the students to fire a couple of pieces at the end of each term. That's ridiculous; students won't come here for that. I couldn't teach an evening class of amateurs like that!'

'Did you tell her that?'

'What do you think?'

'And?'

'She said do it or she'll close the ceramics department. After all, there is a perfectly good one at Bath University.'

'Is there?'

He sighed. 'One of the best in the country.'

'What makes your course different?'

'Theirs is very cutting edge; ours puts more emphasis on the traditional.'

'How traditional?' I asked. I fished out my sketchbook and showed him my drawing of the kiln in the woods. 'That traditional?'

He scrutinized the drawing. I pointed behind me over my shoulder where a mere ghost of the kiln had made it on to my big canvas. 'A wood-firing kiln,' he said. 'No, not that traditional, we don't have one of those. Where did you draw this?'

I pointed over his shoulder. 'About five minutes' walk that-a-way.'

Dan nearly choked on his shortbread. 'What? I had no idea! No one ever mentioned it. You must show me where it is. Can you do it now? I mean, finish your tea first, of course. How big is it? Is it in good repair? When has it last been used? Have you looked inside?' Dan was as excited as a kid.

So much for getting some painting done. It was back to the woods for me to show Dan the kiln. I took my sketchbook; I might as well do some drawing while I was out there. And of course while I had it with me nobody else could draw in it.

When we reached the little clearing, Dan stopped and stood in awe. Then he looked at me as though I had given him the nicest present he had ever received before he went and danced all over the ruined heap. It was *wonderful* and *perfect* and *so cool* and he *never imagined*. He was as entranced as though I had shown him a lost city in the jungle, complete with a hoard of gold. 'That's the solution, of course. We'll go *ultra* traditional – and of course burning wood is carbon neutral, how right-on is that?' He cleared some of the debris from the entrance to the tunnel. 'I can't wait to see what it looks like inside.'

'Is that a good idea? You don't know how stable that thing is.'

'It looks rock solid. Oh. You haven't got a torch on you, by any chance?'

Trust me, I'm a detective. I handed him my mini Maglite,

which earned me more aren't-you-a-marvel looks from Dan before he duck-walked into the tunnel of the kiln. Meanwhile I sat and sketched the thing in detail. Dan kept talking to me and though I couldn't make out a word of what he was saying the melody of his chatter was a happy one. From time to time he appeared at the mouth of the tunnel, pushing heaps of broken pots in front of him. 'Stuffed with broken vessels. Last firing must have been a disaster.' Then he'd disappear again. As long as it wasn't the first-and-last firing, I thought.

It was getting late (in art-school terms, anyway) before Dan had had enough. He was covered head-to-toe in soot, charcoal and ceramic dust but right now I was willing to bet that he was the happiest tutor on the campus.

'I'll go out there again tomorrow,' he said back at Batcombe House. 'With a few volunteers to clear up properly, start a few repairs and collect firewood, of course.'

'Great.' So much for my idyllic oasis of peace in the forest.

Dawn had already left but Hufnagel was still working, without Petronela, on the imaginary landscape of his painting. I just dropped off my drawing gear and left. Only a few cars were out front. Matthew, Stottie's faithful chauffeur-cum-boyfriend, was leaning against his immaculately white Ford Focus, looking bored in immaculate leather jacket and designer jeans. He had parked as far away as possible from the rusting disaster area of Hufnagel's ancient Fiesta.

But, I noticed now, not everything about Hufnagel's car was ancient. The I><I tag scratched viciously into the driver's door looked brand new.

SEVENTEEN

Tim and I had never talked much about Annis, and recently, not at all. Right from the start we had decided that exchanging notes would probably lead to disaster. We were blokes, which meant we happily avoided all relationship talk anyway and so restricted our comments about our triangular arrangements to half-ironic remarks of the ain't-it-awful and aren't-women-odd category. In a strange way, however, our unusual connection had driven a wedge between us. Both of us had probably long decided that while we liked each other a lot, we both preferred Annis's company to each other's and as a result now saw very little of each other, except when Tim was helping out with my private investigation 'lark', as he called it. All of which meant that evenings like today's, with the three of us on the verandah with our feet up and beers in our hands, was now a rare occasion. 'That kind of thing always amazed me,' said Tim when I recounted how half the doors and most of the windows at Batcombe House could not be locked. 'I would walk up to a house that cost an absolute fortune. A hundred grand's worth of cars in the garage. But can't be arsed to fit forty quid's worth of window locks to keep me out.'

'That's exactly how Anne Birtwhistle thinks. She's desperate to save money so spending a tenner on each window seems too much to her. The door to our studio can't be locked at all. Every day I go into the refectory and Mrs Washbrook asks me what I have done about the pilfering. What can you do about pilfering if you leave the doors open? And now someone is messing about with our paintings.'

'Or in your case, helping to paint them,' Tim said. 'There's a fairy tale like that, a shoemaker, I think, gets help from the little people. Every morning they have done all his work for him. So he and his wife hide one night to see who makes the wonderful shoes but the little people discover them and never come back. It's obvious: you've got fairies up there.'

'Well, if it happens again I'll seriously consider hiding myself to see who does it. I might kill two birds with one stone and catch the pilferer at the same time.'

'Might be the same one,' Annis suggested. 'Nick some food, get bored, do a bit of painting . . .'

'I get such an ominous feeling when I drive through the gate up there now. According to Kroog, John did too. Something isn't right. And I think it all hangs together somehow, all of it. The murder, the break-ins, the graffiti.'

'What graffiti?' asked Tim.

'It's like a large X, flattened out. I saw it at Landacker's, who had his studio broken into; it's on Hufnagel's car, who had *his* studio trashed; I saw it in the woods and on the wall of the school next to our studio entrance. Here, I'll show you.' I drew it on a bit of paper and handed it to him.

Tim took it and shot out of his chair. 'That? I saw that earlier. It's on your studio door.'

'*What?*' Annis and I said together.

'Annis had left the door open, so when I got here I thought she was still up there. There was no one in there, at least I thought there wasn't. And I closed the door, being a neat sort of guy. *That,*' he waved the piece of paper, 'has been scratched into the outside. Or not scratched, really . . .'

In the dusk we all rushed up the meadow to the barn. There was the tag: I><I. It had not been scratched, it had been sand-papered into the weathered planks of the door. Annis did not stop to admire it. She yanked open the door and turned on what passes for light up here, a forty-watt bulb hanging at the end of a cable from the corrugated roof. Nothing looked out of place but after what I had told her about mystery painters, Annis care-fully checked for evidence of the little people having changed her canvas.

'Anything?' I asked.

'Not a thing, hasn't been touched.'

'Anything else been disturbed?'

'Not as far as I can see.'

'What would you have done if they had had a go at your painting?' I asked. 'If someone had added to your canvas and it was absolutely brilliant. As good as your own. Or better.' Annis's eyebrows shot up. 'If that was possible,' I added quickly.

'Now you're getting metaphysical. It's about authorship, isn't it? And changing someone else's art work is . . . well, I think it's vandalism if it makes it worse but still mischief if it improves it.'

'I agree. But that doesn't answer my question.'

'You know, I'm not sure what I would do. It hasn't happened, therefore I don't know what I would feel when confronted with it.'

An honest answer, as always. But no help at all.

'What about Hufnagel's arrow? They just made it disappear. He has to paint it again, now.'

'That's just plain mean. I do think you'll need to try to catch your painting fairy if it happens again.'

Outside we took another look at the tag on the door. 'It's called reverse graffiti,' Annis enlightened us. 'I've seen it elsewhere. Instead of spray-painting, they clean the stone or wood or whatever. I'm not sure you can be done for cleaning bits of a wall. I doubt there's such an offence as illicit wall-cleaning.'

'Strictly speaking you are stealing someone's dirt,' Tim suggested.

'Ah,' mused Annis, 'but how did it get there? Is dirt on a wall private or public property? And how can you prove ownership of dirt . . .?'

I was suddenly no longer in the mood for banter. Whoever was responsible for the tags had been here, in my realm, and whoever was responsible for the tags might also be responsible for Rachel's death. I took another good look at the symbol on the studio door. It didn't tell me anything new but it gave me a bad feeling. This kind of thing, like scratching cars and doors, is done in anger. And it almost always escalates because it can never be enough. Rachel was dead. I didn't know if the symbol had appeared around her place too. I might try and find out, although it was too late for Rachel. But not for others.

'I'll have to go out again,' I announced.

'Oh?' It was getting dark. Annis frowned and checked her watch.

'Yes. This worries me. I'm going to pop round to Landacker's place.'

'Your number-one fan; he'll be delighted.'

'I know, I know. But that's where I saw the symbol first and I want to at least warn him that it may be connected with a death. I don't know, I'm beginning to get a bad feeling about this.'

'I'm not surprised,' said Tim. 'Someone was definitely here and did that on your door. Must mean *something*.'

'You want us to come with you?' Annis asked.

'No, I'll be fine. And I won't be long.' How wrong can a man be?

'I gotta go too,' said Tim, 'I have a presentation to make first thing tomorrow.'

I felt ashamed for being relieved about that, but I didn't think about it long. I suddenly had an eerie feeling that I was late for something, that I ought to hurry, that I was in the wrong place. I drove with the window open, despite the cool evening air that began to bluster through the lanes. The I><I symbol had somehow imprinted itself on my matrix; I was beginning to see it everywhere, like it was following me around. I was driving too fast down a narrow lane near Motterton, Landacker's village, when a thought struck me that made me take my foot off the accelerator. I let the car roll to a stop. What if it really *was* following me around? Until tonight, when the graffiti had appeared on the barn door, I had comfortably assumed that it had nothing to do with me, that I was merely a witness. It could equally be that I saw the symbol everywhere because I was meant to, because it was meant for me. Just because it appeared on Landacker's gate and Hufnagel's car didn't necessarily mean it was meant for them. It had been carved into a tree by the old kiln when it was still only me out there, apart from the occasional naked man in the undergrowth. But what could I do about it? I could not anticipate where it would appear next and get the jump on the tagger . . . I could conceivably go away and stay for a week a hundred miles away and see if the sign followed me. But realistically I would have to find other ways of making sense of it, if there was any to be made.

I drove on, more slowly now, still mulling it over, through the village and out the other end, down the lane to the Old Forge. Landacker would probably shrug it all off, as he seemed to have done with the break-in. I didn't even like Landacker, so why was I bothering? I couldn't have said. All I knew when I parked the car in the dark lane opposite his gate was that I now felt I was in the right place, while when I was standing outside my own studio I had felt that I wasn't.

I could smell it as soon as I got out of the car: raw petrol. By the time I had crossed the road I could see it too. The petrol was on fire.

The light of it glowed eerily, yellow and blue on the other side of the gate. I tried to open it but the lock had been repaired. I jumped, grabbed the top and pulled myself up so I could see over it. A long line of fire was running along the outside of Landacker's studio, with the core of the fire centring on the entrance door. Mostly it was petrol burning – a thin yellow tongue of it was running towards me – but the wooden door and door frame had already caught. The barn was part stone, part timber and would be a fireball in minutes. I dialled 999 and asked for the fire service. No, sorry, I did not know the sodding post code, but you could hardly miss it since the damn thing was on fire! *Honestly*. I heaved myself over the gate and dropped down on Landacker's drive. I tried opening the gate for when the fire brigade arrived but it was locked. Well, they had ladders, didn't they?

Whoever had set the fire had to have done it literally seconds before I arrived, yet there was no sign of anyone. Landacker's BMW was not here. Some of the petrol on the drive was slowly burning itself out, but fire was beginning to take hold on the door and doorframe and was creeping up a beam on the side. I knew from my first visit that the path between the barn and the house led into a substantial back garden and where there's a big garden there's usually a hosepipe. The fire hissed and spat as it consumed the varnish on the door. Squeezing past it, I averted my face; the heat and fumes caught in my throat. It was dark back here. A terrace with furniture and plant pots lay to my left; a paved area with a shed at the far end to my right. All else was lawn and trees. At last I found a stand pipe near the corner of the house but no convenient hose attached, not even a bucket or a watering can. I grabbed one of the plant pots and turned it over. The plants in it stuck firm. I shook. Nothing. I banged it on the patio and the pot broke in two. I grabbed the next one and shook that. Nothing. I banged it on the grass this time and eventually shook most of the plants and soil from the pot. It had a hole in the bottom, naturally. I stuck a finger in it and began filling it. The light from the fire increased as it spread. The plant pot was of thick glazed ceramic and got quite heavy but my finger managed to plug the hole. I filled it to the brim and ran towards the fire with it. The crash of the glass blowing from the half-glazed door nearly made me drop it. I stopped, hurled the water at the fire and nearly ripped my finger off in the process. The water made little difference that I could see. I ran back, filled the pot, chucked it at the door. And again. Now that the glass had blown, the fire had found something interesting inside and had started consuming the varnish on an interior beam. I was sweating from the heat and the exertion and was panting. But I couldn't stop. I'd never put it out but I could perhaps buy a few seconds' time for the fire brigade. I staggered back and forth with the flowerpot. My right side was now sodden with spilled water, my left was bone dry from the heat of the fire. I took a breather to drink some water from the tap. When I straightened up I could hear the glorious sound of the sirens wailing their way toward me but I might as well go on. I filled the flowerpot. It seemed to get heavier every time. The fire was roaring now as it sucked air through the shattered window into the vestibule behind it. At last there were the growling diesels of the fire engines outside the gate, flashing blue beacons reflecting off the house and a couple of firemen climbing over the gate. Two uniformed police came after them. Soon a hose was being dragged across and the pumps started to shoot glorious, high-powered water jets on to the fire – it collapsed in less than a minute. The police came over to me. One of them looked familiar. Then it came to me: he was the one who had attended the scene when the dead John Birtwhistle had nearly run me down. He recognized me too. And promptly arrested me.

'. . . on suspicion of arson. You do not have to say anything but it may harm your defence . . .'

'Wait a *second*! I was the one who called the fire brigade.'

'Oh yes, after you set the fire.'

'Rubbish.'

'I'm afraid you were seen climbing over the gate and the witness called us. Apparently the fire started soon afterwards.'

Seen? By whom? 'I climbed in *because* there was a fire. I was trying to put it out.' I held up the flowerpot in my defence.

'Yes, please put that down.'

'I'm afraid I can't.' It was true, I had tried. The finger in the drainage hole had swelled up beyond the second joint and the more I tried to pull it out the more painful it became.

'Please don't make this difficult, sir; put the pot down.' He reached a hand out for it, but I withdrew it out of reach.

'Would you just listen for a second . . .'

'Put the pot down, sir.'

'Very well.' I sat down so I could at least rest the damn pot on the damp ground.

'This is not helping. Please get up, sir.'

'You asked me to put the pot down,' I said childishly.

He called across to his colleague, who was talking to a fire officer. 'Terry, give us a hand here.'

'Look, my finger is stuck . . .'

'Up you come. Let go.' The other officer tried to prise my hand off the pot. It hurt like hell.

Apparently it is not the done thing to call a police officer a 'complete and utter pillock'. Ditto 'deaf moron'. 'Educationally subnormal' is also frowned upon these days, while 'ow, my finger, you stupid arse' got me additionally arrested for swearing at a police officer. I eventually got enough elbow room to smash the pot on the verandah's railing, which the arresting officers mistook for a prelude to a fight. One squirted pepper spray into my eyes and the other handcuffed me. This didn't improve my mood (or my language). Most of the pot had disintegrated now but I was left with a jagged saucer-sized piece of the bottom part with my finger still stuck solidly in the hole. This was the moment Greg Landacker chose to make an appearance in his BMW. He was wearing an expensive dark suit with a cream rollneck jumper and picked his way carefully across the broken glass and potsherds in his handmade brogues to inspect the damage. Then he spotted me between the two policemen. 'You!' He stared at me in bewilderment.

'Is this person known to you then?' one of the officers asked.

'Yes, that's Honeysett. I constantly find him here, but . . .' He looked astonished at the damage to the barn.

'Right, in the car,' said the officer, pulling me away.

'I was trying to put it out,' I called to Landacker, but he gave no indication that he had heard me and stood with both hands on the top of his head in an attitude of despair. I let myself be dragged off. The sooner I got to a police officer with more than two brain cells, I told myself, the sooner I'd get out of this mess.

Surely.

By now I was handcuffed, had one hand stuck in a potsherd, my hair was wild and in my face, my trousers and shoes were sodden and I had an itch on my nose I couldn't reach due to my handcuffs. I sat muttering darkly to myself in a self-righteous cloud of antipathy and misery.

'We'll get the police doctor to take a look at your finger once you've been processed,' the officer called Terry promised. In the state I was in, he'd probably have me sectioned as soon as look at me. I pulled myself together, stopped muttering, rubbed my nose against the window frame, shook the hair out of my face and sat up and took notice.

I was getting far too familiar with the booking procedure at Manvers Street station. I only very briefly lost my temper again when I was told that the jagged edges of the broken pot were considered dangerous and I would have to remain handcuffed until a doctor had been found. 'For your own safety, sir,' said the other officer, who I most wanted to slice into small pieces with it.

A doctor was eventually found, who ummed and ahhed and suggested we try lubrication first. 'This might hurt a bit,' he said with remarkable presentiment and pulled. It did. I really had little to add to my previous expletives so I just gritted my teeth. Eventually he freed me by breaking the shard with a pair of pliers.

The relief! 'Thanks, Doc. How are you with handcuffs?'

They came off next, since I was no longer in possession of anything sharp. Or shoelaces, phone or much else apart from my clothes. Arson was a serious crime, I was told, and there was no question of me going anywhere until I had been interviewed and a decision had been made whether to charge me or not.

If you have never spent a night in a police cell, imagine a lot of nothing at an unnoticeable temperature with an indestructible red mattress, and a surveillance camera plus monitor high up in the wall. The TV is not tuned to your favourite show but if you make enough of a nuisance of yourself the ugly mug of Sergeant Hayes will appear on it and you'll hear him say sympathetically: 'I'd just try and get some sleep if I were you, Mr Honeysett.'

Other guests of the custody suite appeared to include a drunk who made an awful racket, banging and shouting for half an hour, then appeared to fall asleep in the middle of a word, and a rattling drug addict who kept screaming about his rights and that he needed a fag and a doctor, both of which he eventually got. It's hard to believe but despite the whining, injured voice in my head that went *on and on* about how mean and stupid everyone was and how dare they do this to me – *me*, Christopher Honeysett, painter, PI and all-round good egg – I fell asleep.

They told me it was breakfast: a slice of white toast plus cornflakes and tea in red plastic containers on a red plastic tray. 'The punishment has started already?' Then I became amazingly polite and asked if it would be at all possible, at their earliest convenience, to speak to Superintendent Michael Needham when he had an incy-wincy minute to spare?

No, that wasn't possible. I lost some of my *politesse* when I enquired why the hell it wasn't. Because he was in Bristol all day, being chummy with the ACC. The Assistant Chief Constable, the officer translated for me.

Being stuck at an airport waiting for an indefinitely delayed plane home with no money and no conversation left is paradise compared with kicking your heels in a police cell. It was mid-morning when I was allowed to leave the custody suite and was marched all the way to Interview Room Two – the one with the unnerving stain, as you may remember – and handed over to the now equally familiar DI Reid and his bland sidekick with his suit full of static.

For some strange reason, DI Reid seemed to dislike me. He was one of those overeager types whose confidence was as thin as the ham in his sandwich. He was desperate to prove himself and do something praiseworthy while his boss was away but I'd have thought even he would have realized that I couldn't possibly be the one who had set fire to Landacker's studio.

'And why not?' he asked, smiling as though he had said something clever. 'Unlike you, it seems, Greg Landacker is doing pretty well with his aunt.'

'Is he?'

The DS nudged him. 'Art, sir.'

Reid frowned at the interruption. 'What?'

'Art, sir. You said "his aunt".'

'Right . . . *art*. From his *art* . . .' He seemed to have lost his thread for a moment. 'Yes, we spoke to Mr Landacker. He had a break-in not so long ago and found you on the premises then, too. It seems to me then that you are jealous of Mr Landacker. He seemed to think that it was possible too. He said you had been, and I quote, "reduced to teaching".'

'Did you find the petrol can?' I asked.

'Let me ask the questions, Mr Honeysett,' he said with a practised sigh.

'I didn't see one either. Yet it was definitely petrol.'

'You should know, since it was you who set the fire.'

'And presumably I carried the petrol there in my pockets.'

'You could have thrown the plastic can in the fire and it would have burnt.'

'Is that what the fire officer told you?'

There was just a hint of a pause. 'No. They said there was no sign of it. But you could have . . . had an accomplice, of course. Who left.'

'And I stayed behind to get myself arrested? I went there to speak to Greg, found the place had been set alight and was throwing water on the fire when you lot turned up!'

'Perhaps you changed your mind. You set fire to it . . .'

'With an accomplice.'

'. . . and realized it was a stupid thing to do and tried to put it out again.'

'Having told my accomplice, "You go, I'll stay and put it out with this here flowerpot." Having called the fire brigade.'

This ding-dong nonsense went on for long enough to get boring even for Reid. He terminated the interview, then let me wait for another age before I was released.

'On bail!' I complained to Annis, who was waiting outside. 'I had expected an apology, at the very least for the food they made me eat, if not for arresting me. The bed in the cells was appalling, the noise in the place . . .'

Annis knew how to handle a fulminating Honeysett. She steered me round the corner into Demuth's restaurant where they had just begun serving lunch and by the time I had got stuck into roast aubergines with miso and sunflower seeds (and crispy new potatoes with pickled mustard greens, very nice), I was beginning to shake the episode off.

'Break-in is one thing,' I suggested. 'Burning the place down is in a different league.'

'It's in the same league as murder,' said Annis while jabbing a fork into her salad. 'But from what you told me, the first one wasn't much cop as a burglar. They may have come back and tried to burn the door down.'

'And it got out of hand with petrol going everywhere.'

'And with you turning up.'

'And with me turning up in my car which is still parked in the weeds opposite Landacker's gate.'

'I'll take you.'

It was still there. I walked around it once to make sure it hadn't acquired any tags or scratches and then, for the first time ever, rang Landacker's bell next to his gate like a normal person. We could have just wandered in since the gate was open. Greg already had the menders in; there was a van in the lane and one on his drive. The intercom squawked: 'Yes?'

'Aqua Investigations,' I informed him.

'You have a nerve, Honeysett.'

I let Annis, the acceptable face of Aqua Investigations, go in first. Landacker came sailing out of his front door to start the inevitable tirade, saw Annis and at once changed his mind. I could see immediately that he had become more interested in smarming her than bellowing at me.

'I don't know why I'm not throwing you back out in the lane,' he said indulgently.

'Because you didn't have time to thank me last night. For calling the fire brigade and chucking water on your fire until they got here.' I would have mentioned my swollen finger but annoyingly it had already gone completely back to normal.

Landacker buried his hands deep in the pockets of his sand-coloured corduroys and looked a bit more at Annis, then at the two workmen carrying charred timber away. 'Oddly enough, I believe you, Honeysett. It's just that you always appear just when rubbish happens around here.'

'How about the last time you burnt supper? I was nowhere near the place,' I said reasonably.

'Yeah, yeah, you're right. But what on earth *were* you doing here last night?'

This time we didn't have to talk on the doorstep, though I had no doubt that this was purely due to Annis's presence. 'Nice place,' she said when we walked through his preposterous house. 'Imaginatively done.'

'Thank you. It was a wreck when I bought it.'

'Love the staircase. Is it real glass?'

'It is actually. The architect has a brother who runs a specialist . . .' Etcetera, etcetera.

He had a huge espresso machine with enough pipe-work to heat a house and made cappuccinos for us and found me an ice-blue Murano glass ashtray when I asked if I could smoke. 'Just this once,' he said. I was really warming to *please-call-me-Greg* Landacker.

I finally got to explain to him that the tag I had first seen scratched into his gate now made the rounds up at the college and that I was afraid it might have to do with Rachel's death. Did he have any idea what it meant?

'None at all, I'm afraid,' he said. 'I would have said.'

'Who's got it in for you?' Annis asked him.

He smiled serenely and opened his hands as though in supplication. 'I'm an extremely successful artist. I'm beginning to think it might simply be professional jealousy. After all, it was the studio that was targeted both times. It's simply the price of fame, I expect. I'm having my security beefed up as soon as the workmen are finished.'

'It's a possibility,' said Annis. 'Which is worrying, because the tag appeared on our studio as well.'

'Our?' Landacker asked. 'Are you an artist as well?'

'Annis Jordan,' she offered.

'Of *course*,' he said unconvincingly. 'Where was it that I saw your work last?' Two minutes later he was refreshing his memory by studying her work on his iPad, making all the right noises.

'I do love your work,' Annis reciprocated. 'Now that I am *actually* here, you can't possibly send me away without showing me your studio.'

Landacker stopped ogling Annis and her paintings. 'I'm afraid that won't be possible. I never allow anyone into my studio while I am working on a painting. I cannot *bear* anyone seeing my work until it is *absolutely* perfect. I'm quite superstitious about it too. I'm sure you'll understand.' He got up, signalling that it was time to go.

He walked us halfway to the gate, then stopped and looked worried. I could see that an effort had been made to sand away the I><I tag on his gate but it had been scored too deeply. 'The sculptor who was killed. Was there a tag at her place as well?'

I kept walking. 'I don't know, Greg. I'm going there next.'

'Well . . . let me know, OK?'

'Well, I'm not going,' said Annis back at the cars. 'Shame he wouldn't let us have a look at his studio. He's a worried man underneath all that price-of-fame rubbish. He terminated our audience rather quickly when I asked to see his studio.'

'Yes, I didn't know the form, was I supposed to kiss his signet ring?'

'He's definitely a worried man,' she said, climbing into the cab of her Landy. 'I wonder if he knows why someone is doing this to him?'

'If he knew, wouldn't he say? Tell the police? Tell us?'

'Perhaps. But maybe not if the person who's doing it has a really good reason,' she said and drove off.

Good reason! You'd need a pretty good reason to set fire to a painter's studio, I thought as I drove towards Limpley Stoke where the late Rachel Eade had lived with her solicitor husband. Then I thought of the X-symbol sanded into the door of our studio at home and wondered if I should not worry about my own. Only I could not think of a single thing that would make our rattling clapped-out barn with its bodged-in windows more secure. Our three acres were bordered by fields and woodland. It would take a twelve-foot security fence and patrolling Alsatians to keep out a stranger carrying matches. And what had we done to deserve to have our studio torched?

And what had Rachel done to deserve being electrocuted, I asked myself for the umpteenth time as I let the DS roll to a stop in front of the house. Rachel's car was standing in the open double garage and a sober, grey Lexus was parked in front of it. The reason I had not come here before was of course cowardice. I had hoped not to find anyone here so I would not have to deal with the grieving husband but it was too late now; a curtain was moving and even before I had managed to lock the car the front door opened.

The dark-haired man who stood on the doorstep looked a young forties but his eyes were hard and ancient. He looked like he hadn't slept for days, or if he had, he had done it in his suit and with the help of a bottle of Scotch. No, gin, I mentally corrected as I got close enough to smell him. He looked unmoved as I walked up to him, giving no sign whether he was going to be civil, fall over or head-butt me.

'Mr Eade?' I asked.

He took a deep breath and looked towards the heavens to grant him patience. 'My name is Dominic Swift. My late wife kept her maiden name for her artistic identity. Who are you and what do you want?'

Who was I, private eye or painter? 'I teach up at the Bath Arts Academy. I'm Chris Honeysett.'

His voice was bitter. 'Are you the chap who invited her up there to do her installation?'

Cowardly, I said: 'The invitation came from the late John Birtwhistle. But I delivered it, yes.'

He looked away from me down the lane and sniffed, as though not sure what to do with this information.

'I am extremely sorry about your wife's death . . .'

'Murder. Her murder, Mr . . .'

'It's Chris. Yes, her murder. I am worried that there might be another killing. Strange things are happening around other people who were invited to exhibit. I came to ask you whether you had seen any graffiti around your place. Specifically something like a flattened X, almost like a stylized butterfly.'

He wordlessly stepped past me and walked over to the garage. He pulled down the metal door; it banged shut in front of Rachel's car. In the centre of the door was the tag, scratched into the pastel-green paint with vicious strokes. The scratches had already begun to rust. 'Is that what you are looking for?'

I nodded. 'When did that appear?'

'Soon after she went up to the school for the first time. What does it mean?'

'I don't know. It could be just a tag. Like the idiots who spray-paint their tag all over town, marking their territory like dogs.'

'Looks different to me.'

'What does it look like to you?'

'Just four slashes. It looks angry. In retrospect I'd say it looked like a warning.'

I agreed. There was very little else to say and Swift did not ask me inside. I asked him one more question. 'Your new garage in town . . .'

He gave me a suspicious look. 'How do you know I have a garage in town?'

'Rachel mentioned it in passing. Did you know it had been a painting studio for some years before you took it over?'

'Was it? I knew it wasn't used as a garage for a while. Is that relevant somehow?'

'I'm grasping at straws.'

'So are the police.' He walked back to his front door, paused, looked at me over his shoulder. 'They said it may have been a prank that went too far.' He pressed his lips tightly together and nodded curtly with wide eyes that were losing their focus. Then he said stiffly: 'That I may have lost my wife to a prank.' He went inside. The slowness and gentleness with which he closed the door behind himself expressed his hopelessness more completely than anything else he could have said.

A prank, I thought as I drove towards Batcombe House. It was still possible, of course, in which case this feeling of impending gloom that had been growing on me would all be wasted. What I couldn't decide was what would be more tragic – Rachel's life taken deliberately or wasted accidentally.

When I reached the school I was greeted by the strange sight of students doing manual labour. There were about a dozen of them, some on ladders, climbing all over the rusty wrought-iron gates. I could only just squeeze my car through a gap in the cloud of rust and flaking paint. On closer inspection I found it was a selection of sculpture students who were sanding and filing the rust of ages from the ironwork. The gates also appeared to have been returned to a useful state by having their hinges unwelded, if there was such a word. 'We're going to paint it too,' said Alex, who was wearing a folded newspaper hat to keep the rust out of her hair and had an unlit roll-up in the corner of her mouth.

'And do you get to keep your welding gear?'

'Only just,' she admitted.

'What colour are you going paint it?'

'Whatever is the cheapest one the Dementor can find. But I really think it ought to be the painting students who paint it.'

'Sorry, my lot are too busy,' I said. 'Besides, it definitely wasn't a painter who welded the hinges solid.'

She acknowledged this with a wry smile and went back to work. I saw that while there was still a police car parked by the entrance, Rachel's sheep pen and the incident tape had disappeared from the lawns. Hufnagel and Dawn were both still working in the studio, despite the lateness of the afternoon. It was getting dark noticeably earlier now and there was hardly any point in me starting work this late. There was strip lighting, of course, but fluorescent light distorts your sense of colour and is pretty useless for painting by.

'I only really came to tell you why I wasn't here all day.' I quickly sketched the recent events for them.

'Couldn't happen to a nicer guy, I'm sure,' said Kurt. I wasn't sure if he meant me or Landacker and didn't ask. He had made a lot of progress on his canvas and the arrow was now back in place. He was just letting Petronela go. Looking at his superb brushwork, I could not help noticing that, like Modigliani, he had lavished most of his artistic attention on his model's perfect breasts.

Dawn was more thoughtful. 'OK, my studio is gone. Kurt here first had his place broken into, then his studio trashed soon after. Landacker had his studio broken into and now someone tried to set fire to it. How safe is your studio?'

'It's a hundred-year-old barn on top of the meadow behind my house.'

'Wow, listed?'

'No, listing. Of no architectural value whatsoever. Of course, I'm not working there at the moment. But I did find the tag on the studio door, and that worries me.'

'I got one on my car,' said Hufnagel.

'Yeah, I saw.'

'Did Rachel have a studio somewhere?' he asked.

'No. But she had a garage door,' I said. After that we all sat gloomily in the darkening studio for a while, with our private gloomy thoughts.

It was beginning to fall into place but in no shape I could recognize. 'I'm going home,' I said eventually. 'It's too late for me to do any work.'

'No need to anyway,' said Hufnagel, who had a bottle of wine open and was drinking from the neck. 'Your phantom painter has done a bit more.'

I swung around. So far I had paid little attention to my own painting, not having worked on it today. I skidded to a halt in front of it. He was right. It wasn't much, but a beautiful slant of sunlight was now falling across the top of the old kiln where before it had only been sketched in. 'How about yours?' I asked Hufnagel. He pointed meaningfully with the top of his wine bottle across the studio at Dawn.

'Yup,' she admitted.

'Added or subtracted?'

'Neither. Just changed it. See that bit here, the edge of the cloud? It's a deeper shade of pink than I had left it and here on the underside too. It's rose madder. I don't even own a rose madder; they must have used yours.'

'How do you feel about it?' I wanted to know, since I still hadn't completely made up my mind about my own painting.

'I think it's presumptuous,' Dawn said through a cloud of cigarette smoke. 'Whoever is doing it is basically saying, "I'm a better painter" or "I know better". And, I mean, how could they be? *I* saw it. *They* weren't there.' She took a breath to continue but slowly deflated as doubt crossed her face.

And I knew what she was thinking. 'They could have been, you know?'

'That's even more creepy!' she said with an unhappy frown. 'That they could have been following me around while I was sketching.'

'Someone was certainly creeping around me a couple of times while I was drawing in the woods.'

'Ugh.' Dawn got up and rubbed her arms as though she suddenly felt chilly. She looked out at the gathering darkness. 'I'm packing it in for today.'

'I was just leaving too.'

'You're not leaving me here by myself,' Hufnagel said, grabbing his wine bottle and sweeping out of the French windows ahead of us.

'Do you think he actually still has a driving licence?' Dawn asked.

Before I closed the door behind us I took one last look at our three paintings, trying to fix them in my mind so I might recognize any mysterious overnight changes, however small. As it turned out, I needn't have bothered.

I checked my watch. The only thing I wanted to do now was to go home, crack open some beers, stick a Béla Bartók CD on the hi-fi and wash the last two days out of my system, but it would be chucking-out time at Mantis IT Solutions soon and, however much I wanted to, I couldn't let Susan Byers down. Whether I would dare send her a bill for my lacklustre performance was another matter. At least I had given Martin Byers plenty of time to forget about the black Citroën that had now returned to the double yellow lines down the road from the Mantis car park. I hadn't been there five minutes when he emerged from the building, together with his friend. But lo! He didn't get into the chap's Audi with him. They parted and Martin got into a big, wine-red Alpha Romeo. He might be working in IT but in his spare time he was a man of taste. Was he going to do anything else today that was noteworthy or was he just going to follow his Audi friend up the hill?

I followed at a safe distance. It soon became clear that he was neither following his friend nor taking the quickest route to his city-centre flat. Instead we joined the clutch-grinding late-afternoon procession along the Pultney Road, moving ten car lengths at a time, then coming to a stop again. The Citroën DS being ancient, the only in-car entertainment to be had was to twiddle the radio tuning knob and confirm to myself my violent dislike of pop, hip-hop and opera and my complete indifference to all types of sport. The traffic crawled past Sydney Place, where Jane Austen used to live and complain about the 'noise and bustle' of the city. I managed to squeeze across the junction without getting separated from my prey, then the traffic began to flow again as the A36 took us past Claverton and out of town.

Now, the A36 goes to many places but eventually it'll take you to Southampton, where Martin Byers' pink family would horribly clash with the colour of his car. I pulled into a layby near the aqueduct and called Susan Byers.

'Is your husband coming to visit you in Southampton?' I asked her.

'He is. He's coming to stay for three days, lucky us. He's got his car back from the menders at last.'

'Oh good. That means I don't have to follow him all the way down the A36. Could you tell me next time he's leaving Bath? I just spent half an hour sitting in traffic behind him.'

'At least I know you're doing your job now,' said Susan. 'I don't suppose you've found out anything I should know?'

'Not so far. I followed him to his colleague's house a couple of times, that's all. Are you sure you want me to continue with this?'

'Yes. I need to know.'

EIGHTEEN

'She needs to know, she says,' I complained. 'But at least he's away for a couple of days and I don't have to worry about it. Pass the jam when you've achieved the impossible.'

'In a sec.' Annis was busy challenging conventional physics by piling a Matterhorn of rose-petal conserve on her last little piece of croissant. Why that woman wasn't twenty stone by now remains a literary mystery. 'Don't let it slide,' I think she said after she had closed her mouth over it. 'She's getting more pregnant by the day and you can't tell her anything.'

'More pregnant? Rubbish. You're either pregnant or you're not.'

'I think Susan Byers is all too aware of that.'

'Why don't you have a go if you're so concerned?'

'Nope, too busy. Too busy painting and I have a lecture to write.'

'You do?'

She got up from the breakfast table and picked up her steaming mug of coffee. 'Kroog talked me into it. She wants me to give your lot a spiel about my work.'

'You don't have to write a lecture for that – you can wing it, surely.'

'No thanks. I have sat through too many of those when I was a student. I'm going to do it properly.'

'Of course.'

Not like me, then, I thought as I drove up to Batcombe House, although I had in fact given the assignment for my students quite a bit of consideration. I was gratified to see, when I walked into Studio Two, that the place was littered with the results. The walls were lined with small paintings, lively ones, colourful ones, dark ones, even monochrome ones. Some students had painted great detail, others had reverted to impressionist idioms, two had rendered their chosen view in abstract colour blocks. I recognized Hiroshi's canvas without having to ask – it was a painting of a mossy stone, rendered in startling detail. Phoebe's style had taken on a definite turn towards the pastel clouds of Dawn's paintings; she had begun to let her hitherto neat hair go wild too.

One or two students had produced terrible daubs but on the whole the crop looked good and I told them so. This appeared to please most of them but I noticed that Hiroshi seemed beyond such feeble praise and Ben's face clearly said that any painting that didn't have Petronela in it was a complete waste of his time.

'OK, this looks really good. Now for the last two parts of your assignment. So far you have drawn your subject from life, then painted your subject from life. I now want you to go and photograph your subject, from the same place where you were when you painted it, and at the same time.'

'What do you mean, the same time?' asked Ben.

'Well, I can see that some of these paintings have a very bright afternoon feeling to them; there's a sunset scene over there, and I presume it wasn't done at the crack of dawn?' The author of the paintings shook her head in horror. 'Thought not. And Phoebe will have to wait until dusk.' Phoebe had painted an uncharacteristically crepuscular painting of Batcombe House, seen through the foliage of a low tree branch. She had exaggerated the menace of the ancient facade to the point of parody. 'Please do not use your mobiles to take the pictures. They need to be decent quality, as we'll print them out. Mobile phones have lenses made from broken pop bottles and make up for it with cheap electronic trickery. And they don't have an optical zoom so as you zoom in you lose quality. If you don't have a camera, borrow one. There are about half a dozen simple ones in the graphics department for students to use. If you ask Stottie – I mean Catherine – if you ask Catherine nicely she'll lend you one. And take some care over the photograph, don't just take one, take many, make sure you have a good photo to work with.'

After an exhausting twenty-five minute stint of teaching I was ready for a quiet day of drawing and painting, especially since last night I had possibly overdone the beer-and-Bartók therapy.

The weather had turned autumnal; cooler and cloudier, with sudden showers that washed the last taste of summer out of the shortening days. I stood on the lawn outside Studio Two and lit a cigarette. It was my new smoking rule, with which I was hoping to curb my recently re-acquired twenty-a-day habit – I would only allow myself to smoke outside, whatever the weather. I had invented it that very moment and naturally it wasn't raining just then. What *was* happening just then was that inside Batcombe House something heavy crashed to the ground and the door of Studio One flew open, spitting Hufnagel out on to the lawn. Without looking left or right he marched across the grass to the big hollow steel sculpture rusting there and began kicking it all over in a fit of rage. The rusting hulk boomed like a cracked bell and drowned out whatever Hufnagel was shouting. Then he abruptly stopped kicking the thing, turned around and limped back, hands balled into fists by his side, stringing together random swear words until he seemed to run out somewhere near me. But he wasn't looking at me; he was staring murderously at the house. 'What's happened, Kurt?'

He looked down at his feet. 'I think I just broke my sodding toe.'

'I'm not surprised. I'd have kicked something softer.'

'If I catch who did it I'll kick them until they're mush,' he said fiercely. 'With the other foot,' he added.

I thought I knew what this was about. 'Is the arrow gone again?'

The question turned Hufnagel rigid with anger. 'The *arrow* gone? Yeah, it is, actually. But that isn't the half of it! Go! Go inside and take a look!'

Reluctantly I stepped into Studio One. I could now see that the noise I had heard a minute ago had been Hufnagel overturning his painting table in a fit of rage. Brushes, paints, bottles of painting mediums everywhere. The smell of spilled turpentine was thick in the air. My eyes met those of Dawn, who was sitting in front of her own painting, smoking a roll-up, her face screwed up with suppressed laughter.

I approached Hufnagel's big canvas with caution. Yes, the arrow was gone again. And so was the bow. Petronela's fists were now both empty, giving her the look of an awkward pugilist whose threat could not be taken entirely seriously since an enigmatic smile played on her face. Yet I was sure this was not what had provoked the explosive reaction. What had brought Hufnagel to the brink of apoplexy was that the phantom painter had given Petronela a bra.

I thought it was a very nice bra too, in a shimmering bronze and green, lacy, with delicate straps and a tiny green bow in the centre. It suited her complexion and was painted with great realism and in Hufnagel's style, fitting seamlessly into the composition.

Hufnagel appeared at my elbow, letting out a fresh groan. 'Why me?' he asked. 'You? You get helpful elves. Me? I get bastard goblins.'

'What's Dawn got?'

'Pastel pixies. It's not fair. They were such beautiful tits, too,' he moaned.

'Very true,' I commiserated. I didn't tell him what I really thought: that the painting had been improved immeasurably by the addition of the bra and by losing the bow and arrow nonsense. It was now a contemporary, rather enigmatic image of a young woman in a belligerent pose rather than a nineteenth-century allegory chosen as an excuse to paint a half-naked girl. I helped him right the table and pick up his paints. 'Honestly,' he said, 'if it wasn't for the free canteen food, I'd be out of here. You know what I'm going to do? I'm going to hide myself here tonight with a cricket bat and wait for the bastard.'

'No, please don't. I have a much better idea.' I wasn't sure it was a *much* better idea, but the last thing we needed was one of the students being worked over with a cricket bat by an irate and possibly drunk Hufnagel, no matter how justified his rage. 'We're going to install a spy camera. Once we have them on tape we can confront them with the evidence. But even then cricket bats will definitely not be a feature.'

'And where are you going to get a spy camera? Oh, I forget, you're also a private eye.'

'Sometimes I do, too. Fortunately I have a couple of associates who remind me from time to time. And one of them is rather good with all this electronic surveillance stuff.' I walked outside and called Tim. He was less than enthusiastic.

'Do you remember what happened last time we did that?' he asked.

'I poured a mug of coffee into the rugged laptop.'

'Oh yeah, that too. I spill stuff over keyboards all the time, that's why I chose a rugged laptop, otherwise we'd be on the fifth replacement by now. Actually, leaky jam donuts are the worst, there's no way back from those unless you're very quick.

No, the last time you set up the cameras to catch a night prowler, someone ended up left for dead on the ground.'

'It's fresh in my mind. But if I don't do something it'll be cricket bats in the dark. Anyway, why should it happen again?'

'Because this stuff always happens around you. When do you want it?'

'As soon as.'

'You surprise me. I'm busy this afternoon but I'll come up as soon as I can get away. What's your postcode there?'

'No idea but Batcombe House is marked on the A to Z.'

'What's an A to Z, you luddite?'

The more I looked at Hufnagel's painting, the more I liked the changes the phantom had made. But how to tell him? And even if I could convince him, could he possibly pass it off as his own painting if the phantom had completely altered its meaning? I made a token effort to help him mop up the spilled painting mediums but his anger still throbbed in the air and any suggestion that the phantom was a better painter than him would not have gone down too well. 'Are you going to repaint your bow and arrow?' I asked eventually.

'Well, I would, but guess what?' he said through clenched teeth. 'They have disappeared as well.'

I couldn't bring myself to mention the bra.

The phantom seemed to have had no time to do any work on my own canvas in the night; changing Hufnagel's image so radically must have taken some time. When I searched my painting and found no additions or changes I had to admit to myself that I felt a tiny bit disappointed. The phantom was improving it, tweaking it, like a Photoshopped photograph has its colours adjusted, its shadows deepened, blemishes removed. No matter how much I puzzled about it, I could not decide which student was my favourite suspect. Hiroshi was an obvious candidate for improving on my canvas, Ben Creeling the obvious choice for the Hufnagel canvas. I doubted Phoebe would dare tweak Dawn's painting, since Dawn seemed to be her new painting hero, but I had to admit to the possibility that the phantom was a team effort.

I had hours before Tim's promised arrival, which I decided to spend drawing in the woods since the atmosphere in the studio was too heavy with Hufnagel's frustration and thick with fumes from spilled painting mediums, and if I had to listen to one more tirade by Hufnagel I might just blurt out that the phantom had at least managed to drag his painting into the twenty-first century. Or thereabouts.

I had almost forgotten about Dan's unquenchable enthusiasm for the rediscovered kiln in the woods but it was all too obvious when I got to my little clearing. He had managed to infect some of his students too and a couple of them had joined him out here in his restoration efforts. One of them was a tall bloke with a stoop, which a lifetime at the potter's wheel was unlikely to improve, the other was Abbi, the blonde potter who had greeted me so sagely on my first day at the school. She remembered it well. 'What did I say about the future? From Dumpy to Dementor in a hop, skip and a jump. Shame Boris the spider didn't manage to drown her at her dad's funeral.'

'Yes, what a time for the thing to malfunction,' agreed Dan. He was already covered in ash and dust again and so were his two students, but it's fair to say that potters don't mind getting their hands dirty. And these three at least seemed happy in their work. They shifted the mountain of broken pottery from inside the kiln, discussed the repairs needed, discovered an overgrown woodpile and generally danced around the thing with noisy enthusiasm. Because it had been me who showed him the kiln, Dan seemed to think that I wanted to be kept informed about every bit of progress while I tried to draw the place. They also had an amazing knack of standing just in front of what I was trying to sketch. I almost regretted not having kept the kiln a secret until after I had finished with it, but Dan's transformation from depressed adult to excited kid had been worth it. I was relieved when they ran out of steam before I did, though the light was beginning to fade a little by then. I carried on. There was plenty of rain forecast and while I had played the hard-nut painter for the benefit of my students, I couldn't really see myself doing much drawing in the wet. The wind was driving dark clouds across the sky with the odd startling flash of brightness when the sun found a gap in the clouds, golden as it approached the western horizon. It was in one of those sudden, golden moments of sunlight that I looked up and saw him: my wild man of the woods. His white skin too just caught the sun, some hundred and fifty yards into the forest. His body looked streaked with mud. He was standing quite still, facing me, with both arms lifted

shoulder-high, palms towards me. The figure stood too far away
for me to be sure, but my first thought was that I was looking
at Hiroshi, except that this creature's hair and beard were wild
and matted and Hiroshi was always immaculately groomed. It
looked as though he was praying, or perhaps meditating. Whether
his eyes were open or closed I couldn't see. I stood up, sketchbook in hand, intending to draw him. No sooner had I put pencil
to paper than my mobile started to chime. Immediately the figure
bolted like a startled deer, running in full, headlong flight, jumping
obstacles in its path. I could see that the man's feet were bare
too and winced at the thought of running barefoot across the
forest floor. I could not be sure that it was Hiroshi, but of one
thing I was absolutely certain: the wild man of the woods was
not carrying a knife with which to carve signs into tree trunks.
I answered the phone.

'I'm here, where are you?' said Tim's voice.

'Deep in the woods where the Yeti roams. Stay where you are,
I'll be there in five.'

Tim was standing in the car park, drumming his fingers on
the roof of his black Audi. There was no sign of the police now
but no arrest or announcement had been made, which meant that
possibly there were certain police officers out there still thinking
that I might be behind Rachel's death and the fire at Landacker's.
Tim dug a tiny piece of paper from his jeans pocket, which he
now unfolded and unfolded and unfolded – it turned out to be
A4. 'You asked me to look into some of your folks up here?'

'And?'

'Do you realize, some of these people have never left school?
They went from playschool to primary to secondary to university
and straight into teaching at art school, like Catherine Stott.
Institutionalized, I'd call that. They probably couldn't survive
outside the school gates.'

'Yeah, that happens.'

'The sculptor, Kroog, too, she's been here forever but at least
she's exhibited her work all round the world. Some I couldn't
find anything on at all, like the administrator, and your potter,
Dan Small? I doubt he could survive anywhere else because he
doesn't have any qualifications.'

'Must be a mistake. It says in the school's brochure he did an
MA in ceramics in Stoke-on-Trent.'

'Never went there, I checked with them. So I dug around a bit more. Turns out he has no qualifications of any kind, not to teach and not in ceramics.'

'That could make life quite tricky if he were forced to leave here. No wonder he was doom-struck when he was told his department might get the chop.'

'Are you going to tell them?'

'What would be the point? If Birtwhistle and Kroog thought he was doing a good job, who cares about the MA? Any other revelations?'

'Everything else checks out. I can't find anything incriminating on your cheating husband, he's just an ordinary overworked IT chap like me.'

'Right, let's get the gubbins installed and catch ourselves a phantom before Hufnagel starts digging Heffalump traps all over the lawn.'

Hufnagel and Dawn both greeted Tim's camera installation with interest. 'Is it in colour?' Dawn asked. 'Will we be able to watch it live over the internet?' Hufnagel wanted to know. The answer, disappointingly, was no to both questions because apparently Aqua Investigations' boss was too stingy to invest in decent, up-to-date equipment and software.

'We'll lock the laptop in the cupboard and we can check it in the morning, that's early enough,' I told them. 'I don't know, young people today, always wanting instant results . . .' I stood outside to smoke and distract any potential visitors until Tim had finished setting it up. It was getting dark by the time it was done and we all left together. It occurred to me that if the mere installation of the cameras put a stop to the phantom then it probably was Dawn after all and she had added that bit of rose madder to her own canvas to throw me off the scent.

When we four walked out into the little car park it suddenly seemed crowded. Stottie's immaculate boyfriend Matthew was waiting by his immaculate car to pick her up, and Anne Birtwhistle burst out of the front door, on some kind of mission, followed by Stottie herself.

Anne marched past us, fuming with indignation. 'It is after dark and the gates are wide open! Does nobody – *no*body – bother to look at the noticeboard? It says quite clearly . . .'

Anne never finished the sentence; instead she shrieked. So did

Matthew, and I might have too, because the arrow that whistled through our group missed me, him and Anne by inches before slamming into the door of Hufnagel's car where it stuck fast.

Hufnagel's rage was instantly rekindled. 'Oh *great*! What next, a meteor strike I suppose!'

'Where the hell did that come from?' Dawn yelled. She was taking shelter behind my car now and everyone else was joining her there.

I guessed the trajectory from the way it had missed us and hit Hufnagel's car door. 'It came from those trees on the edge of the lawn, near Kroog's cottage,' I said. 'I'll have a look.'

'Are you mad? You could get shot!' Anne called from behind my car.

'I don't think so. I'm pretty sure that it's the bow and arrow that vanished from our studio and there was only one arrow.'

Relief spread through the group and they came out from hiding. 'Still, be careful,' Dawn warned.

'I will,' I said and started jogging towards the trees, hoping to get a whiff of the assailant, or at least hear his footfall. Which one of us had he aimed at? One in particular? Or the entire group?

The second arrow came whistling out of the dark and slammed into my left shoulder. The impact was so hard I staggered sideways. Then my legs decided I should sit down on the grass and yelp with pain for a bit. So I did.

'He's been shot! Oh my God, oh my God!' I could hear Dawn shouting.

'Someone call an ambulance!' Anne demanded in a voice that sounded more annoyed than frightened.

Next thing I knew it was Tim kneeling next to me. He was talking on the phone, calling an ambulance. 'Someone's been shot. Bow and arrow. So send the police too. Hang on, I'll ask.' He turned to me. 'Do you think you're about to die?'

'Die, no. Scream, yes.'

'Not life-threatening; he was hit in the shoulder.' He terminated the call. 'They'll be here pronto. That looks nasty. Did it go far in?'

'I've no idea but it hurts like hell.' The arrow had gone through the leather of my old motorbike jacket, through the double thickness of the shoulder pads and the padding inside into the shoulder muscle. 'I wonder if I can pull it out?'

Dawn had come over too, walking in a crouch in case any further arrows came flying over. 'You're not supposed to do that! It can do more damage.'

'The arrow Kurt painted had quite a simple point. I mean, no barbs, or anything.'

'Still, I wouldn't touch it. Let them take it out in hospital. They'll carefully cut away the jacket around it and take it out under anaesthetic.'

'Cut away the jacket? *My* jacket? *This* jacket? No way!' I gritted my teeth, grabbed the shaft of the arrow and gave it a good pull.

Ouch.

'You madman!' Dawn shrieked.

It came out much more easily than I had imagined and from the blood on the tip it looked as though it hadn't gone in all that far. Far enough to bleed quite a lot, as I discovered when I reached inside my jacket. Dawn handed me a whole packet of tissues, which I pressed against the pain. Perhaps it had been stupid to take the arrow out myself but I felt better. The sight of the thing sticking out of me had made me feel quite weak at the knees.

There were no more arrows coming out of the dark but a figure staggered drunkenly towards us from between the trees. I thought I recognized the blonde-haired figure as Phoebe. She stopped to vomit on to the lawn, then sat down heavily.

'Do you think it was her?' Tim asked. 'Looks like she's drunk as the proverbial.'

'Go grab her,' I urged. Tim loped across. 'And see if you can find the bow!' I called after him but shouting made the pain in my shoulder worse.

'Do you want to get out of that jacket?' Dawn asked.

I did, only I didn't relish the prospect. I supposed that once the ambulance arrived they would drag me out of it anyway so I might as well yelp in relative privacy. 'Okay, give me a hand with it.' I found my legs had firmed up again as I stood up.

'I'll be *really* careful,' she promised.

Now that the arrow was out, moving didn't hurt half as much, which I found was still quite enough for me. The packet of tissues had turned into one scary wad of blood-red sogginess and more blood trickled down my t-shirt. Hufnagel appeared by my side with a nearly clean torn bedsheet that hadn't yet been cut into oil rags and Dawn, even while tutting over the dubious hygiene of the thing, tore it into strips like a movie heroine and bandaged my shoulder with them.

Tim came over from where Phoebe was sitting on the ground, head in hand. 'She's not drunk. She's concussed and dizzy and her head's bleeding. Says someone hit her over the head while she was trying to take pictures for some project.'

'Damn, that'll be my project.'

Ambulance and police arrived together. By that time I was surrounded by a mob of people; Kroog being concerned, Alex fascinated, Hufnagel morose, Stottie and her boyfriend whispering to each other, Dawn fussing with my bandage that was slipping, Dan the potter looking shocked and Claire trying to make a gangway for the ambulance men.

But it was Anne's voice I heard above all the others. 'That's it, that's the last straw. This place is a complete madhouse and someone here is killing people.'

'I'm not dead yet,' I pointed out, but Anne didn't hear me.

'That's it,' she said again. 'This school is closing. I'll sell this madhouse, no matter what it says in the will.' She stomped off towards the flashing blue beacons of the ambulance and police.

The paramedics both went to work on me but I directed one of them to Phoebe who was now just a dark lump on the grass. More and more police arrived in the grounds, including an armed response unit, waving torches. They started fanning out across the grounds and towards the area I pointed out to them as the most likely place that the arrows had come from. They soon returned with the bow and after that people visibly relaxed. The PC who had found it slipped it into a large evidence bag and waved it proudly at Superintendent Needham, who had just walked on to the lawn.

'It was *you* who was shot!' Needham said as he found me sitting in the ambulance.

'Yes, it's marvellous,' I told him. The paramedic was undoing the bandages and was slicing away at my t-shirt.

'Marvellous, is it?' Needham studiously avoided looking at my messy shoulder by keeping his eye on what was happening elsewhere.

'Yes. Plus I have witnesses that will swear that I didn't do it. Being the victim appears to be the only way to convince you lot one isn't the perpetrator and I managed it. Ow!' The paramedic was doing things to my shoulder. Since I wasn't looking I don't know what; I can only report that it was properly painful.

'Will he be all right?' Needham asked.

'It'll need stitches and the shoulder will need to be x-rayed but I'd say he was very lucky. A few inches either side would have been a different story.'

'Oh no, does that mean I'll have to go to the hospital?' I moaned. I do hate hospitals.

It turned out Phoebe wanted hospitalization too, for severe concussion, and she needed stitches in her scalp. She ended up on the stretcher next to me in the ambulance with an oxygen mask over her face, holding on to a kidney dish in case she needed to puke some more. She was lying down with her head sideways, facing me. Her eyes were wide open but not focussed on anything much.

'Any idea who hit you?' I asked.

She pulled the oxygen mask away from her face. It hissed quietly. 'None. I heard something behind me but before I could turn round – bang. Woke up lying on the ground feeling like shit.'

'What's it like now?'

'Lying on a stretcher feeling like shit. Never been in an ambulance before,' she added.

'Were you out there taking photographs?'

'Yup.'

'For my project?'

'Yup.'

'See anything suspicious?'

'Not a thing. Sorry.'

When we arrived at the A & E department of the Royal United, Phoebe was wheeled away on her stretcher and I was invited to sit in a wheelchair. My arm was in a sling to keep it still and I could have walked, but I was suddenly feeling very tired and gratefully sank into the chair. Being carted about in one of those hospital chairs turns you instantly from a person into a patient, with no responsibility for anything, not even self-propulsion. It was only the pain that kept me awake.

An hour later even that had disappeared under local anaesthetic. I had been x-rayed, cleaned up, had received six stitches and several times been declared 'a very lucky man' for not being dead and was released back into the night. Did I need a taxi? I didn't, because Annis was waiting for me. So was Needham. Such concern; I was touched.

Annis carefully put her arms around me. 'I knew it would happen sometime. You could so easily have been killed. You were damn lucky.'

'So I'm told.'

But Needham wasn't there to hug me. 'I need a statement off you before you disappear,' he insisted.

I checked my watch; it was after ten. 'I'm not sure I can manage a statement, too groggy. But if you're really keen I could possibly manage a chat if you pay for the beers for myself and my accomplice here.'

Fifteen minutes later we were sitting in a corner of the St James's Wine Vaults, Needham sipping post-industrial lager, Annis her gin and tonic and I was hoovering up a pint of Guinness. I was planning to drink enough of them to send me to sleep when the anaesthetic wore off.

'Who shot you?' Needham wanted to know. 'Did you get some idea of who killed Rachel? Does someone want to shut you up?'

'No idea. And no, I haven't got a clue who killed Rachel. Tell you who didn't shoot me, though: Tim, Catherine Stott, her boyfriend Matthew, Hufnagel, Dawn Fowling and Anne Birtwhistle. They were with me. And the girl Phoebe was in the trees taking a photograph. I don't suppose she hit herself over the head.'

'Why not? We get offered self-inflicted injuries as fake alibis all the time. What was she photographing? Surely it was a bit dark for photography?'

'The house, for an art project. Did you find the camera?'

'No, no camera. If someone was lying in wait with bow and arrow waiting for the opportunity to kill the intended victim then the girl . . .'

'Phoebe.'

'Thanks, Phoebe may just have been in the way.'

'That's how I see it. Shame you didn't find the camera. You might want to look in the pond. I'm not sure the arrow was actually meant for me. The first arrow went right through our group. I then jogged off towards the trees . . .'

'Like an idiot,' Annis supplied.

'. . . just as all the others stood up again. It was already dark. I could just have got in the way.'

'I'll bear that in mind. We found the bow. And two more arrows.'

Annis looked up from playing with her slice of lemon. 'Two more arrows? Then it was definitely not meant for Chris.'

'And why not?'

'Chris was jogging along and the arrow stopped him running. He would have made a much easier target after that. He was closer and he was stationary. With arrows to spare it would have been easy to finish him off.' She put a hand on mine and squeezed it. My other arm was in a sling again. Affectionately she held on to my hand while we discussed this new aspect of the events, which meant I now had no hand free to drink with. I left it for what I judged to be a decent interval before wriggling free and going for my drink.

'Okay,' said Needham. 'Let's for a moment assume the arrow wasn't meant for you. Which one of the others is the most likely target?'

I didn't even have to think about it. 'Anne Birtwhistle. She's trying to turn the place into a borstal. She's petty and overbearing. She doesn't understand that art schools are different from other institutions. They need to be places where people are free to create, dream, experiment, break moulds, and above all, waste huge amounts of art materials until they arrive at some kind of artistic understanding. She's managed to alienate practically everyone.'

'Enough for someone to want to kill her?' Needham looked doubtful.

'We're mostly dealing with young people here, passionate young people and also perhaps some strange young people. Arty people can get quite obsessed, messianic, even, about their mission in life.'

Annis confirmed it. 'It's a religion. And every religion has its extremists.'

'You're saying that to some, art is more important than people?' Needham asked.

'Oh, much more important,' Annis said. 'There's loads of people in the world, billions. Always more where they came from. But there's very little art. And even less *good* art.'

'Anne has been going around threatening to close down whole departments or to confiscate materials and machinery,' I said.

'I think she's going further than that now. From what I heard earlier, she's closing the place down,' Needham said.

'Yes, I think I heard her say something like that but I was somewhat distracted at the time. If she had already decided to close the place and someone knew about it, that may have pushed someone to extreme measures. There's only one problem with all that.'

'Which is?' Needham queried.

'It doesn't at all fit in with Rachel's death. She has nothing to do with it.'

Needham drained his beer. 'Not necessarily. People who kill once, at least those who kill with premeditation, might find it easier to kill again. They are less likely to feel remorse than someone who, let's say, killed a person in a brawl or in a red mist.'

'Yes, but . . .' Annis tried to interject.

'Let me finish. The other possibility is that Rachel's death was a prank gone wrong and has nothing whatever to do with tonight's shooting. And that means Chris here could well have been the intended victim. It was dark. The arrow had found a home, Chris went down, our archer thinks he's achieved what he came to do and flees the scene. And that means you need to look over your shoulder.'

'That still leaves a lot of other possible targets,' Annis argued. 'We can probably rule out Tim.'

'Yes, what was he doing there?' Needham wanted to know.

I couldn't be bothered to explain it. I suddenly felt tired. Very tired. 'Just stuff, nothing important.'

'You look all in, Chris,' Needham said. 'You better take him home, Annis. And make sure you lock your doors tonight.'

NINETEEN

'Of course you couldn't have cereal for once,' Annis moaned.

'Powdered grass seed rehydrated with cows' milk, let me think . . . mm, no thanks, I'll pass.' It would, admittedly, have been a lot easier to eat one-handed than soft-boiled eggs and croissants with jam but I felt like being difficult. For some reason my shoulder hurt more today than it did yesterday. Getting dressed had been a challenge.

'And I suppose apart from feeding you boiled eggs I'll have to chauffeur you up there,' Annis complained. 'Wouldn't it make sense to take a few days off? Stay away from the shooting gallery and wait for your shoulder to heal?'

I was doing pretty well with the croissants so far. I had hacked them into pieces on my plate and decorated each piece with a dollop of quince jam. 'I can't. The exhibition is coming up. I have a painting to finish and the phantom to catch.' I was doing pretty well with the egg, too. I had smashed the top and peeled it – normally I decapitate mine – and jabbed my spoon into it. Ah. A certain amount of spillage had to be expected, of course. I did manage to get some on my spoon and into my mouth.

'Then promise me one thing.'

'Mm . . . what?' I said, distracted by my breakfast battle.

'Don't wander off into the woods up there on your own. That's just asking for it.'

'It's all right, the police have the bow and arrows in custody. Bum!' I had plunged my spoon into the egg and when I tried to pull it out the whole egg rose out of the egg-cup. I was stuck.

'So what? So far it's been high-voltage electricity and bows and arrows. Next it might be chainsaws or spears. You have no idea who's behind this. If they walked up to you in the woods with a smile and a poisoned HB pencil, you'd be smiling back until it was too late. Promise you'll stay inside.'

Gravity refused to help free my spoon so I had to massacre the thing. 'Poisoned pencils, eh? They could just as easily stick one in my ear inside as outside.' I hacked what was left of my egg into pieces and shovelled it into my mouth.

'I've seen two-year-olds make less mess when they're eating. Get cleaned up and I'll drive you to Batcombe.'

It was a misty day and a fine spray of rain drifted across the hill above Batcombe and hung like a veil between the trees of Summerlee Wood. It didn't look that inviting anyway, I thought, as I promised Annis again not to enter the wood alone. 'I'll drive you back after I've given my presentation,' she said. 'About sixish.'

I had forgotten it was today. 'That's late for a lecture. Students usually go home around four.'

'I know. This way I'll only have students there who are really committed.'

'That's one way of looking at it.'

Had the phantom been in? That was the question on my mind as I walked into the studio. The answer was immediately clear. The phantom had been. And the phantom had been busy. Hufnagel's painting was untouched; I wasn't sure about Dawn's, but my painting had been moved on considerably. Most of the trees had been worked on, detail added to passages I had started and the background sharpened up. Had I painted it myself, I'd have been proud of it.

'Okay, let's have you,' I said out loud and opened the cupboard just as Dawn came into the studio, closely followed by Hufnagel.

'You're here!' said Dawn. 'They didn't keep you in, then.'

'Walking wounded.'

'Has the phantom been?' Dawn wanted to know straight away.

'Mine hasn't been touched,' Hufnagel said. 'It's so completely ruined I suppose he thought his job was done.'

'Or hers.' Dawn reminded him.

'Ah, but Chris's canvas got the treatment,' Hufnagel said. 'Let's see the recording. I can't wait to wring his or her neck.'

'Steady on,' I warned as I disconnected the laptop and put it on a table. I clicked on 'view last recording'. 'Here goes.' The screen showed the studio from a high angle, a little fish-eyed at the edges. Mounting it that high had been necessary to get in the French windows and all three canvases, with mine roughly in the centre. There being practically no ambient light, only the French windows showed clearly, the rest were darker shapes in the darkness. Numbers ran in the bottom-right corner of the screen, displaying the time to within a hundredth of a second, the manic digits being all that moved on the screen. 'Okay, I'll fast-forward.' The numbers went into overdrive but all the rest stayed the same.

'This feels really creepy,' Dawn whispered. 'What if it's a real ghost? Invisible?'

'There!' Hufnagel and I called out at the same time.

I returned the viewer to normal speed. A light had appeared in the corner of the screen, the corner the camera didn't cover.

Our phantom had entered not via the French windows as I had expected, but from inside, through the door from the corridor.

'How did they get into the building then?' wondered Dawn.

'Any old sash window,' Hufnagel said. 'I did tell Anne to nail them shut but she called me an idiot.'

'Well . . .' Dawn conceded.

'The conservatory door to the ceramics department doesn't lock either,' I said, 'and you can get down into the basement and up again into the house from there.' The figure was wearing a hooded top that was surrounded by a blazing halo.

'That's one of those hands-free head lamps,' Dawn said. 'I can't see who it is, can you?'

I couldn't. None of us could make it out. The light illuminated everything and anything but not once did it allow us to see the face. Whenever the phantom painter turned towards the camera, which was rare, the light created such a glare that the face remained hidden. Most of the time however the figure had its back turned to the camera while it sat and worked on my painting. It was infuriating in more ways than one.

To actually see it happen made me deeply resent the presumptuousness of the phantom. 'Cool as a cucumber. It's unbelievable. I can tell you who it isn't, of course, and that's Phoebe.'

'Why not?' Hufnagel asked.

'She's in hospital.'

'Oh yeah.'

'And it doesn't look like Hiroshi.'

'No, Roshi is taller,' Anne agreed. 'And has broader shoulders. I think it's a bloke, though.'

Hufnagel didn't go along with that. 'I think it's a girl.'

'Chris, you have the casting vote,' Dawn said.

'I abstain. It's definitely one or the other.'

'Listen to the great detective.'

It was true. One minute I thought the phantom looked female, then there was a movement or an angle that made me think it was a bloke. Knowing how excellent the result of the phantom's work was made me wish the CCTV images were in colour; I might even have learnt something. I irritably fast-forwarded the tape. Two solid hours the phantom had spent painting last night, then spent another ten minutes cleaning the brushes and my palette.

'A very tidy phantom, I must say,' Dawn said.

'I think the phantom cleans the palette each time because it might reveal its identity. Every painter has certain habits, ways of laying out the paints and so on. This ghost painter has thought about that, I'm sure.'

As I rewound to look at the footage one more time there was a knock on the door and Claire came in. 'Morning. You haven't seen Anne anywhere, have you? Oh, hi Chris, didn't expect you in, how's the shoulder?'

'Spiffing. No Anne so far, long may it last.'

'Normally I'd agree but the police want to talk to her again.'

'You heard of our phantom painter?' I asked. 'We have fuzzy footage. Want to have a look?'

'Yes, please.' I ran the recording for her. 'Is that it?' she asked. 'Dark shape with a halo?'

'That's as clear as it gets. What do you say – boy or girl?'

'I'd go for girl. Are you running a book?'

'For that we'd have to catch the phantom first.'

'Well, my money is on girl. And of course eighty per cent of our students are girls. And most of the staff are female. It's a girl. If you see Anne, tell her she's a wanted woman.'

'That'll be a new experience for her,' Dawn bitched quietly.

I shoved the laptop back in the cupboard and stood in front of my canvas for a while. 'It's coming along,' I said, mostly to wind up Hufnagel. 'How about you, Kurt? Are you going to reverse the phantom changes?'

Hufnagel was just opening a bottle of supermarket plonk; he was reinvesting the money he was saving by eating in the canteen in liquid inspiration of the screw-top variety. 'I've not decided. Until then I'll concentrate on the background.'

'Good thinking. I'll go and round up my students.'

Once I had herded them all into the studio I found that their main interest was no longer painting but death by electrocution, deadly arrows in the dark and Phoebe's head injury. Parents were understandably upset. Two students had apparently already decided it was too much and were preparing to leave.

'Did you see who shot you?'

'Do you think there'll be another murder?'

'Is it true the college is closing down?'

'Do we still have to do this project?'

'No, I didn't see the archer. The place is full of police again
so I think another murder is unlikely. I have not heard anything
about the college closing but if I see Anne Birtwhistle I will ask
her about it. And yes, you definitely have to continue with the
project. I want you to print out the photographs, on cheap paper
in the graphics department, preferably when neither Catherine
nor Anne are looking because printer ink is expensive. Then I
want you to paint your subject again, working only from the
photograph. And while you are doing it I want you to pay attention to your mental processes, and to notice to which extent you
are drawing on memory and the detail you observed when you
were drawing the same view and what kind of information you
get from your photograph, how it differs from direct observation.
Pay attention because there might be an essay in it later.'

General groans. 'Is there any chance the phantom will come
and do the painting for us in the night?' asked Hiroshi.

'I don't know,' I said, looking around the room. 'But there's
a very good chance that the phantom is in this studio right now.'
Excited murmurs all round. 'And all I want to say to the phantom
painter is this . . .' I paused for effect and was rewarded with
complete silence in the room. 'Excellent work! Keep it up.'
Laughs and cheers.

By the time I was queuing for lunch in the canteen I had been
asked three times if I had seen Anne. Apparently everyone needed
to talk to her about this or that. Only Mrs Washbrook couldn't
have cared less; all she wanted to know was what I had done
about the pilfering.

'I'm making progress,' I told her. Had she heard about the
phantom painter? I explained what was happening night after
night in our studio. 'And I think your pilferer and our phantom
painter could be one and the same. We have now caught him on
CCTV but the images are inconclusive.' Mrs Washbrook seemed
to agree that this was progress and rewarded me with an extra
sausage in gravy.

By the afternoon it was becoming clear that Anne was not
around. Nobody was heartbroken but DI Reid wanted to interview
her about the 'arrow incident', as attempted murder was apparently now called. There was also a community police officer on
the warpath about security at the college; I saw him pass the
windows several times, stopping to stare in, taking photos around

the grounds on a phone and then scratching his neck while staring at the thing.

It was now just two days before the paintings were to go up, with the doors opening for the anniversary exhibition the following evening. For once even Dawn worked quietly at her atmospheric canvas and I saw that Hufnagel was adding a semi-abstract background of contemporary urban greys to his painting. Despite the phantom's helping brush I had plenty of work to do. Eventually I was the only one still left in the studio, fussing over values, tightening things here, blurring things there. As often happened in my own studio too, I didn't stop until the natural light became too dim for work. I did not bother putting on the lights, just sat by the window with my feet up on another chair, watching my forest scene dwindle into the darkness just as it would now be doing outside. A real autumn chill had replaced the unseasonal warmth of the last month. I laid a hand on the old-fashioned lump of a radiator under the window; it had no heat to spare for radiating if it wanted to keep itself from freezing, probably another result of Anne trying to make the school profitable. The image of the naked man in the woods came into my mind. He was shivering. I quickly kitted him out in knitted woollens and a beanie. While I was at it I combed out his beard and it was obvious that I was looking at Hiroshi. Perhaps he was taking his own research into his subject more seriously than I had given him credit for. Anyway, with the weather turning much cooler now I expected his man-of-the-woods phase would be drawing to a close soon.

It was nearly completely dark now. From upstairs came the distant sound of scraping chairs, signalling that Annis had finished the presentation about her own work. Soon there was footfall and I heard voices in the corridor; it seemed Annis had attracted a fair number of students to her lecture, certainly a lot more than I could have mustered had I dared to schedule a lecture for this hour. Soon the voices dwindled away, some car engines started up, then just the sound of a single bicycle squeaking away down the lane.

A moment later the door opened and a little light fell into the room from the dim corridor. Annis found the light switch and flicked on the neon light. I squinted against the sudden glare.

'Oh, sorry,' she said and flicked the lights off again and closed the door. 'Are you in a dark mood?'

'Not at all.'

'Oh, good.' She came and found my mouth in the dim light and planted a kiss on it.

'Good lecture?'

'Full house. Kroog, too, smoking her pipe in the back row. I do like her. What happened with the phantom vid?'

I told her. 'The way it was done it was almost like the phantom knew about the camera. Not one glimpse of the face.'

'No suspects at all?'

'I ruled out Hiroshi but I have him down for the wild man in the forest now. Most people who saw the CCTV think it's a woman.'

'Are you sitting in the dark to catch the phantom then? One-handed with your other arm in a sling?'

'It's a thought. I'd only have to turn the lights on; I don't want to wrestle with the phantom.'

'I'll keep you company. What time did the phantom turn up last night?'

'Half past ten.'

'Some time to go then. What'll we do till then?'

'Oh, I'm sure we'll think of something.'

Dear reader, we did. In the absence of Anne it was Kroog who locked up the front doors. We heard her talk to someone as she walked away towards her cottage; I guessed it was probably her companion Alex. While the building fell completely silent we huddled together for warmth and discussed in murmurs the events of the last two weeks – break-ins, trashed studios, fires, wild men in the woods, Rachel's electrocution, the attempt to frame me for it, the tags scratched everywhere, the phantom painter, the pilfering, and now Anne's disappearance. 'You don't think she's just had enough and stomped off in a huff?' Annis asked.

'Not Anne. That would be completely out of character. She is desperate to make herself heard, she wants people to listen to what she has to say. Last thing I heard her say was that she had had enough and was going to close down the school.'

'Can she do that?'

'Don't know. Not immediately, I don't think; people have contracts, students have paid fees. It would be hugely costly, and money is her number-one interest, it seems. But she might do it eventually.'

'That would be a shame. There aren't many independent art school about.'

'I wonder why?'

Annis grabbed my arm. 'Did you hear that?'

I had – the distant sound of something being broken, like a pane of glass, somewhere in the building. 'Sounds like a break-in.'

'Why break windows? Most of them open easily. The phantom would know that.'

We stole towards the door. With great care I opened it a crack. There were more distant clinking sounds. I thought I could now make out the direction: it came from the corridor leading off on the other side of the entrance hall. We tiptoed across like cartoon burglars but the soles of my boots squeaked on the floor. 'Stop squeaking,' Annis hissed. I halted, undid my laces and took off my boots in almost complete darkness. If it hadn't been for a thin dribble of moonlight falling through the windows we'd have been unable to see a thing without using a torch. We could still hear noises when we entered the other corridor, but whoever was there did not use a light either. Annis and I both saw it at the same time – a dark, bulky figure walking towards us. I was about to challenge it when it too must have noticed there were three of us in the corridor. It ran towards us, then took a sharp right down the stairs to the basement. Annis, wearing trainers, was quicker off the mark than me but once up to speed I could slither and skid wonderfully on the polished floor. It was the braking I had problems with and I had to grab Annis to stop myself from skidding into the wall. Padding down the stairs was easier but there was no light here at all. The stairs curved to the right and for a moment the bluish flash of an LED torch reflected from further down, then left us in utter darkness. I stuck my hand in my jacket pocket, through the hole in it and furtled about in the lining until I found my mini Maglite. We proceeded by its eerie concentric beam to the bottom and found ourselves in a narrow service corridor that smelled damp, with an unusual top note.

Annis smelled it too. 'Now, why do I suddenly feel like a cheese sandwich with Branston pickle?' she murmured.

I knew where this would eventually lead us – to the bowels of the ceramics department where another set of stairs would lead us back up to moonlight again. The floor was bare concrete and I soon wished I had carried my squeaky boots with me. There were several narrow doors off, all to one side, looking in this light like a medieval dungeon. I tried the first one; it looked and smelled like an old coal hole. In the next two we found mouldering books in tea chests and the utterly silent central heating. Getting closer to the other side of the building now I found one door that put up a certain resistance to being opened, which could have something to do with the strong smell of cheese and pickle lingering here. I put my shoulder against it and pushed it open against the resistance of whatever had been piled against the door from the inside until I could squeeze through the opening. The beam of my torch revealed a large storeroom where thirty years' worth of old furniture, props for still lives, broken easels and drapes were being stored. There was a small, dim skylight right at the back. We made our way past the dusty drapes, forgotten student paintings and a headless, one-armed skeleton to the other end where, below the skylight, someone had built a nest. A mattress, sleeping bag and blankets, candle in a jam jar and a couple of paperbacks. In the middle of it all, under a grey blanket, hid a human-shaped lump, keeping very still.

'Okay, let's have you,' I said, keeping my torch focussed on the shape.

The blanket was pulled back and the lump looked up. 'Is night time,' said Petronela irritably. 'What have you doing here so late?' Then she looked at the sandwich in her hand like she had forgotten it was there. 'I get the hunger,' she added and stuffed half of it into her mouth as though she thought we might take it from her. Petronela was wearing pink fluffy slippers, flower-print pyjamas, a pink cardigan and her faded pink dressing gown, the ensemble that had made her appear so large in the dark. 'I broke cup, you heard. Pity.'

'Annis, meet Petronela, the life model.'

'What are you doing camping in here?' Annis asked. 'It's a rubbish place to build a nest.'

'I know, getting cold now. I thought of blowing heater but nowhere to plug.'

'Why are you here in the first place?' I wanted to know. 'You didn't always hide down here, did you?'

'No, two weeks only,' she said. 'My boyfriend . . .' She

swallowed the last of the sandwich. 'He threw me out of flat. Was his flat,' she added, shrugging her shoulders, 'so I must go.'

'Why?'

'He is very Catholic. I am slut to him. He finds out I take clothes off when sitting for students. This makes me slut and get out, not come back.'

'Bum,' I said eloquently. 'You should have said. You can't live down here, you'll catch your death. We'll find you somewhere else tomorrow.'

'You think? I don't have deposit.'

'Don't worry about that. So at least we've solved the mystery of who was doing all the pilfering. Mrs Washbrook will be pleased.'

Petronela groaned at the mention of Mrs Washbrook. 'I know is really wrong but sometimes I get hungry late. And I am not only one making the pilferings.'

'Why, who else?'

'Anne Birdwhistler. She does pilferings *every* night. Big plate-fuls. I always watch out for her but she always hums by herself and goes with noisy feet, so easy avoidance for me. Please don't tell Mrs Washtub about my pilferings? I'll stop. Promise.'

'I won't tell her. I'll tell her about Anne instead.'

'Okay, enough about food, my stomach is growling,' Annis complained. 'What about the phantom, Petronela. Is it you?'

'What, me? Be phantom painter? Very funny. I cannot paint stickman. And I would not have put green bra in my painting. I don't like wearing green underlings, all my underlings pink or white.'

I looked about the room by torchlight. It was a miserable place and it smelled musty. 'I don't really like leaving you down here; this is no place for you to be sleeping.'

'You find better place for me tomorrow?'

'Definitely,' confirmed Annis.

'Then one more night no problem. I'm fine. I have torch with windings up and sometimes moonlight.' She produced her torch as evidence and wound its crank handle noisily.

Back upstairs I shuddered at the thought of her sleeping down there but when we got back to the studio to pick up my things the French windows were wide open. I thought I could hear running footfall outside and I could tell someone had used turpen-tine in here. I flicked on the lights. There was an abandoned brush on my palette next to a mixture of greys and pinks. I rushed outside but the moon had disappeared behind clouds and all I could see was the dark band of trees and Kroog's cottage beyond the lawns.

'Curses, foiled again.'

'You want to check the CCTV?'

'No point. I forgot to turn it on again.'

TWENTY

I found Kroog in the canteen having a serious breakfast talk with Claire and joined them with my scrambled eggs, grilled tomatoes and corrugated sausage (a Washbrook special). The two were discussing the forthcoming exhibition. 'Nibbles,' Claire said forcefully as I sat down.

'Nibbles to you too,' I offered.

Claire ignored me. 'I've ordered the drinks but I think we should have some nibbles too. I suggested it to Mrs Washbrook but she instantly went into some kind of 1970s trance about mini sausage rolls and cheese and pineapple cubes on cocktail sticks.'

Kroog shuddered theatrically. 'I remember those. You get whatever you see fit but don't let Washtub find out.' She turned to me. 'Morning, Chris. How's your shoulder?'

'Much better already.'

'Good. I see we now have a permanent police presence here to make sure no one else gets attacked.'

'I'm not sure it'll put them off. It may have been dark but there were plenty of people around when I got hit. Talking of which, how's Phoebe doing?'

'They are keeping her in for another day then she's going home to recover. Have you caught your phantom yet?'

'No, but I caught the pilferer.'

'Oh? Who?'

'According to a reliable source our nightly pilferer is none other than Anne Birtwhistle. Stealing from herself, really.'

Claire couldn't contain herself. 'And at the same time giving Mrs Washbrook a hard time about balancing her budget? That's terrible.' She stabbed her fork at a piece of bacon on her plate. 'This is not the same college I joined three months ago. I knew Anne was trouble the moment she walked in here with that "mine at last" air. Sorry, Liz.'

'Not at all,' said Kroog, 'I'm on your side, Claire. But now she's disappeared. As soon as I realized she was missing I snapped into action – I turned the heating up. No one is looking very hard for Anne, I assure you.'

'She still hasn't turned up?' Kroog was right; if it was anyone else I'd be worried but as far as I was concerned Anne could go missing all she liked.

'Actually it's not true, the police *are* looking for her. Anne has a flat in Bristol but apparently she hasn't been there since her father's death, or since she came to stay upstairs in his rooms, I should say.'

Claire had finished savaging her plate of bacon and eggs and sat up primly. 'Perhaps she's flipped her lid and the next time we see her she'll be a bag lady or something. Best thing she can do for the college.'

Kroog gave me a shrewd look. 'Want to look into it?'

'No, I'd be afraid of finding her. Do we need her? What if she stays disappeared, can't you just run things?'

'I can run things but I don't own this place. And I don't want to run things; that's her business. And Claire's.'

'The place is jolly easy to run without constant interference,' Claire said, smiling.

'That's why I have already contacted Henry. He'll be here this afternoon. *Her brother*,' she added when she saw our questioning looks.

I remembered. 'Ah yes, you mentioned him. I thought he was in Tibet or Norway?'

'Goa. But he's back. He ran a little theatre company out there but it got into financial trouble and it folded. Turns out he's been sleeping on people's sofas in London for the last few weeks. If Anne doesn't show up soon, he'll take over. It's his place too.'

'What's *he* like?' Claire asked in a doom-laden voice.

'The exact opposite of his sister. He's more like his father though more extrovert. He'll happily throw money out of the window with both hands and worry about nothing until it's too late, then claim it's *kismet*. You'll have to watch him, Claire, but he'll be a lot more fun to watch than Anne.'

'Oh good, the place could do with a bit of cheering up.' Claire picked up her plate and left for her office.

'I did find something else last night while I lay in wait for the phantom,' I said. 'Petronela. She's been kipping in the cellar in a sleeping bag for the last two weeks since her boyfriend chucked her out.'

'In the cellar? Can't have that; she'll catch all sorts down there. Split up with her boyfriend? Are they likely to get back together?'

'He objected to her nude modelling on religious grounds. She chose the college over home and boyfriend.'

'Girl after my own heart. Yes, I'll put her up. That is what you are asking me, isn't it?'

'Yup.'

'Plenty of bedrooms at my place. Remind me, does she smoke?'

With that sorted I went to round up my students to look at the results of the painting project. There were one or two duds and cop-outs but as a group they had worked extremely well and I told them so. Only very few of them preferred the results that were based on photographs, most reported that drawing the subject first made them look harder, in more detail, and remember the scene more clearly than the photograph could show. When they worked from their photos they often fell back on their first impressions and memories.

'You'll be glad to know that this project is now finished. I have one *more* painting project for you before I leave you to get on with your own work.' Stony silence. *You must be kidding*, is what their looks conveyed. 'I want you to go and rip all the ancient paintings in the corridors off the walls, paint the walls white with emulsion – Claire has a few gallons of it in her office – and when it's dry hang a selection of your own best work on it for when the visitors arrive.' The room came back to life. This was more like it. Painters are exhibitionists, after all. 'There is one prominent place in the entrance hall, opposite Claire's office, the first thing anyone sees when they come through the door. At the moment there's some bland 1980s nonsense hanging there. It's a prime spot and I think you should decide by vote whose painting gets pride of place there. That's all. Get to it.'

I had made sure that there were a few litres of white emulsion

for us tutors and was carrying a tin of the stuff into the studio
where the significant looks my fellow artists gave me clearly said
that the phantom had been again.

'I thought I scared the phantom off last night.'

'Must have come back,' Dawn said.

'I think your painting is finished,' Hufnagel said. He had a
point. Looking at it closely I couldn't think of anything I wanted
to change. 'It looks to me,' he went on, 'like the phantom likes
you, hates me and feels so-so about Dawn.'

'I'm not sure that's true. The phantom changed all our paintings
in one way or another. The phantom doesn't hate you, Kurt, or
your painting would have been cut to ribbons or whatever. And if
you don't mind me saying so, I prefer your painting the way it is
now. Dawn said herself that she approves of the changes to hers.
I think mine has gained too. What it all means is that the phantom
believes he or she is better than all of us. And it could be true.'

'Just different,' said Dawn. 'I don't mind critics, but buggering
about with other people's work is just arrogant. No matter how
good you are.'

'Oh, arrogance is right at the heart of it. But I'm also sure the
phantom has a lot of fun and it's not malicious fun.'

Even Hufnagel grudgingly agreed, hidden under much grumbling – grumbling that became louder when I told him we were
going to paint the walls today. 'Can't we get students to do that?'

'Nope, they're already doing the corridors and entrance hall.
This one's our baby.'

Never ask a painter to paint anything but paintings; you'd be
better off asking a five-year-old. We cleared paintings, painting
tables and other furniture into the centre and started daubing the
walls like three utterly dilettante decorators, each tackling one
wall as high as we could reach with brushes that were far too
small, dripping paint everywhere. In the middle of this delightful
mess Kroog appeared and ushered a man through the door. Brown
as a nut, wearing rings, earrings, bracelets and a necklace of
Indian silver, Henry looked exactly as you'd expect an old Goa
hippy to look but he had the features of his father and I was
immediately prepared to like him. Introductions over, he showed
interest in everything, asked intelligent questions about our work
and the students and after half an hour hadn't said a single
annoying thing. I could see he was an immediate hit with Dawn,

too, who painted over her own knee because she couldn't take her eyes off him. Eventually Kroog left and Henry took me aside.

'A lot of strange things have been happening around here,' he said. 'You haven't got my sister locked in a cupboard somewhere, have you?'

'Not guilty.'

'It would serve her right; she locked me in a cupboard once in Lizzie's cottage. I missed strawberries and cream on the lawn. You were shot with an arrow, Lizzie said.'

'Yes, but nothing vital damaged,' I said heroically.

'And you were there when my father died?' he said, inviting me to tell the story.

It was at that moment that the door opened again and two students appeared, carrying a large canvas, professionally boxed up in museum-quality protection, followed by its illustrious creator, Greg Landacker. He came straight across to address – no other word for it – Henry.

'Ah, I take it you are the new man in charge, John's son. Henry, isn't that right?' Henry said it was. 'Well, I'm glad you are setting these layabouts to work on the walls.' He delicately pushed a bottle top out of the way with the tip of his brogue. 'I do hope you are also going to do something about this floor before tomorrow. I think *that* wall would do,' he said, indicating the place where I had been painting my own canvas. 'The lower edge of the painting must be seventy-two inches off the ground. The lighting in here is wholly inadequate for showing artwork. Can you make sure there are spotlights installed, erm, here,' he walked as he pointed, 'and here?'

'Of course, no problem, Mr Landacker,' said Henry cheerfully.

'Call me Greg. I'll leave it all in your hands, then, Henry.'

'You have to excuse him,' I said. 'I think he grew up with servants.'

'Yes, never mind. I've met plenty like him in India. People still have servants there, you know? Most of course *are* servants. We'd best postpone our chat until tomorrow and get cracking. I'm still not used to the pace of things here; everyone's in such a hurry. I'm also still a bit stunned to find I have this behemoth of a school on my hands now.' He waved his arms theatrically towards the ceiling, then let them fall by his side. 'Of course I thought the old man would live forever,' he added quietly and walked out through the French windows into the cool midday sun and crossed the lawns towards the cottage.

'I've never seen such a tan on a white man,' Dawn said in an awestruck voice.

'It'll fade,' Hufnagel said.

'Yes, but until then . . .'

'Get some more paint on the walls,' I moaned, 'or we'll still be here at midnight.'

I was nearly right, too. Preparing a room for showing artwork always takes longer than you think, even without having to dance around a taciturn electrician on a huge ladder fiddling with spotlights. The students had long-finished hanging their work. For pride of place in the entrance hall they had chosen, as I thought they might, Hiroshi's forest painting. It wasn't just the painting that was huge, his talent was massive too: the composition, the execution, the startling detail here and there gave the painting an old master feeling. I was pretty sure I had very little to teach Hiroshi. Had he really done his research in the nude, I wondered? Perhaps I was missing a trick.

When it was done it looked good. Claire and Henry had managed to find a few framed examples of John Birtwhistle's work, sensitive little etchings of nature subjects and views of Batcombe village. The freshly painted walls and waxed floor set it all off well and the spotlights that had now replaced the strip lighting made all the difference.

Landacker's canvas had taken pride of place opposite the French windows and was looking superb. I had only seen the very first beginnings of it on my uninvited inspection of his studio, now it hit me with the full Landacker broadside that his canvases always delivered. They had a depth and emotional ambiguity that was hard to pin down. Mysterious, was how many critics described his abstract compositions. The contrast with the man's personality was as stark as ever.

I was the last to leave. When I turned off the lights I was sure tomorrow could be a success, provided we kept shootings and other maimings to a minimum.

If you're a painter and you've been doing it for a while then I'm sure you'll agree that it can be difficult to find enough items of clothing without paint stains on them to make an ensemble. When you're a student, spatters of oil paint on your clothes can still be worn as a badge of honour, and if you're desperate, a talking point. Later on in your career it may simply denote a lack of funds, as it did in mine. Annis was doing rather better than me, which is easy if all you're wearing is a pair of tights, shoes and little black dress, but when that evening I stepped from my shiny DS 21 in an almost spotless black suit and rollneck and without my arm in a sling, I thought I would not let the side down as long as no one slapped me heartily on the shoulder. We knew the anniversary exhibition was well-attended even before we got there since cars were parked all the way up and down the lane, which meant that the little car park was full to bursting. The sky had threatened rain all day but none had materialized, just a blustery wind that tore at suits and dresses and was noisy in the trees.

'I think rather than keeping them away,' said Claire, handing each of us a glass of red by way of a greeting, 'Rachel's death and your near miss have had the opposite effect.' Claire looked splendid in a dark, sequined outfit, and I could tell Henry, hovering near her, thought so too.

'It's the English murder mystery effect,' I agreed. 'Country house, stormy night, plenty of suspects, all we need now is a power cut.'

'Oh no, not that, I don't think there are any candles,' said Claire seriously.

'Petronela has a wind-up torch. Any sign of Anne?'

'None. We are truly blessed.'

'And look, we are blessed with a police presence too.' Hard to overlook, DSI Needham was mingling down the corridor towards us. He was fond of a drink or two, which meant the orange juice in his fist was probably a sign he considered himself on duty. He noticed me, acknowledged me with a nod but parked himself at the bottom of the stairs. There was a trickle of traffic up and down the stairs – parents going to check out the offerings of the printing and graphics department – but the bulk of people and students were on this floor, close to the paintings and the drinks, dispensed from behind a table by a couple of sculpture students. Kroog, who had made no secret of her loathing for this kind of occasion, had dutifully turned up but was puffing so furiously on her pipe that only the most determined parents (and of course Alex) went anywhere near her.

I recognized none of the parents and none would know who

I was unless I stood next to my painting which was just as well since I shared Kroog's aversion to polite chatter. By contrast, and despite his limited capability for politeness, one who didn't seem to mind as long as the booze lasted was Hufnagel. He had been even less successful in finding any paint-free clothing but looked happy as a sandboy carrying two glasses of red through the crowd towards Studio One.

'Studio One looks really excellent,' Claire said. 'You should go and have a look while there is still some daylight.'

'Oh, all right then . . .'

'No sign of Greg Landacker yet,' I heard Claire say to Henry as Annis and I walked away. No one had told either of them that Mr Landacker never even came to his one-man shows any more. Quite a few people, students and parents, were admiring some kind of exhibit on the wall near the door to Studio One. It turned out to be a long, narrow noticeboard covered with photographs of the last thirty years of the college: students, tutors, art works, exhibitions, arranged by Kroog who had dug around in the hundreds of pictures John Birtwhistle had taken of the life of the academy. I caught a glimpse of a younger Lizzie, with more hair but otherwise the same Kroog, down to the notorious pipe. Annis dragged me away into Studio One. Ours was the best-lit room and attracted most of the attention. I refused to feel guilty about this since that was what the show was about, showing off the work of the tutors, past and present. Landacker's painting had pride of place but the canvas attracting most of the attention was Hufnagel's. He was being eagerly quizzed by earnestly nodding people and photographed by a press photographer in front of his painting.

'It is a good painting,' Annis admitted.

'Yes, but how much of it is his?' I sniped.

'And how about yours?'

'Yes, good point,' I admitted as we walked across to my own painting. 'But at least the phantom didn't completely change the theme of my canvas, he just . . . erm, hang on.' I nearly spilled my wine in my haste to elbow my way closer to the canvas.

'What?' Annis asked irritably.

'It's changed again. The phantom has added to the painting since last night, since we finished the hanging.'

'Oh, yes, I can see it, it's a working kiln now.'

In what I had hoped was my finished painting the mouth
of the kiln had been open, showing the shady and slightly
mysterious-looking entrance to the dark interior. Now the front
entrance was closed up with firebricks and there was smoke
and haze issuing from the domed part of the kiln. Next to the
entrance the phantom had added something else. I had to get
in close and go down on my knees to identify it. 'It's a pair of
shoes, women's shoes, kitten heels.'

'You know what that reminds me of?'

'Shoe shops?'

'No, dummy. Hansel and Gretel. After they shoved the witch
in the oven.'

'The witch in the oven . . . where is Dan? I have to find Dan!'

Annis gulped her wine and left the empty glass on a table.
'Who's Dan?'

'Ceramics tutor,' I said. We were outside, marching along the
side of the building to the brightly lit conservatory.

'The one with the fake CV.'

'And the one whose department Anne threatened to close.'

There were so few people in the ceramics department that the
place looked forlorn, though there were plenty of exhibits, mostly
by students of course. Dan was there, looking quite chirpy nevertheless. 'I think we're a bit far away from the bar,' he said by way
of explanation.

'The kiln – the kiln in the woods. Have you used it yet?' I
asked urgently.

'No, we're nowhere near done restoring it. And we need bone-
dry wood and what's out there isn't—'

I cut across him. 'You wouldn't know anything about Anne's
disappearance, would you?'

He looked around to see who might be listening before
answering. 'No. But I'm jolly glad she did disappear. That woman
was a disaster. I hope her brother takes more after his dad. Why
are you asking me all this?'

'Not sure yet. You haven't got a torch here, have you?'

'I have as it happens, I got it for working inside the kiln.'

It was rapidly getting dark outside as Annis and I crossed the
lawn towards the black streak of woodland beyond. 'We are
looking for a dead body, aren't we?' Annis asked.

'I don't know.'

'Because I'm not really dressed for it. That's more a paper-overall kind of job.'

'I'm aware of it. You don't have to come, I just have to check; it might be nothing.'

'No, I'm coming,' she said when we reached the trees. 'Just hang on one second.' She popped her shoes off and slipped off her tights. 'They won't last two minutes in there, I remember woods.' She stuffed them into my jacket pocket. 'Ready now.'

We hadn't gone more than a few yards into the trees when we needed the torch. The leaves were turning but there were enough of them on the branches to make it dark and murky down here. The wind was loud in the bows above us and everything in sight moved and shifted, with the torch beam adding jumping shadows to the picture.

'This isn't much of a path, you know?' Annis complained as we staggered on.

'I know, but I'm pretty sure we're on the right track.' It wasn't easy to find, but eventually I recognized the approach to the place. 'If you see a naked man, throw a pine cone at him where it hurts, I want to hear his voice.'

'I didn't bring any and there's no pine trees.'

'Use your imagination, woman. There's the clearing.'

And there was the kiln, a dark, mysterious hump in the bank that bisected the clearing. I focussed the spider's web of the torch beam on to the entrance of the kiln. As in my painting it had been bricked up.

'Chris, look,' Annis whispered. *'The shoes.'*

'Exactly as in my painting,' I whispered back.

'Shh, I can hear something,' Annis hissed. 'Singing?'

We tiptoed closer to the looming dome of the kiln. Annis was right, someone was singing, deep inside the kiln, in a thin, slightly flat voice. As we got close to the bricked-up entrance I was able to pick out the words:

> *Oh you canna shove your Grannie off a bus*
> *Oh you canna shove your Grannie off a bus*
> *Oh you canna shove your Grannie*
> *'Cos she's your daddy's mammy*
> *Oh you canna shove your Grannie off a bus*

It was sung to the tune of *She'll be Coming Round the Mountain*.

We crouched down by the entrance. Annis picked up the shoes to inspect them, then set them down again with a what-the-hell shrug. I called: 'Hello?'

The answer was a shriek, loud and prolonged, then Anne's voice, hoarse but unmistakable. 'Get me out of here! You get me out of here, you hear? Who are you?'

'It's me, Honeysett.'

'About bloody time. I am *starving*! The *bastards*!'

'Right, keep away from the entrance, we'll try and bash it in.'

'I can't get *at* the bloody entrance or I'd have bashed it in myself by now, you stupid man.'

'On second thoughts perhaps it would be easier if we waited until daylight . . .' I suggested maliciously.

'You get me out of here now, you hear? *Now!*'

'I'm not sure why but let's do it,' I said to Annis. I didn't have far to look for a suitable rock to hit the bricks with. They gave almost immediately. 'No mortar; they just stacked them up, it's just symbolic.' Like so much else recently.

We pushed and pulled until the entrance was more or less clear, then I crawled through the short tunnel until I reached the chamber.

Anne, in a frazzled and filthy business suit and with a blanket over her shoulders, sat at the furthest end, hands cuffed at the front and with a chain around her waist. The chain ran to the wall and out through a gap. She looked miserable, furious and ever so slightly mad. She was surrounded by empty plastic containers, sandwich boxes and bottles of water. The place smelled bad.

'About bloody time! Did none of you nits notice that I was missing? How could it have taken you this long to find me? I screamed myself hoarse.'

'We thought we'd leave it to the police,' I said sweetly. 'Who locked you in here?'

'How would I know? They put a filthy sack over my face. They threatened to drown me in the pond if I screamed.'

'What did they sound like? Would you recognize them again?'

'I doubt it. They spoke in Micky Mouse sort of comic-strip voices. But definitely students. They smelled like students. I hate the smell of students.'

'I'm sure. I wonder what they've got against you? Okay, I'll have to go out again to see where that chain leads. Won't be a mo.'

'You'd better not be long. I am *sick* of this place. Sick of the dark, sick of the smell, sick of my voice . . .'

'How is she?' Annis asked.

'In fine fettle. They chained her up, the other end is round the back, wait here.'

'You really know how to show a girl a good time.'

'Ah, but you'll never forget tonight, will you?'

'Not for want of trying. It's freezing out here.'

At the back of the kiln I found the chain running out from the chink in the wall; it had been wound and padlocked around a brick. It took a few blows but eventually I managed to break it into three pieces and pull the chain off. It was still a tight squeeze with the padlock on but Anne managed to drag the thing through to the inside. By the time I had made it back to the front she was already emerging from the entrance on all fours, cursing fluently and dragging her chain like a ghost in a castle. 'My shoes!' she greeted them like lost children and wriggled inside them. 'Prison is too good for them. When the police find them I want them flogged. I'll kill them! When I get my hands on the criminal creeps I'll make them pay. Where the hell are we and how do we get out of here?'

Suddenly the impulse to shove her back inside with a fresh supply of sandwiches was overwhelming. I took a deep breath. 'This way for Batcombe House.'

For someone who had spent days chained up in the dark, Anne Birtwhistle displayed surprising vigour. She seemed a touch deranged at that moment but a bolt cutter, a hot bath and a quick raid of Mrs Washbrook's fridge would probably restore her to her old self, more was the pity. She stormed ahead of us across the lawns and disappeared into the house through the conservatory. Moments later a loud crash made it pretty clear that she had taken out her anger at being chained up in a kiln on the nearest piece of smashable ceramic.

The evening was now in full swing. Some of the parents had left but there was still a good crowd, and naturally the students would hang around until the last of the booze was gone, of which there was presently no danger; with Anne safely locked up a

decent amount had been ordered. Annis wriggled back into her
tights and we dived back into the studio. Almost immediately I
was accosted by Claire, who looked like she had drunk just the
right amount of red wine to be jolly, only she clearly wasn't.
She seemed agitated and angry. 'Has Greg Landacker arrived
yet?' she asked. 'Do you have any idea when he might get here?'

'I doubt he will, Claire,' I said carefully. 'These days he doesn't
even turn up to some of his one-man shows.'

'What? You can't be serious!' She was nearly shouting now.
'But then it's all pointless!' She stormed past the approaching
Hufnagel, knocking his brimful glass of wine over him with a
deliberate slap.

'What's eating her?' slurred Hufnagel, his pale blue shirt dripping with red wine. 'Look at me. That was my last shirt with all
the buttons on it. I'm ruined now. Hold that.' He thrust his now
empty glass at me and stripped off his shirt. The vest he was
wearing underneath had seen better days and had soaked up some
of the wine too. It made him look like the victim of a
stabbing.

'You'd best soak the shirt in the sink,' I suggested.

'I'm going to,' he said and turned away.

That's when I saw it. I grabbed Annis, who had been talking
to a painting student, by the arm to get her attention. 'What
now?'

Hufnagel had squeezed through the throng towards the Belfast
sink in the corner; I dragged Annis after me. 'Look. There. The
tattoo on Hufnagel's shoulder. What do you think that is?'

The tattoo was simple; a small, crude home-made thing.

'It looks like an hourglass. Yes, it is an hourglass, not very
well done. And if you look at it sideways . . .'

'Then it looks like our ubiquitous I><I tag. Kurt!' I grabbed
him by the arm.

'Yeah?'

'Your tattoo.'

'Which one? I've got two, only one is a rose and I couldn't
possibly show it to you here – think of the scandal.'

'The one on your shoulder blade. What is it?'

'Meant to be an hourglass; it's pretty rubbish.' He craned his
neck to try and look at it. 'Not finished either.'

'Who gave it to you?'

'A girl.'

'What girl?'

'That student girl, you know? The one that I got chucked out of here for. She had one too. We were very pissed and infatuated. It was meant to be a symbol of how we counted the hours and so on.'

'Who was she? What was her name?'

'Erm . . . Sara. Sara Horn. And I can tell you she certainly did . . .'

'Come with me.'

'My shirt,' he complained as I dragged him away from the sink and out into the corridor.

I shoved him towards the wall of pinned-up photographs. 'Find her.'

'What, in this lot? There's hundreds of pictures. What makes you think she's even in one of them?' His eyes flitted over the display.

'Do it methodically, left-to-right.'

'I prefer right-to-left. *If* you don't mind. How come she's so important all of a sudden?'

'I think she's behind the tag we see everywhere. It's an hourglass knocked over. Time is up, is the message.'

'Jeez, you think Sara fried Rachel? What's she got to do with it?'

'I don't know.'

'Anyway, it's, what, twelve years ago now? This is nonsense, Chris, it's utter – oh there she is.' He tapped a square photograph. It had three girls in it, standing in front of a large partially visible canvas. 'That's her on the right. She was quite pretty. Bit weird, of course.'

I was too busy staring at it to pass sarcastic comment. The picture came off the board easily, being held on by double-sided tape. Sara Horn was a thin, blue-eyed girl with long blonde hair and an intense look about her. Her clothes were black. Now she preferred greys, had a pudding basin haircut and pink spectacles.

'I'm going to get a drink,' Hufnagel said and tilted away.

On tiptoe I scanned over the heads of the visitors and saw Kroog's smoke cloud disappear through the front door. When I caught up she was just turning the corner towards her cottage with

Alex. They appeared to be arguing about something but I was too obsessed with my discovery to notice what it was about.

'Lizzie!' I caught up with them and held out the photograph. It was dark now but I was still holding the torch and illuminated the snapshot for her. 'Sara Horn.'

'What about her?'

'That's her, isn't it? On the right.'

She took the photograph from me, raised her eyebrows high and produced a pair of spectacles from her waistcoat. 'Ah yes, poor girl.'

'What happened to her?'

'She had a breakdown while she was here. She was very highly strung; I think she may have been taking drugs. There were all sorts of things going on at the time. She was sectioned, I believe. Never came back.'

'She did, you know? Sara Horn turned into Claire Kilburn.'

Kroog opened her mouth as though to say something to the contrary but instead she went back to the picture. She steadied my torch hand; I hadn't even noticed I was shaking.

'Think twelve years on,' I prompted. 'She's over thirty now, put on about six stone in weight – medication does that to you – has very short hair and big pink glasses. Which she probably doesn't even need.'

'It's her,' Kroog agreed.

Alex took the photo, looked at it and said, 'Blimey.'

'I think Sara Horn came back because she had a less than happy time here and she came back angry.'

'Do you think she shot you?'

'Yes, but I think she was aiming at someone else. An ex-tutor of hers. I had long left when she studied here. Where did you last see Claire?'

'She ran out the door,' said Alex, 'a short while ago. In a real hurry.'

'What car does she drive?'

'Not sure. Small blue thing,' Kroog said. 'They all look the same to me.'

'Right. I have an idea where she might have shot off to.' I was already jogging towards my car. 'Oh, by the way, I found Anne,' I called back.

'Did you have to?' called Alex.

I was glad of my torch as I hurried along the lane to where I had left the car; in my hurry it felt miles away. Claire or Sara, I didn't know how to think of her, had been very agitated when she realized Landacker wouldn't be coming. Why? It now seemed that everything had pointed to this day, the exhibition. When she managed to get a job here she may have hoped that all her old tutors were still working here and disappointed that three of them had left. She might even have put the exhibition idea into John's head in the first place as a way of bringing them all back. I fumbled with the keys to my ancient car, then with the ignition, but once on the road I flicked my headlights to full beam and set the controls for The Old Forge, Motterton. Sara-Claire would be at Landacker's place, and not for the first time. As far as I could tell she had started with Landacker, on the very day of my first visit. Who had the arrow been for? Hufnagel? If she had been behind the break-in and trashing of his studio then she could have killed him in private there and then. I could only presume that it was meant for Stottie, the graphics tutor.

As my headlights illuminated the bottom of the hill in Motterton I could see a small blue car parked awkwardly opposite The Old Forge's front gate. The driver door was half open. Someone had been in an even greater hurry than me. I locked my car, climbed up Landacker's front gate and let myself drop down on to his drive on the other side.

TWENTY-ONE

The house lay in complete darkness, the security light on the drive did not react as I cautiously approached the only dim source of illumination there was. It came from the open door of the studio. Somewhere inside a lonely lamp was burning. I had left the torch behind; quite apart from the light it might provide, its rubberized weight in my hand would have given me a little more confidence than I was feeling at the moment. Getting shot doesn't do much for your poise. As noiselessly as possible I sidled into the dark vestibule and from there slid into the studio proper.

A lonely anglepoise lamp was the only illumination in the place, lighting the sad remains of a shattered computer and splintered projector. The printer, too, would print no more. The large studio easel had been knocked over, the painting table overturned. The resulting cascade of expensive tubes of French oil paints had been partially trampled. A bright trail led away from the devastation, across an expensive rug and to the foot of the spiral staircase, as though a wounded animal with multi-coloured blood had dragged itself across the room. That is how wounded painters should bleed, I thought as I put my foot on the bottom rung of the iron stairs: in many colours. Would I find a bleeding painter at the top of the staircase?

Or would he have already stopped bleeding? I took one step then froze: I could hear a voice. A voice was good news, a voice meant life. What I really wanted to hear was two voices. I took step after step as quietly as I could.

It was very dark up here on the gallery but it was immediately obvious that the voice did not come from here. I remembered a door at the furthest end, dark, yale-locked, devoid of a door handle. I felt my way towards it; I heard murmuring voices, then, just as I laid the palm of my hand against the cool, smooth surface, a shrill, ironic laugh – Claire's. I pushed gently but the door was locked.

In films private eyes usually say at this point: 'Stand back!' and then charge at the door, barging it open with their shoulder, but having tried it once with a spectacularly painful lack of success, I wasn't about to try it again. I knocked with my open palm, like police officers like to do. 'Open the door!' I added unnecessarily.

'Who are you?' asked Claire, close to the door.

'It's Chris.'

'Go away.'

I heard Landacker's voice from further away but I couldn't catch what he was saying. 'I can't do that. Open this door, Sara. You shot me, you owe me an explanation.' After a pause the door was unlocked and opened.

Painters bleed mundanely monochrome in a bright, lively red. Claire – she always remained Claire in my mind – was pressing a small blue hand towel against her stomach to stem the blood that was still spreading from there, soaking into her mouse-grey top. On the floor, leaning against the leg of a writing desk in the small square room, sat Landacker. Beside him stood an old green safe, the door wide open. On the desk stood a large canvas bag bulging with a dozen or so sketchbooks, large and thick and spattered with paint.

Landacker looked very pale. In his left thigh stuck an old-fashioned bayonet. He was bleeding even more heavily than Claire, though not, I thought, from an artery. 'Call an ambulance, Honeysett. And the police. The bitch tried to kill me,' he said without taking his eyes off the bayonet.

'You lying, thieving, disgusting toad! *He* tried to kill *me!*' she shouted. 'With *that*. He had it hidden in his safe. Along with my sketchbooks. *My sketchbooks!* Mine! Every single bloody Landacker canvas comes straight out of my sketchbooks.'

'How?' I said, groping blindly for my mobile. I couldn't take my eyes off the two bleeding painters. There was a baseball bat leaning by the door, and that bat had seen some action too recently, though mainly downstairs. I had no luck with finding my mobile.

'I thought you knew? You know my real name, anyway. I had a breakdown. I went completely mental, completely hyper. I didn't sleep, I had visions of paintings day and night, I was convinced they came straight from God. I filled sketchbook after sketchbook with oil sketches of abstract paintings. Brilliant paintings, mysterious paintings, gorgeous, surprising, *extraordinary* paintings! Help yourself, Honeysett, have a look.'

I reached across and picked up the top sketchbook. As soon as it fell open it was obvious – here were Landacker's paintings, one solo exhibition after the other, in A3 format; every surprising compositional detail, every colour study. All he had done was project them on to his canvases and copy them. There was a lot of manic writing, scrawled notes and squiggles on the back of each study. He could never have pretended the sketchbooks were his.

'Yes,' I said. 'Looks very familiar. You're one hell of a painter. I can't find my mobile, is there a phone downstairs?'

'There's no hurry,' said Claire. 'That's the only good thing about being fat, if a scrawny bastard like him sticks a knife in you, the first few inches are just blubber. I don't think he got anything vital though it hurts like hell as soon as I move.'

'So does this,' Landacker complained. 'There's a phone down-stairs, but I don't want you to leave me alone with her, she's mental.'

'Nearly ten years I spent in one psychiatric institution after another. But now I'm utterly sane, my friend. And I've come for you. All of you.'

'What have the others done to you?' I asked.

'They were all at it, they were all responsible. My boyfriend couldn't cope with my mental state, and he dumped me when it kicked off. Dumped me to shag Stottie instead, the antiseptic posh cow. I'm sorry you got in the way; I was aiming at her current boyfriend. I thought it would do her good to find out what it's like to lose one. Then Kurt hit on me when I was already quite bad. For a while I thought I had found a soulmate but he was just pretending so he could get his leg over. I was going to mess him up a little too but then the phantom painter did that for me.'

'You're not the pantom painter? I could have sworn . . .'

'Work all day and paint all night? No thanks, that's how I had my first breakdown. I have no idea who it was but he did me a favour. Hufnagel was livid.'

'Why did Rachel have to die?'

'She didn't have to die, the stupid woman. I don't think I wanted her to die. Not sure. Not that I cared much either way, really. She was my "personal tutor" at the time. The person you come to if you are troubled; everyone has one assigned to them. She told me to pull myself together or leave the college. "Not everyone is cut out to be an artist; not everyone can live with the tension" was what I got from her. So I thought I'd bring some tension to her life. I'm not sure I wanted her to drop dead but it's no great loss to the art world, is it? Oh, this really hurts now.' She lifted the blood-soaked hand towel.

How sane or disturbed Claire was I couldn't tell, but I agreed with Landacker: I would feel uneasy leaving the two in that blood-stained room together. It was beginning to affect my own equilibrium. I picked up the bag from the desk, shoving the sketchbook in with the others. 'Let's you and I get downstairs. I'll carry these for you. Then I'll call an ambulance.'

'All right,' she said and picked up the baseball bat.

'What do you want with that?'

'Brain you with it if you try and make off with the bag, Honeysett. That is my life you are carrying. I had it stolen once but not again.'

I looked her in the eyes. She looked completely sane. 'Leave it here. You won't need the bat.'

'You're not that cute, Honeysett. Go on,' she said, giving me a gentle poke with the thing.

'Watch out for her, she's vicious, that woman, and completely mad. The sooner they lock her up again the better!'

Claire took one step at a time. I made sure to stay close so as not to alarm her. 'What did you have in mind for Landacker originally? Were you going to kill him?'

'No, I was going to expose him. You were all supposed to bring your sketchbooks and I had the press invited and they came, too. I was going to expose him in front of the journalists and destroy him. And then the bastard didn't show at all.'

'You wouldn't know who chained up Anne in the kiln in the woods, would you?'

'Is that where she was? What a good idea. No, not the foggiest. But she was asking for it. God, I thought those stairs went on forever. There's an old dialler phone over there, I didn't smash it,' she said. 'I like those old phones.'

I dropped the bag at the foot of the stairs and went to the back of the studio. Next to the wreck of the laptop stood a shiny black 1960s dialler phone. The line crackled a little but it worked; I enjoyed the sound of the dial running through the three nines of the emergency number. I asked for ambulance and police. Two stab wounds, I explained. 'No, I have no idea of the bloody postcode but it's the same place that caught fire the other day.' Was it me that was hurt, the operator wanted to know next. Was the attacker still on the premises? Hard to answer that, really. I turned around. Claire was nowhere to be seen. The bag with the sketchbooks had gone. So, on further inspection, had Claire's car. The baseball bat was leaning against the bonnet of mine.

The mention of a knife attack swiftly brought an armed response unit down the hill and the mention of my name brought Superintendent Needham with similar haste. The armed response guys patted me down for weapons, not knowing who was who and Needham, who did know who was who, grabbed me by the arm that hurt and dragged me into his car and asked me a million questions. 'Why, when you knew it was Claire or Sara, didn't you say anything?'

'I didn't really know for certain, I just had a sudden brain-wave. You probably wouldn't have got here any quicker and what could you have done? Police hammering on the door would hardly have calmed things down in there. It was all over when I arrived.'

Landacker, the bayonet still sticking in his thigh, was being carried out to the ambulance, a drip in his arm. Needham went over to arrest him for attempted murder. The look Landacker gave me told me he was considering his next one.

'Shame you didn't get the index number of her car,' Needham said as the blue beacon of the ambulance disappeared up the lane. 'Still, we have a description and she needs medical treat-ment, so I'm sure we'll pick her up soon. Follow me to Manvers Street to make a full statement.'

'Have a heart. I've had a long day. Can't it wait until tomorrow? I found Anne Birtwhistle for you.'

'So I heard just as I left the college.'

'Kidnapped and chained up in an old kiln in Summerlee Wood.'

'By whom?' Needham asked sharply.

'Don't know yet. I might find that out for you too if you let me sleep on it.'

'All right, bright and early tomorrow, though, *my office*.'

Early it was, bright it wasn't. Naturally I didn't get an early night. Annis and I had endlessly talked it all out over a few glasses too many, then there were the phone calls that had to be made. It meant that when I eventually stepped out of Manvers Street police station, having made my statement and drunk too many coffees, the grey blanket of cloud overhead mirrored my state of mind perfectly. By the time I had rolled through the wide-open gates at Batcombe House, I had come to a definite conclusion about it all: I had been right from the start; teaching was not for me.

All seemed eerily quiet compared to last night. There was no sign of any students – they'd all taken the day off to nurse their hangovers presumably, and of course there was no Claire in the office. I let myself into the studio through the French windows.

There were empty bottles and glasses everywhere – well, mostly around Hufnagel's painting. It had acquired a red dot, I saw now, which made me feel good because it meant I hadn't made too many false promises when I dragged him up here.

I went out through the other door, along the corridor, to check on the rest of the place. The photo wall had been removed and some of the student paintings were gone. The centrepiece, however, Hiroshi's large forest landscape, was still in place. And the phantom had been very busy on it during the night.

Hiroshi's painting was as mysterious as ever, a dark and tangled forest scene through which a faint footpath wound into a vaguely guessed-at, misty distance. But now on the path, hand in hand, walked two naked people, seen from behind. One was my wild man of the woods, Hiroshi himself; his companion was Alex, looking back at me over her shoulder with a half-smile, perhaps of uncertainty, perhaps of regret. On the floor in front of the painting, carefully folded, lay their clothes; their shoes stood neatly beside them.

I could smell Kroog's pipe. Lizzie was standing in the door to the admin office behind me. 'They're gone,' she said in a voice a little gruffer than usual. 'There's a Japanese legend, or is it Chinese? Who cares. Of some painter. He was imprisoned for something. Asked his guards if he could have his paints to decorate his cell. He painted a beautiful landscape on the wall and then walked into it, never to be seen again.'

'It's a very good painting,' I admitted.

'Alex is a very good painter.'

'I thought she was a sculptor? Working with you?'

'Yes, that too. But that was just a bit of infatuation with an old tutor; she was a painter to begin with. She'll be very good at both.'

'Where will they go?'

'Who knows? Japan? They'll make a success of it wherever they go.'

'Won't Anne send the police after them for chaining her up in the woods?'

'Henry and I will talk her out of it. She's already gone back to her old life and Henry is moving in upstairs. He's thinking of adding theatre design to our course program. I don't suppose I can persuade you to stay on with us?'

She couldn't. Just because you're a painter doesn't mean you
can teach the stuff. And I had other things to do. Didn't I say
that right from the start?

The events of the last few days had absorbed me so much I
had failed to notice that it was the weekend. Martin Byers would
not be at work. Martin Byers was not at his impersonal little
studio flat. Martin Byers was never at his little studio flat. You
probably got there long before me, but as I said, I had been a
little distracted. I drove up the hill towards Bear Flat and
Bloomfield Road with a heavy heart. This type of private detective
work – and there's a lot of that – was my least favourite. A good
result always meant a lot of pain for someone, often for everyone.

Byers' car was parked in front of the pretty house in St Luke's
Road. It was there because that was where he lived. My ringing
of the door bell was answered first by a small child's shout of
'Door!', then the door was opened by the woman I had seen
open it before. She was about the same age as Susan Byers and
there was nothing pink about her.

She frowned at me. 'Yes?'

'Hi, is your husband in? Sorry to disturb you. I'm from Mantis,
just need to ask him something.'

'You can ask him but you're not allowed to drag him away.
We're about to go out. I thought you were the babysitter.'

'I'm sure you're glad I'm not.'

'Martin?' she called back into the house. 'Someone from
work to see you.' She managed to put quite a bit of danger into
her voice.

Martin came to the door and went pale when he saw me. He
pulled the door to behind him. 'It's you,' he said. 'You've been
following me. Did Susan send you?' I nodded. 'Does she know
already?'

'She doesn't yet. But she suspects you. Care to explain?'

He walked me away from the door into the front garden so
we would not be overheard. 'Whatever I say now is going to
sound stupid to you.'

'I think that's the least of your worries.'

'It just happened. The long separations because of the job,
we had just bought the place in Southampton and had Mel when
I was sent here for months on end. And I met Maria. I didn't
tell her about Susan, obviously . . .'

'Obviously.'

'And then she got pregnant. Almost straight away, in fact. I couldn't . . . I couldn't bring myself to tell her then, she was so happy about being pregnant and I should have been horrified but I found I was happy too.'

'And you married her?'

'No, we're not married. We pretend to be for the company's sake.'

'So now you have two families? Two houses?'

'Yes. Yes, for the last two years. Look, it's not something I planned, you know, it's not a frivolous thing, either. One can love two people at the same time, believe me.'

I could well believe it. My own domestic arrangements weren't exactly standard issue either, but there was a difference. 'It's not about love,' I told him. 'You're allowed to love as many people as you like in as many ways as you like. *As long as you have their consent.* You might love them but you're also lying to them. All of them. All of the time. And it won't work.'

'Can't you tell Susan you found nothing? Can't you say you think I am faithful to her? How much is she paying you? It can't be much. I'll double it if you don't drop me in it.'

'You dropped yourself in it. You know this cannot last. It will come out some time. There are other private detectives. You'll make a mistake and it'll all collapse around you. You'll lose all of them. Both women. Both children. I know it's very late but you have to come clean. To both of them.' Martin Byers looked past me with a thousand-yard stare. He was plainly terrified. 'I'll give you one week to do it. I can't keep Susan waiting longer than that.' I handed him my card. 'Call me. But I warn you, I'll check up on whatever you tell me.'

I hadn't told him that Susan was expecting another child. That was for her to hit the man with. When the week had run out I let it slide a bit, but when I hadn't heard from him nor from Susan in Southampton another ten days on, I drove up to St Luke's Road. There were no plastic toys in the front garden but a For Sale sign had been rammed into the little bit of lawn. I didn't contact Susan Byers either. In the circumstances I could hardly demand a fee from her.

But I could afford not to. I had some pay coming to me after all and I had been commissioned to paint a large rural canvas by one of the visitors to the Batcombe show, so I was doing well.

Not as well as Hufnagel, though. It wasn't just that he had sold the Batcombe painting, he had also been hailed in the press as a new Delacroix for the twenty-first century. His painting of the pugilistic Petronela was likened by the critics to Delacroix's *Liberty Leading the People* and Hufnagel found himself greatly in demand. Of course, with the sudden retirement of Greg Landacker the art scene was now ready for a brand-new star.

And Annis was ready for a month of breakfasts in bed.